AMBUSH AT FIG TREE GULCH.

The True Story of Butch Cassidy, Che Guevara and the Sundance Kid the Day They Died in Bolivia.

By

M. WARD LEON

For information, or to order additional copies, please contact:

Beacon Publishing Group
P.O. Box 41573 Charleston, S.C. 29423
800.817.8480| beaconpublishinggroup.com

Publisher's catalog available by request.

ISBN-13: 978-1-949472-49-3

ISBN-10: 1-949472-49-3

Published in 2022. New York, NY 10001.

First Edition. Printed in the USA.

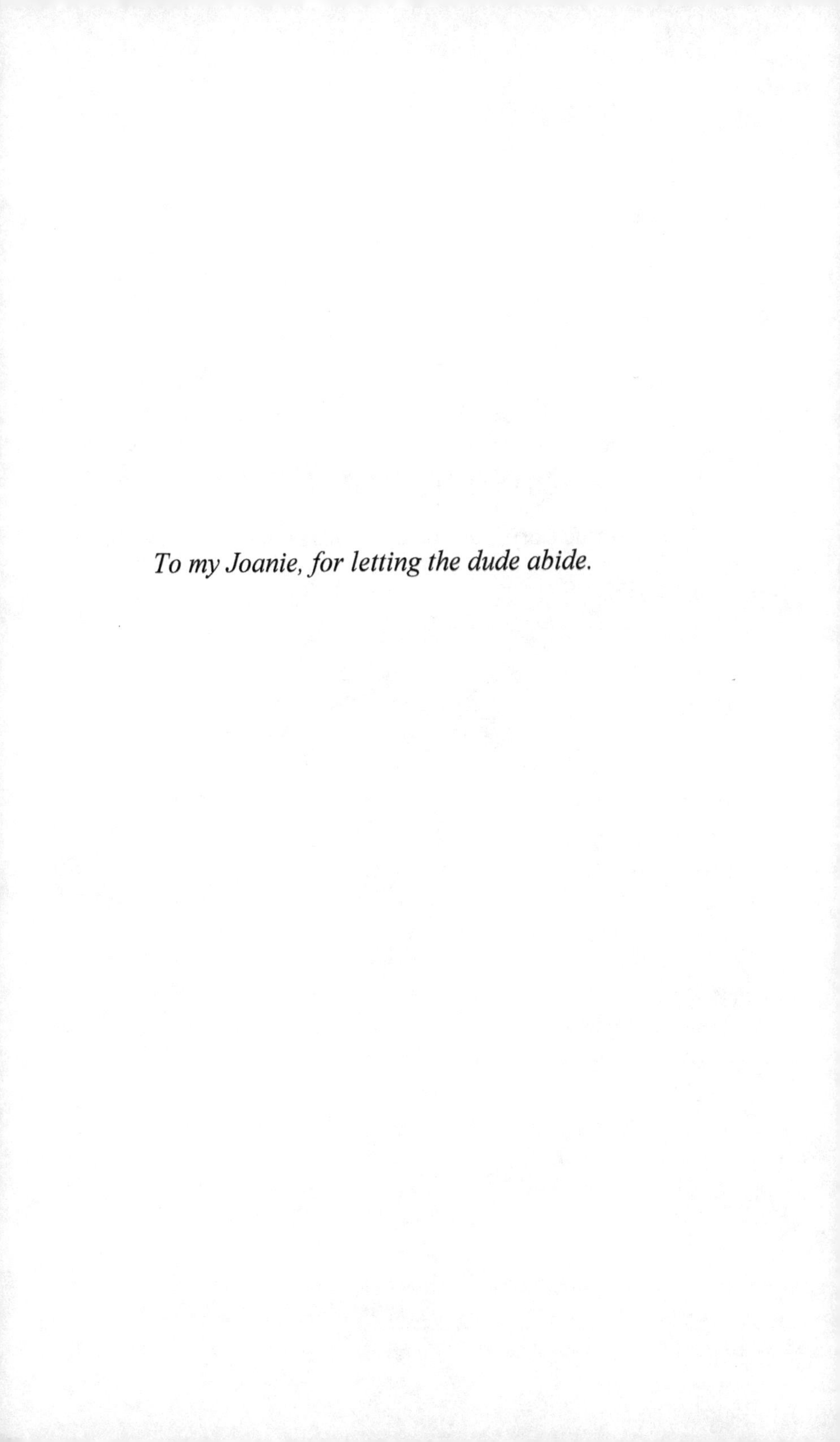

To my Joanie, for letting the dude abide.

Ambush at Fig Tree Gulch [©]

A true story based on actual historical *alternative* facts.

Front Row: The Sundance Kid, Ben "The Tall Texan" Kilpatrick, Butch Cassidy

Back Row: William "News" Carver, Che Guevara, Harvey "Kid Curry" Logan

My name is William Carver, but everybody calls me "News" because I always enjoyed seeing my name in the newspaper stories about my exploits with the Wild Bunch.

I am the sole remaining member of Butch Cassidy's "Hole in the Wall Gang" who's still living to tell the tales of Butch, Sundance, and the Wild Bunch.

I know that there's been a lot of yarns told about Butch, Sundance and the gang, most of them are just that, tall-tales made up by dime-store novel writers or by the moving pictures studios. This here's the real story of real desperados, Wild West outlaws, thieves, bandits, and killers. We were called the Wild Bunch for good reason.

I'm 103 years old now, and I guess I'm ready to finally tell the real story about the early days of the Hole in the Wall Gang in Johnson County, Wyoming and the final days of Butch and Sundance fighting alongside and dying with Che Guevara in La Higuera, Bolivia.

What you're about to read is the truth, not history book truth, but Wild West truth, so help me God.

Signed

William 'News' Carver

Both Butch and Sundance laid there in the ravine assessing their wounds. Butch had been shot in the left shoulder and right thigh, Sundance had sustained a bullet to his left side, a grazing wound to his right forearm, and a minor laceration to his forehead.

They both knew deep down they weren't going to survive, that this was the end of the line, but they couldn't bring themselves to admit it to the other.

"Hey, we've been in tougher jams than this, right Butch?"

"Ah, piece of cake."

"It reminds me of that time when we had that posse, General Miles, and his troops surround us outside Las Cruces."

"Yeah, we just held out until dark and then gave them the slip."

"And, they were a tougher lot than these guys."

"There can't be more than a couple dozen of them out there."

"How you doing on ammo, Butch? I'm down to fifty rounds for the BAR and four clips for the pistol, you?"

"Bout the same, plus I have two grenades."

"Hell, that should last us until it gets dark. What time is it anyway?"

"9 am."

"Damn, seems later."

"Listen, Sundance, after we get out of here, we got to meet up with News and head down to Australia."

"I liking the sound of Australia."

"Yeah, they love Americans, and they speak English. You know we've been down here over twenty years, and we still have trouble speaking the language, plus we stick out like a couple of gringos."

"That's because we are a couple of gringos."

The bullets started up again. They were taking fire from all sides.

"Butch, we gotta move! See those fig trees on the edge of the forest? Let's make a break for them. We can probably lose the soldiers in the jungle."

"Man, I'm really getting too old for this shit."

"You and me both, brother. You ready?"

"No, but let's go!"

They both starting firing in all directions, as they started running, Butch lobbed the two grenades, one to his left and one to his right.

As a result of their wounds and their age, they fell short of making their goal by ten feet. A group of twelve Bolivian Rangers had been hiding in the thicket of fig trees and opened fire point-blank, killing Butch Cassidy and the Sundance Kid.

Not far away, down in the ravine, surrounded by his dead comrades, Che had been wounded twice. With his gun out of ammunition, he surrendered.

He put up his arms and shouted to the Rangers, "Do not shoot! I am Che Guevara, and I am worth more to you alive than Dead."

I guess I should start at the beginning by telling you a little something about the man named Robert Leroy Parker. Of course, you all know him as Butch Cassidy. Butch never did like his real name, he would always say it was too cumbersome; it didn't roll off the tongue.

He told me once that he picked the name Butch Cassidy because he liked the way the ladies said it. Thinking back on it now, I think the real reason was because when we went into a bank to rob it, and he would shout out who he was, the name Robert Leroy Parker sounded more like a lawyer than an outlaw, and besides Butch hated lawyers. But, the name Butch Cassidy, well it just has grit.

Butch was born on April 13th, 1892 in Beaver, Utah Territory. There's been some dispute about when he was born, some say it was 1866, but they would be wrong; it was 1892. He was the oldest of thirteen children. His parents were British immigrants and had a small ranch near Circleville, Utah, a couple hundred miles from Salt Lake City.

Both of his parents couldn't write or read, so there weren't any books in the house. Butch always jokingly said the reason his folks had so many kids was because there wasn't anything else to do at night.

Butch led a cowboy's life after leaving home, with his childhood friend, Matt Warner. They worked on ranches primarily around Telluride, Colorado, but roamed as far as Wyoming and Montana.

When Butch turned twenty-three, he and Warner returned to Telluride after working in Montana. One day they rode up to the San Miguel Valley Bank and proceeded to withdraw close to twenty-one hundred dollars using their guns as withdrawal slips (which is the equivalent of $6,000 today), after which they fled to Hole-in-the-Wall.

Butch took his share and bought a ranch on the outskirts of Dubois, Wyoming. He found that he had no real desire to be a rancher, too much hard work for him. He did keep it as a façade for his covert and fraudulent activities with the Hole-in-the-Wall gang.

Hole-in-the-Wall is a remote pass in the Big Horn Mountains of Johnson County, Wyoming not far from Butch's ranch, the Reverse-E Box, E Ranch. It wasn't long after he bought the ranch when he got arrested in Lander, Wyoming for stealing horses. He was sent to the Wyoming

State Prison, sentenced to two years and that's where I met him. I was doing a three stretch for cattle rustling, and we soon became fast friends, Butch got out after only 18 months, and I joined up with him eight months later.

By the time I hooked up with him, he was putting together his gang, which would be later known as the Wild Bunch. Now, let me see, there was Harvey "Kid Curry" Logan, Ben (the Tall Texan) Kilpatrick, William Ellsworth "Elzy" Lay, Black Jack Ketchum, "Laughing" Sam Carey, George "Flat Nose" Curry, and me.

Harry Alonzo Longabaugh, better known as the Sundance Kid, was born in Mont Clare, Pennsylvania on November 7th, 1893.

Sundance was the youngest of five children, his parents, Josiah and Annie Longabaugh were poor dirt farmers. When Harry turned 15, they sent him and his cousin George west in a covered wagon to Wyoming to find their fortune.

He got a job at a ranch in Sundance, Wyoming where after a short time, he stole a gun, horse, and saddle. He was captured by the local sheriff, stood trial and was sent to prison for 18 months, it was at that time he adopted the name Sundance Kid.

While doing time in the Wyoming State Prison, he met Butch and me. In the beginning, we didn't hit it off, being that they were both alpha dogs, who aren't followers, but leaders, and when you're trying to be the leader of a gang, it's tough if you got two leaders.

After a while, we grew to like and respect each other and became friends. When Sundance was released from prison, he got a job as a ranch hand up in Alberta, Canada at the Bar U Ranch, one of the largest commercial ranches around.

But, ranching wasn't for Sundance, it wasn't long until he and a couple cowpokes robbed a train and a bank in Canada and were pursued by the Royal Canadian Mounties. So, they hightailed it down to Hole-in-the-Wall, Wyoming to seek shelter and refuge. And that's when he reconnected with Butch Cassidy and joined the Wild Bunch.

Having been the leader of his own gang, Sundance found it easier and less headaches to let Butch do the figuring, and thus began one of the Wild West's most legendary outlaw teams, Butch Cassidy and the Sundance Kid.

My niece, Laura Bullion was as good an outlaw as Butch, Sundance, Kid Curry or any of the other members of the Wild Bunch. In fact, she was so good that she was the only female member of the gang ever.

Me and her pa, Henry, started out stealing cattle and horses when Laura was just a baby. We'd alter their brands and sell them back to the same ranchers we stole them from. After a while that got boring, so we eventually graduated into robbing banks.

It just so happened that when Laura was fifteen, she left home after her mother died. She had had enough of home-life. She headed down to San Antonio, where, just by chance, she sees me and Henry standing outside the bank, contemplating weather to rob it or not.

Well, Laura walks right past us, without so much as a howdy-do, pulls out a six-shooter and proceeds to rob the bank.

She comes running out whooping, and a hollering jumps on her horse and rides off, with Henry and me right behind her.

"Girl, what was you thinking?" Her father asked.

"I'm thinking, this sure beats taking in washing." Laura said as she held up a fist full of dollars.

I told her she could walk away now and not live her life running from the law.

"What and be a seamstress, a wife, or a whore? No, thank you." She said.

So, the three of us started robbing banks and even a train or two. I think it was when we was hiding out in old El Paso, that Laura met Ben "The Tall Texan" Kilpatrick and was smitten. Kilpatrick had been robbing trains and decided to move up to Utah and hook up with Butch Cassidy and the Wild Bunch, so that's what me and Laura did. Henry decided he preferred Texas, so he said good-bye to his daughter and me, and that was the last time we laid eyes on him. Two months later, Henry Bullion was shot in the back by a couple of bounty hunters, they got five hundred dollars reward.

Being part of the Wild Bunch, Laura did her share of robbing and even shooting. She also helped the gang by fencing goods and money. She was known as the "Thorny Rose." Everyone knew you didn't mess with Laura. Butch said that Laura was a natural-born outlaw.

It was on Wednesday, August 13th, 1913 that the Wild Bunch rode into Montpelier, Idaho to rob the town bank. We were looking to get enough money to bail Butch's old friend, Matt Warner out of jail.

Montpelier was a sleepy backwater town on the border with Wyoming, so we figured it would be a piece of cake.

Let's see, there was Butch, Lay, Logan, Bob Meeks, Sundance and me. It was a gray day, a slight mist in the air. We were all wearing dusters, which didn't draw much attention, due to the wet conditions. Plus they helped disguise the fact that we was all concealing rifles and shotguns underneath them.

We tied our horses up to the hitching post outside the bank, Meeks stayed outside watching the horses and kept a lookout. Inside, there were two male tellers, both looked to be in their sixties, four customers waiting in line, and behind the cage, there were three bank executives doing paperwork.

Butch opened his duster, pulled out his 45 Colt Single-Action Army revolver from his holster, and shouted, "This is a stick-up! Don't nobody try anything stupid, and no one will get hurt. Everybody get on the ground. Now!"

Me, Lay, and Logan jumped the teller's counter and started filling the saddlebags that we brought in with us. Sundance kicked in the door on the cage and shoved a shotgun in the manager's head and forced him to open up the safe.

As we're leaving Butch announced proudly, "I'm Butch Cassidy, and this is my gang. If'n we see anybody sticking their heads out after we leave, we'll shoot them off."

It only took a few minutes before the whole gang comes strolling out of the bank, each one of us $7,000 the richer.

We hightailed it out of there and headed back to Hole-in-the-Wall, where we all got equal shares of the loot after we put money aside for Matt Warner's bail. It was easy pickings; no shots were fired, and no one got hurt. We never went in looking to hurt anyone, but sometimes people do foolish things, then all Hell breaks loose, and people die. But not today.

Butch and Sundance rode off to the La Barge jailhouse to see about posting bail for Warner. La Barge sat on the banks of the Green River about 300 miles from Hole-in-the-Wall, so they would be gone a good month or so.

Meanwhile, me and the boys headed off to Buffalo City to do our fair share of drinking and whoring. Buffalo City sits at the foot of the Bighorn Mountains, about 100 miles from the Little Bighorn Battlefield. When we got to town, we checked into the Occidental Hotel; it was mighty highfalutin, Butch and Sundance had stayed there many a time and told us to stay there until they returned with Warner.

By the time they returned with Matt Warner, Butch had hatched a plan to hold up the Union Pacific Overland Flyer.

We all were summoned to Butch's room for a big pow-wow. When everyone arrived, Butch announced, "Boys, we're taking a ride on the Overland Flyer."

"Where we going, Butch?" I asked.

"Down in history, News. Down in history."

"The Union Pacific Overland Flyer carries the payroll for all those workers in the Chicago slaughterhouses, Butch figures the haul could be close to seventy thousand dollars," Sundance said.

Needless to say, we were all speechless, $70,000 in 1913 would be close to 2 million dollars today.

Butch pulled out a train schedule and laid it out on the bed in his room. "Okay, gather round, here's the plan. Me and Sundance will board the train here in Ogden, Elzy; Laura, and Black Jack will get on at Granger, and finally Flat Nose, Sam, and News you'll join us at Laramie.

"By the time we get to Laramie, all the big money will be on board, so right after we stop in Cheyenne and cross over into Nebraska, that's when we force the train to stop. Matt, Kid Curry, and Ben will be waiting for us with fresh horses.

"We then split up, everyone riding in different directions and meets back at the Hole-in-the-Wall. Questions?"

"Yeah, I got one, when do we get our cuts?" Kid Curry asked.

"When we all get back to the Hole." Butch said.

"And who's carrying all the loot?"

"I am, you got a problem, what, you don't trust me, Kid?"

"No, nothing like that Butch." Curry answered.

"Anybody got a problem with the plan?" Butch asked, looking around the room.

"Why can't we split the money and get our cut before we all ride off?" BlackJack asked.

"Cause afterward, we got to move and move quick. Every lawman and Pinkerton agent within a thousand miles is going to looking to get a piece of that reward." Sundance answered.

"Look, I know you all, once you get your cut, you're going to want to go showing it off, or go drinking and whoring and that's how you land in prison or end up dead. This way if someone stops you, you won't have any evidence that you were part of any robbery." Butch said.

"And besides by the time we all meet up, things will have cooled down." Sundance added.

So, it was agreed, we'd all meet up back at Hole-in-the-Wall.

Flat Nose, Laughing Sam, and myself got to the Union Pacific train platform in Laramie two hours before the Flyer was due in. The station man said she was running right on time.

Standing among all the other passengers waiting, I felt very uncomfortable. We was all wearing our Sunday go to meeting clothes; we had just bought them from the Sears Roebuck store. Mine was too big on me, Sam's and Flat Nose's were too small and tight. I never felt right wearing them types of clothes, unlike Butch who felt right at home all duded up.

Looking at the other men walking around in suits, we surely stuck out. None of us could figure out how to tie those damn neckties, and not wanting to look like idiots we stuffed them into our pockets.

Flat Nose wore a bowler hat, whereas Sam and I both sported a flattop straw hat, sometimes known as skimmers. Of course, we brought along our everyday clothes that we planned on wearing after the heist, not wanting to look like a bunch of dudes riding around. We didn't want to stick out like a sore thumb, especially when you're on the run from the law; you got to be at ease in your duds.

It was strange seeing what people were wearing in the big city. Everyone, men and women were mostly all dressed in what we would call fancy wear, and most men didn't wear side-arms. I don't know about the others, but I felt like a fish out of water. I couldn't wait to get back to Hole-in-the-Wall.

I had been on trains before, but never one so splendiferous. They had rooms where people could sleep in beds. The walls in all of the cars were made from polished wood, and they even had chairs in one car that were covered in green velvet. There was a restaurant car with fancy china plates and crystal glasses with waiters and a chef.

Seeing all the rich folks, Laughing Sam poked me in the ribs and whispered, "News, these high-rollers ain't going to be rich for much longer."

After the conductor came by and punched our tickets, Flat Nose said, "I'll be back, I'm going to go look for Butch."

He was gone for about twenty minutes before he came back and signaled for me and Sam to follow him back to the bar car, where Butch and Sundance were sitting at a table, drinking beers and playing cards.

"Hey, Butch." I said.

Butch looked up at me and said, "News?"

"Yeah., Butch it's me."

"Jeez, News, I didn't recognize you with the beard."

"Thought it would be a good disguise. What do ya think?"

"Well, you fooled me. How 'bout you Sundance?"

"I never would have known it was you. But, News I thought you liked publicity, now no one's going know to put your name in the paper if they don't recognize you."

"Well, then I'm just going to have to announce who I am."

Butch gave a short nod and said, "Good idea, you got to make sure that you get your fair share of the credit. Say, what time does your watch say, News?"

I pulled out my pocket watch and saw that it was 11:48, so I said, "11:48."

Butch looked at his watch sitting on the table next to his glass of beer and nodded in agreement. "Right, 11:48. Now, listen boys at exactly 2:00, I want you three to start at the back of the train and work your way up to the mail car, collecting all the passenger's valuables and guns; don't forget the guns.

By the time you get to the mail car, me, Sundance, Black Jack, Laura, and Elzy will have gotten the payroll. You should plan to be at the mail car no later than 2:30, understand?"

"Got it, Butch. What should we do until 2:00?" Asked Flat Nose.

"Go get something to eat and have a beer, Flat Nose. Remember, 2:30."

I said, "2:30."

At 2:00, the three of us moseyed on back to the buffet-library car, it was the last passenger car on the train. When we entered the car, we got a whole bunch of disapproving looks. Sam and Flat Nose walked to the back of the car where the male librarian was seated. Sam tapped on the wooden counter where the man was sitting and asked, "Do you have any of them girlie magazines?"

"Certainly not, sir."

"Well, how about any of them Wild West dime store novels?"

"No sir, I'm afraid not."

"Got a book on train robbers?'

"No."

Sam said as he pulled his gun out from his holster, "Well, maybe you could write one."

Both Flat Nose and I pulled our revolvers as Laughing Sam shouted, "Everyone, this is a hold-up! Don't nobody try anything!"

"We're the Butch Cassidy gang, and I'm News Carver!" I yelled.

While Sam held everyone at bay, Flat Nose and I walked the length of the car collecting people's cash, wallets, watches, women's jewelry and any weapon they might be holding.

We did the same thing for the next six cars; meanwhile, Butch and the rest had somehow finagled their way into the mail car and held the guard at gunpoint.

"Open the safe." Butch said, pointing the gun at the man.

"You go to Hell." The guard said.

Sundance held his pistol up against the man's head, cocked the hammer back and whispered, "See ya there."

The man relented right there on the spot, Black Jack told me later that he actually peed his pants. The guard knelt down in front of the safe and dialed the combination unlocking the Chandler Bank Vault specially made for the Overland Flyer.

As the guard slowly opened the safe door he reached inside and grabbed a hidden Colt revolver; he died in a hail of bullets. The hand that was holding onto the vault door handle as he fell backward swung the door open, revealing two sealed Pinkerton payroll bags and several safety deposit boxes full of passenger cash and jewelry. They opened that once me and the boys met them at 2:30.

At exactly 2:45 Butch pulled the train's emergency stop cord. By the time the train had completely stopped, and Butch had opened the mail car's sliding side door, there sat Matt Warner, Kid Curry, Ben Kilpatrick on their mounts, each holding the reins to the horses, seven for riders two for supplies.

As me and the gang were mounting our horses, shots began to ring out, which appeared to be coming from the direction of the passenger cars. We returned fire, our aim being more accurate, as we are more experienced in gunplay than most civilians. As newspaper articles would later report we were responsible for killing at least four and wounding six. As for us, our only casualty was a minor gunshot wound sustained by Kid Curry in his left arm.

As planned, we rode off together for about a mile then split off into all different directions, taking care to avoid any contact with towns, ranches, and soldiers.

Butch had said to ride slow, not like we were in a hurry, and don't try and outrun the law if they happen upon us, since we wouldn't have any evidence of the train robbery on our person, they wouldn't have any reason to suspect us. And be sure to use an alias, something simple and easy to remember. I chose Timothy Scott.

"Put your hands up!" Sheriff E.S. "Lige" Briant said.

I did as I was instructed, I raised my hands. I had shaved off my beard and discarded my fancy duds hours after the robbery. I was hoping that I wouldn't fit the description of myself that I 'm sure had been telegraphed all over the country.

"Now get off your horse, easy."

I did as I was told, I slowly dismounted.

"What's your name?"

"Timothy Scott." I answered.

"Where ya coming from and where ya headed."

"Red Feather Lakes, I'm headed to Boulder to look for work."

"Do I know you? You look familiar. Charlie, look in his saddlebags." Sheriff Briant instructed his deputy.

"I ain't ever been in trouble with the law, sheriff. I'm just looking for ranching work is all."

The deputy emptied out all my things onto the ground and poked around for a few minutes then said, "He's clean sheriff."

"Okay cowboy you can go."

"What's it all about, sheriff?"

"The Union Pacific Overland Flyer was robbed by the Butch Cassidy gang 'bout a week ago, and we're checking everybody passing by. There's a big reward out for the members of the gang, dead or alive. You be careful now, don't be messing with them, they'd sooner slit your throat than give ya a howdy-do."

"Thanks for the heads up sheriff." I said.

I kept on riding south, I figured when I reached Boulder, I'd head west until I got to Utah and then go north to Wyoming. You can make all the plans you want, but then things happen to change your plans.

By the time I rode into the town of Meeker, Colorado, I was nearly dead broke, so I figured I had two choices, get to jobbing or get to robbing. And since I was never one to enjoy the fruits of physical labor, I chose robbing.

I went into the Pinnacle Peak Saloon for a beer and something to eat. I had been eating nothing but hardtack for over ten days, and I needed something that would stick to my ribs. I sat down at a table in the corner, so as to keep my eye on the goings-on. After what happened to Bill Hickok, I never would sit with my back to a door.

The barmaid came by to take my order, I said, "I'll have the pork chops, fried potatoes, order of buckwheat cakes with syrup and a beer."

The total was almost fifty cents, darn near cleaned me out, I only had forty cents left.

At the table next to him, the man had finished paying for his meal. He stood up and was leaving a copy of the Salt Lake Herald on the chair.

"Excuse me, sir, would you be done with that paper." I asked.

He handed it to me as he walked away, saying, "Help yourself, pardner, sorry to say it's a week old."

"Thanks, mister, that's okay old news is often the best news."

I started scanning the front page, and there in the lower left-hand corner was in bold type, 'Butch Cassidy's Wild Bunch struck again last Tuesday, looting the Union Pacific Overland Flyer.'

As I was glancing over the article there to my delight, halfway down in the column, "Also known to have participated in the holdup are Flat Nose Curry and News Carver." After I made sure my name was mentioned and spelled right, I began to read the article from the beginning. It was full of inaccuracies and falsehoods, but they made sure that Butch and the gang were all larger than life characters.

As I was finishing up the story, I sensed the presence of someone lurking nearby. I leaned forward over the newspaper laying on the table in front of me, and casually lowered my right hand down and grabbed hold of my pistol in ready in case it was called for.

"Hey, News." The man whispered. "Mind if I join you?"

I looked up to see a ghost, standing in front of me, William H. Bonney, who I had heard had been gunned down years ago by Sheriff Pat Garrett, but there he was.

Now, I had known him many years ago before I ever teamed up with Butch and the gang, when he went by the moniker Billy the Kid.

Since the reporting's of his death, there have been numerous sightings in New Mexico, Arizona and even up here in Colorado, but everyone just figured that's all they were, rumors. And yet here he is standing right in front of me.

"Billy?" I said. "Is that really you?"

He slid back the chair and sat down opposite me. He peered around to see if we were being observed, leaned forward and said in a low voice, "News, it's good to see a familiar face. How the Hell are you?"

"Billy, I thought you was dead."

"Well, as Mark Twain once said, "The reports of my death are greatly exaggerated," he said, laughing.

The barmaid walked up an dropped the plate with my pork chops, potatoes, and pancakes down in front of me like she would as if she was feeding her dog.

I said, "Oye, where's my beer?"

"Keep your shirt on, it's coming." She snapped back as she started to walk away.

"And how about a knife and fork, sweetheart?"

"Yeah, yeah, yeah."

Seconds later, she returned and plopped the eating utensils down along with my beer, spilling half of it onto my plate.

She looked down at the mess she made, then at me and said, "Listen, love, it's all going to end up in the same place at the end anyway." And walked away.

Billy looked at my plate and asked, "News, are you going to eat both those chops?"

I looked across the table and saw just how wanting he was, "Naw, go ahead, help yourself."

He reached over and grabbed the bigger of the two and started devouring it.

I said, "Listen, Billy, I'm on the run, so I'm not going by News at the moment, it's Scott, Timothy Scott."

"Timothy Scott, okay and I'm not 'the Kid' or even William Bonney, it's Bill Roberts, Brushy Bill Roberts."

"Brushy?"

"Well, ever since I grew this wooly mustache I've acquired the nickname Brushy Bill."

I looked at him for a few minutes before answering, "Fitting, very fitting. So, Brushy what are you doing in Meeker, just passing thru?"

He gazed around to see if anyone was eavesdropping then said, "Actually…"

"Timothy Scott." I reminded him.

"Actually, Timothy, I've been scoping out local banking opportunities, if you catch my drift. Interested?"

"Maybe. I mean me and the boys in the Wild Bunch just took down the Overland Flyer last week." I said, holding up the paper with the article.

"Why you should be flush with cash, Timothy."

"Well, not at the moment. We're all meeting up at the Hole-in-the-Wall to get our shares."

"So, you're broke, too?"

"Naw, I got me a whole forty cents."

"Well, now's the perfect time. The sheriff is off giving testimony over in Fort Collins in the trial of Dynamite Dick Clifton."

"Dynamite Dick of the Doolin Gang?" I asked.

"The very same."

"What's he on trial for?"

"Robbery and safecracking, course it ain't the real Dynamite Dick."

"The fingers?" I asked.

"Yup."

You see Dynamite Dick was a member of the Doolin Gang when they robbed a bank in Ingalls, Oklahoma. They got into a gunfight afterward with the law, and three of his fingers were shot off.

They escaped, and the gang eventually broke up. A bounty was put on Dynamite Dick's head for $3500, and for a while he was known as the "most killed outlaw in America", people would kill someone thinking it might be him and turn in the corpse claiming it to be Dynamite Dick despite the fact the body had all ten fingers, while some folks who had heard the story of his misfortune would randomly cut off three fingers of the deceased, usually cutting off the wrong ones.

"So, who's on trial?"

"Buck McGregg."

"Bad for Buck, good for Dick." I said.

"Yeah, he'll hang for sure. Not that he don't deserve it. But, if you're going to hang, at least hang for something you did."

"True."

"So, you interested in the bank?" He said as he was gnawing on the pork chop bone.

"Can I at least finish my meal?"

"Oh, sure."

He looked at the clock over the bar and whispered, "News, the bank closes in forty-five minutes."

We walk into the bank with our bandanas drawn up to our eyes, guns drawn and hats pulled low down on our heads, so all they could see were our eyes.

"Don't nobody move, this here is a stickup!" Billy yells.

"If you try anything funny with them alarm bells, you all die!" I added.

Billy walked past the three tellers with an empty feedbag and collected the cash from the draws. We had decided not to fool around with the money in the safe, figuring it would take too long.

We were in and out of the bank in under six minutes, with close to three thousand dollars. About ten miles out of town, we divvied up the loot and said our goodbyes, Billy headed down towards Texas and me, I went up north to Wyoming to connect with Butch and the gang. All the way north I rode only at dawn and dusk, keeping a watchful eye out for posses and bounty hunters.

As for Billy the Kid aka Brushy Bill Roberts, I never did see him again, although I did hear a rumor that in 1950, a gent who went by the name of Brushy Bill Roberts, at the age of 89 years old sought a pardon from the Governor of New Mexico for crimes that he claimed he committed as Billy the Kid. Unfortunately, before the Governor could sign the pardon, the old Brushy Bill died of a heart attack. Not exactly the stuff that wild west legends are made of.

When I finally got back to the Hole-in-the-Wall, only Laughing Sam Laura, and The Tall Texan hadn't arrived. It had taken me eight weeks to make it back, Butch and Sundance had split the money up into ten equal shares, and it was decided to wait another four more weeks for the two stragglers to appear.

Word spread fast that both Laughing Sam and Tall Texan were captured after a fierce shootout just outside of Casper, Laura too. They were taken to Casper, and after a speedy trial the men were each sentenced to 15 years in prison, Laura had gotten five years.

Butch got word to them all that their shares from the Overland Flyer would be held in a trust at the Wells Fargo bank in Denver under their Christian names.

The ironic thing is that when the depression hit in 1929, both their trusts were wiped out, leaving them with nothing. So, after all the times they robbed banks, it would be the banks that ended up robbing them.

Two months after Kilpatrick got out of prison, he and the outlaw Ole Hobek boarded a Southern Pacific Express in Sanderson, Texas. While during the attempted robbery of the Wells Fargo baggage and mail car, David Trousdale, the bank's express manager, managed to conceal an ice pick behind his back.

Once the Tall Texan cleaned out the safe and other passenger valuables, Trousdale told Kilpatrick that several valuable packages were lying on the ground, like any good thief he couldn't resist the idea of stealing more.

When Kilpatrick rested his weapon on the floor Trousdale pulled the ice pick from behind his back and viciously stabbed the bandit three times, twice in the back of the neck, severing his spinal cord and the third time in the back of the head instantly killing him. Stabbing him so hard that Trousdale crushed his skull. The attack was so brutal that Kilpatrick's brains were splattered all over the walls of the car.

Trousdale then picked up Kilpatrick's gun and shot and killed Ole Hobek, shooting him in the throat causing him to die a slow lingering death. It is said that Trousdale just let him suffer, drowning in his own blood.

Back in the days of cowboys and outlaws, people would buy and send postcards of dead outlaws posed by the men who killed them. A couple years later while I was in a sundry store in Kansas, I spotted behind the counter the photograph postcard of Ben 'The Tall Texan' Kilpatrick and Ole Hobek, who was shot dead during the robbery with six steadfast citizens standing next to and holding the two dead bodies upright. The caption scrawled at the bottom was, "Train Robbers killed near Sanderson, Texas."

Laughing Sam Carey was released from prison a year before Kilpatrick. He then joined Otto Chenowroth's less successful gang, and after a failed bank robbery Sam was committed to a sanitarium in North Dakota due to suffering a mental breakdown, and later released to the care of his mother.

David Trousdale became an instant celebrity and was featured in many a dime store novel. The Southern Pacific railroad company gave him a big reward and a promotion within the company. Eight months after the killings, Ben 'The Tall Texan' Kilpatrick's brother, Toby walked into Trousdale's office and stabbed him in the eye with a Bowie knife killing him instantly and then walked out.

Police never caught Toby Kilpatrick. The stories I heard were that he skedaddled down to Mexico and took up with a Mexican whore and lived the rest of his days running a small cantina in the tiny town of Tres Hermanas.

As for Laura, after Kilpatrick was killed, she changed her name to Freda Bullion Lincoln, moved to Memphis and became a seamstress and dressmaker. I never heard from her again, I read that she passed away on December 2nd, 1961.

After the Overland Flyer robbery Butch and Sundance became inseparable friends, they were more like brothers; you wouldn't find one without the other. It was close to three months after we robbed the Flyer that Butch thought it safe to give everyone their shares. Before we all left camp to enjoy our spoils, Butch said that he had the next job all laid out, so if we wanted in, to meet back at the Hole-in-the-Wall camp two months from now, which would be July.

"Hey, Butch where are you and Sundance off to?" I asked.

"Elzy, Sundance and I were planning to work our way down to Robbers Roost, why you want to come?"

"If'n you don't mind."

"Saddle up we leave within the hour."

Now Robbers Roost was a hideout discovered by Butch and Elzy many years ago, it is in southeastern Utah about fifty miles east of Hanksville where Butch and Elzy would ride out to get supplies.

The hideout was considered to be the ideal spot because of the rough terrain. The Roost was hard to find without being detected, because of the height advantage, it was easily defended; plenty of fresh drinking water from a remote tributary of the Dirty Devil River that flowed thru the canyon. It was the perfect place to relax and rest following an arduous train robbery or bank heist.

They built a couple of cabins to help protect them from the harsh Utah winters. They stored weapons, horses, cattle, and chickens.

Robbers Roost was overall a better and more secure hideout than was Hole-in-the-Wall. Lawmen and bounty hunters of the day never discovered the location of their hideout. That we held one and other to the strictest confidentiality regarding the site of the hideaway.

In fact, outside of the gang, there were only four others; and they were women who were allowed inside the Roost: Butch's and Elzy's girlfriends, the sisters Ann and Josie Bassett, Sundance's lady Etta Place, and my sweetie Della Moore.

It wasn't until Butch, Sundance and myself ended up down in South America that Sheriff Joe Bush and a posse from Salt Lake City made a raid on the Roost killing, the last members of the Wild Bunch who decided not to leave the country with us.

More of that later.

Butch, Elzy, Sundance and I was heading down to Robbers Roost when we stopped at this small ranch, not far the entrance to the Roost's canyon, for some fresh horses and some beef. That's when we met the Bassett sisters, the ranch owners.

Ann, the oldest, was also known as Queen Ann for her ruthlessness in fighting an ongoing battle royale with several of the wealthy cattle barons.

Initially, the cattlemen tried to buy the ranch from her and her sister, and when they refused, the barons began rustling the Bassett's cattle. Ann and her sister Josie, in turn, began rustling cattle from them. This opened up a range war. The cattlemen brought in a hired gun the notorious Tom Horn to try and intimidate the Bassett sisters.

Tom Horn started out as a civilian scout for the cavalry during the Apache Wars, earning him quite the reputation, not only as a scout but fierce warrior.

On one campaign while crossing Cibecue Creek, Arizona, they were attacked by a horde of hostiles that were positioned on the high ground. Their commanding officer, Captain Edmund Hentig was killed, and the troops were pinned down under overwhelming firepower.

Horn and another scout broke away from the main body of soldiers and worked their way up and around the attacking Apaches, managing to repel the attack, killing a number of the red devils. He even helped track down Geronimo. He was present at his final surrender and acted as the interpreter.

After the war, Horn used his earnings to build a ranch in Aravaipa Canyon, Arizona. It consisted of a hundred head of cattle and some twenty plus horses. It didn't last long, since one-night cattle thieves attacked his ranch, killing several of his hired hands and stole his entire stock of cattle and horses, leaving him broke and bankrupted.

He wandered from town to town doing odd jobs. He worked as a ranch hand, a prospector, and a rodeo rider. Then someone offered him a job as a hired gun to protect their cattle and kill anyone suspected of trying to steal their stock. He was so effective that the cattle rustling stopped completely along the North Laramie River, Wyoming.

Shortly after cleaning up the cattle rustling up in Wyoming, he was hired by the cattle barons that were feuding with the Barrett sisters. It was around this time that Butch and Elzy had become romantically involved with Ann and Josie.

I was present when Butch, Elzy, and Sundance met up with Tom Horn outside of Hanksville. Horn was accompanied with six other cowboys heading into town as the four of us was leaving town. Horn's companions all looked to me to be hired guns by the way they wore their weapons.

Elzy had known Tom Horn when they both had tried their hands at prospecting for gold around Tombstone, and he recognized him straight off.

"Tom Horn, you're looking fit." Elzy said.

"As are you, Elzy."

"What are you doing around these parts?"

"Been hired to put a stop to some cattle rustling. You?"

"Me and my compadres are on our way to visit some acquaintances."

"Oh, and who might that be, if you don't mind my asking."

"Miss Ann Barrett and her sister Josie."

Horn said nothing for a few moments while he sized up the three of us.

"Elzy, I haven't had the pleasure of meeting your friends."

"Sorry, Tom, didn't mean to be rude. This here is Butch Cassidy, that's News Carver, and that is the Sundance Kid."

I casually noticed that Butch, Elzy, and Sundance all had accidentally placed their hands on their guns, yet their body language didn't appear to be threatening. But they were definitely sending the message that we're ready to throw down if called upon. I could see that Horn had also noticed this, as he smiled, touched his hat, and said, "Gentlemen, a pleasure to meet your acquaintance. I've heard a lot about you all."

Butch tipped his bowler and said, "The pleasure is ours, we've heard a lot about you as well, Mr. Horn."

"Tom, please. And coming from you Butch that means a lot. Elzy, it's always good seeing a familiar face.

"Gentlemen I'm sorry, but we have errands to attend to. Hope to see you all again. Good day."

Elzy held up a hand as we started to ride off and said, "See ya, Tom."

Once the word got around that Butch Cassidy and the Sundance Kid were friends of the Barrett Sisters, cowboys hired to harass the sisters ceased, and the services of Tom Horn were no longer needed.

There was a time several months later when me and Kid Curry, who was the most feared member of the Wild Bunch gang, came upon several cowboys known to be employed by the cattlemen, sitting around their campsite preparing their dinner.

"Evening boys." Curry said as he was dismounting his horse.

I stayed mounted with my hand on my revolver.

One of the cowboys stood and asked. "Can I help you?"

"Well, as a matter of fact, you can. You boys can stop harassing the Barrett sisters."

"And why would we want to do that?" The cowboy smirked.

"Cause I asked you to."

"And who do you think you are, mister."

The Kid took to a straight posture, lowered his hands down, so they were slightly touching his holsters, looked every one of those cowboys in the eye and then said, "Kid Curry. Ain't that right News?"

"That's right Kid." I said, figuring we was in for a drawdown.

The standing cowboy went all-weak kneed and looked at the others and could tell that none of them had the grit to stand up to the Kid and me.

"We don't mean no harm, Kid. We was just doing what we was told."

"Well, I'm telling you to leave them ladies be."

"Yes, sir."

"You boys just know if'n I hear of any you go trifling with the Barrett sisters, you'll be hearing from the Wild Bunch and me. Understood?"

"Understood."

And that was that, the feud was over.

Many years later I had read that while working near Iron Mountain, Wyoming as a range detective, Tom was accused of killing a sixteen-year-old boy, shooting him from over 300 yards with a .30-30 Winchester.

It was reported that Deputy Marshal Joe Lefors got Horn drunk so as to get a confession from him. While still inebriated, Lefors got Horn to confess to killing young Willie Nickell with his rifle from 300 yards. Lefors claimed that Horn boasted that it was the "best shot that he ever made and the dirtiest trick that he ever done."

Tom Horn was found guilty and hung.

Once the feud had subsided, Butch planned our next caper. They ambushed a group of five men carrying the payroll of the Pleasant Valley Mining Company outside of Castle Gate, Utah.

Now let's see, there was Butch, Sundance, Elzy, Flat Nose, Kid Curry and me. We laid wait on either side of the trail, hidden behind some large rock formations for the men to pass us by. That's when he sprung into action, Butch, Sundance, and Elzy pulled out in front of the riders, while Flat Nose, Curry and I darted out to block their retreat from behind.

With pistols drawn, Butch shouted, "Halt! This a robbery."

As four of the five men raised their hands, one of them drew his weapon, Elzy shot the man dead.

"Stand and deliver!" Sundance said sternly.

"Drop your weapons!" Elzy said.

Me and Kid Curry scurried to the band of riders and riffled thru their saddlebags retrieving three bags of gold and their guns from the ground.

I went to check on the fallen rider and proclaimed, "He's dead."

"Tis own fault." Elzy said.

Butch looked at me, assessed the situation, and said, "We're off."

We rode away with over seven thousand in gold, then hightailed it back to Robbers Roost.

Charlie Siringo was a lawman, detective, bounty hunter, an agent for the Pinkerton National Detective Agency, and for a short time rode with the Wild Bunch.

It was back when we spent most of our time hiding from the law at Hole-in-the-Wall before Butch had found the Robbers Roost, Siringo wandered into camp posing as Charles L. Carter, an alleged Mexican outlaw on the run from the law for murdering a railroad agent while robbing the Colorado and Southern Railroad.

The Wild Bunch was a very progressive thinking gang for the times, in that, when Butch had conceived of a plan, you weren't required to take part. Or if you wanted to participate in a venture of your own, working with other members of the gang, it was considered acceptable, you needn't ask anyone's permission.

Siringo/Carter had a plan to stage a train robbery. Working with agents of the Pinkerton Agency, he approached several members of the Wild Bunch gang, including myself, to rob the Colorado and Southern train out of Santé Fe. He tried to convince Butch and Sundance to be part of the raid, but they opted out.

Unknown to us, after the robbery Siringo and the agents would try to capture us dead or alive, then they would split a substantial cash reward from the C&S Railroad.

It came to pass that Siringo, the outlaw Bronco Bill Walters along with Wild Bunch gang members, Elzy, Black Jack Ketchum and myself, all boarded the train at the Santa Fe station. Once the train was climbing thru the mountains southwest of Raton, New Mexico Territory, we would start commencing the robbery.

Siringo's plan would have worked, except that Black Jack overheard two of the undercover Pinkerton Agents, traveling incognito as passengers, going over the details of the scheme.

BlackJack told each of us what he had overheard. It was Bronco Bill Walters who lured Siringo towards the back of the train where we was waiting for him. A scuffle ensued, resulting in Elzy disarming the villain and physically throwing Siringo off of the moving train.

The train seemed to be traveling at such a high rate of speed that it looked to us that the blackguard had sustained a life-threating injury to his person. But alas it did not; Siringo did suffer a broken arm, ankle, several cracked ribs, a fractured skull. But even after all those injuries he persevered and survived. However, he does to this day still need the aid of a walking stick. I say a small price to pay, considering his villainous ways.

With Siringo out of the way, we decided to go ahead with the robbery. Black Jack held the two Pinkerton men at bay, disarming them and locking them together with their own shackles. We then proceeded to break open the mail car door and persuaded the agent at gunpoint to open the safe. Bronco Bill shot the man's big toe clean off of his left foot for dawdling. We then made our getaway.

It was the next day that a posse consisting of Special Agent Joe Lefors, now working for the Colorado & Southern Railroad, and five of his deputies found our trail and tracked us into Turkey Creek Canyon near Cimarron, New Mexico Territory.

As we were held up by a waterhole up on the high ground, we could see that the posse was advancing upon us, but our horses were in need of water and rest. We had no choice but to stand our ground. It was there at the watering hole that the posse engaged us in a great gun battle, resulting in two of the deputies being fatally wounded. We did manage our escape during the night.

The deaths of the two deputies slowed their pursuit of us, so we decided to split up and head for Hole-in-the-Wall. We had divvied up the shares from the robbery, fetching every man the tidy sum of $4000 each. Me and Black Jack would head north, while Elzy and Bronco Bill would travel due east then turn north after a days ride.

It turned out that a short time after the initial shootout, several members of the posse caught up and cornered Elzy and Bronco Bill, while still in the general area of the Territory. While escaping, Elzy's horse had suffered a minor sprain, forcing them to travel slow.

Special Agent Joe Lefors and his deputies engaged the outlaws in another gun battle, resulting in the wounding of Bronco Bill Walters. He along with Elzy was still able to make their escape, but Bronco Bill was found a few days later by Special Agent Lefors at an abandoned ranch, where he was arrested. Elzy had gone on alone.

"You go on." Bill said.

"You sure, I'll stay here and fight if'n you want to."

"No, I ain't up for another shoot out; I just don't have it in me, pardner. Sides, I'd just be slowing ya down. Now get!"

Bill was taken into custody, brought back to Santa Fe and while awaiting trial in the local hoosegow, a spinster looking woman, who claimed to be Bronco Bill's "cousin," named Jessica Pettibone, came a calling one evening and somehow managed to slip Bill a pistol.

That evening, when the deputy brought Bill his evening meal, he forced the lawman into the cell, hogtied him and to add insult to injury, Bill escaped on Special Agent Joe Lefors horse.

Phoebe Ann Mosey, better known as Annie Oakley, was traveling around with Buffalo Bill's Wild West show, performing as a sharpshooter when she met Butch and Sundance in Denver.

The boys were in Denver at the time enjoying the fruits of their labor. The two of them had just robbed a bank in Missoula, Montana and decided to go and enjoy themselves.

One night while they were dining at Delmonico's Steak House, a group of people from the wild west show came in. It was none other than Buffalo Bill and Annie Oakley along with several others from the show. Sundance was smitten the moment he laid eyes on the famous sharpshooter. He sent over a bottle of champagne to her with a note, "Cheers, Sundance."

"Butch, I think I'm in love." Sundance said.

"Don't you mean lust?"

"No, I mean it Butch, she's beautiful."

"Well, she is that."

She looked over and smiled, she spoke to Buffalo Bill who came by their table, stood there larger than life and asked, "You boys care to join us?"

"We wouldn't want to intrude." Sundance said.

"Come on boys, I'll introduce you to Little Sure Shot, Miss Annie Oakley."

They followed the buckskinned legend over to the table where the wait staff had added two more chairs to accommodate the newcomers.

"Annie, I'd like you to meet Butch Cassidy, and this here is the Sundance Kid." Buffalo Bill said.

"Gentlemen, please won't you sit down." Annie offered.

Sundance doffed his derby, "We'd be right honored, Miss Oakley."

"Annie, please." She said as she motioned for them to sit down.

As they sat down, Butch allowed Sundance to have the seat next to Little Sure Shot.

Buffalo Bill called the waiter over to the table, "Give us eight of the thickest steaks you got, with all the trimmings."

"Yes, sir!" The waiter snapped.

Bill turned to Butch and asked, "What brings you two scalawags to Denver?"

"Strictly pleasure, Bill, Strictly pleasure."

"I ain't seen you boys, since I was riding with Texas Jack Omohundro back in aught nine when we was doing the "Scouts of the Prairie" show. Thems were good times. Say you boys, looking for work? I could use a couple of rapscallions like you in my wild west show."

Butch laughed, "Well, you know Bill there'd be a couple of places that me and the Kid wouldn't be able to go to, if'n we did we wouldn't be able to leave for five to ten years if you know what I mean, and I think you do."

Bill laughed, as did the others at the table.

All the while Butch and Buffalo Bill were talking, Sundance and Annie were deep in conversation.

"How long you are you in town for?" Sundance asked Annie.

"I think three more days of shows, and then we're off to Chicago, you?"

Sundance looked deep into her eyes and said, "However many days you'll be here. May I see you again?"

"I'd like that." She said with a coy smile.

To get Sundance's attention, Bill said rather loudly, "Sundance, I remember you being quite the marksman, am I right?"

Sundance smiled at Annie and said, "I usually hit who I'm aiming at."

"Well, I just had a great idea, how about you and Annie have a contest of marksmanship? Annie Oakley versus the Sundance Kid."

"Bill, I'm no sharpshooter," Sundance admitted.

"And I'm no gunfighter, Bill." Annie professed.

"Okay, then not a contest. How about an exhibition of firearm skills; it will be sensational. What do you think?"

Annie glanced at Sundance, smiled, and said, "What do you think?"

"Aww, I don't know."

Annie gave Sundance a little wink, "Come on, it'll be fun."

"Oh, what the Hell, sure."

Annie reached over and took Sundance's hand under the table, held it and gave it a light squeeze.

Buffalo Bill stepped up to the giant megaphone, held up his hands to quiet the six hundred plus crowd and shouted, "Ladies and Gentlemen, welcome to Buffalo Bill's Wild West Show. Today we have a special treat for you. Not only do we have the world's greatest sharpshooter, Annie Oakley, but today only, we have one of the most famous and infamous gunfighters of all time, ladies and gentlemen, the Sundance Kid!"

The crowd went wild, hooting and a hollering, as Annie and Sundance walked out into the middle of the arena.

Annie was dressed in a plain beige colored dress, with a couple dozen or more medals, all shiny with colorful ribbons presented to her from foreign dignitaries from all over the world. They were given to her for her marksmanship and shooting skills.

She had long wavy raven black hair flowing out from under her Stetson cowboy hat. Annie waved to the crowd as she carried her signature Remington Beal's .32 caliber rifle casually over her shoulder.

Sundance felt a little self-conscience when he strolled out wearing all black, with the exception of a silver decorated vest, silver garter bands around his upper arms and a big, old, oversized silver buckle on his gun belt.

"I feel a might foolish in his flashy duds, Bill." He said to Bill after he got dressed in his costume.

"Nonsense, Sundance, it's all part of the show. Ya see people have this image of a gunfighter from all of the dime store novels they read. Just go out there and have some fun."

Annie set a playing card with the edge facing her. She then took 30 paces, turned, aimed and fired splitting the card in half. She then tossed dimes in the air and hit them in midair. She shot a cigarette from Buffalo Bill's lips; next Bill threw playing cards into the air and Annie would riddle them before they reached the ground.

For an encore, she lifted her rifle and fired at a lit candle, and with one shot she snuffed out the flame with the whizzing bullet. Finally, she knocked the corks out of champagne bottles without breaking the bottles.

Now it was Sundance's turn to shine. The plan was to have challengers come and stand by Sundance, and on the count of three, they would draw their weapon and see who could hit the target fifty paces away, not only the fastest but with the most accuracy.

As Sundance would always say, "Boot hill is full of fast guns. But it's the ones with the cool heads that are accurate and the ones still walking around."

Things were going good. People were having fun when things turned ugly, a young hothead wanting to make a name for himself, jumped out of the stands and headed towards Sundance shouting, "Come on old man, let's you and me go for real!"

"Son, I got no quarrel with you." Sundance said, holding up his hands, trying to calm things down.

The man walked over to where the target was opposite Sundance and took a stance for a gunfight.

Sundance looked around to see if anyone was going to step in, but no one did. He slowly took out his revolver and reloaded it, slid it back into the holster, and said, "On the count of three, you call it, Butch."

In a crowd of over six hundred, you could hear a mouse squeak a hundred yards away when Butch started the count.

Sundance had seen his kind before, wanting to make a name for themselves by killing a name. He also knew that most of the time these dime-store desperados like to cheat, Sundance was ready.

"One…Two…Thr…"

The little hoodlum went early, but Sundance was had anticipated the cheat, and even though the culprit drew slightly faster, it was accuracy that won the day.

Sundance slowly walked over to the dead man, shaking his head in disgust. Annie came to his side and asked, "Are you okay, Kid?"

"Yeah, what a waste."

Butch and Bill came over to them, Bill said, "I'm sorry Sundance, I should have figured something like this could happen."

"Don't worry about it, Bill. I'm okay. This is going to boost your sales through the roof." Sundance said, half-joking.

"I'm sorry to say you're right." Bill agreed.

"I think I could use a drink, Sundance, Annie care to join me?" Butch asked.

"Maybe later, Butch."

"Okay, Kid."

As Sundance and Annie walked out of the arena, she took his hand and said, "Shall we go to my place?"

"I'd like that, very much."

Sundance and Annie spent the next three days in Little Sure Shot's hotel room in the luxurious Brown Palace located in downtown Denver. They never left the room, they decided that after the incident trying to leave would be madness with all the reporters and photographers just waiting for them downstairs.

After three days, Annie had to go, she was scheduled to travel with the Wild West Show to Chicago.

Buffalo Bill came around to collect her early that morning.

"Are you ready, Annie?"

"Just give me a minute, Bill, I'll be down soon."

Sundance was standing by the window, staring out onto the bustling street below.

"Sundance, I'm sorry that things didn't turn out. I really am." Bill said apologetically.

"Not your fault, Bill."

"Well, tell Butch goodbye for me, you boys take 'er easy pardner, see ya'll down the trail."

"See ya, Bill."

Bill gave a quick salute, and he was gone, Annie walked over to Sundance and gave him a big kiss.

"Why don't you join the show?"

"What, kill someone every night and twice on Sunday's? No, I ain't cut out for show business."

"Will I see you again, Sundance?"

"Oh, probably not, Annie."

"Well, Sundance, it was fun."

"That it was."

"You take care now, you hear."

Annie picked up her rifle case and walked out, closing the door behind her. They never did see each other again. Annie married Frank Butler, an Irish American marksman who also worked in the Wild West Show. She died of pernicious anemia in 1926, Annie Oakley was 66. Years later, her grand-nephew, while examining her Remington rifle, he noticed scratched into the wooden stock the word 'Sundance.'

BlackJack and me finally made it back to the Hole-in-the-Wall, tales of our exploits proceeded us and were widely accounted in all of the newspapers across the west. Sundance saved me a copy of the Tombstone Epitaph, so I could read about our exploits.

A Desperate Fight Between Officers of the Law and Members of the Wild Bunch. Two Dead.

Santa Fe, March 31 – The news of a robbery of the Colorado and Southern Train perpetrated by several members of the infamous Wild Bunch gang in the New Mexico Territory about 30 miles from here has been received.

Pinkerton Agent Charlie Siringo and two others were waylaid by the gang and made off with more than sixteen thousand dollars in cash. Siringo received severe injuries but is expected to recover having been thrown from the train.

The mail car agent, Frank Hoyt was shot in the foot, resulting in the loss of a toe.

The members of the Wild Bunch included Bronco Bill Walters, William Ellsworth "Elzy" Lay, Black Jack Ketchum, and William "News" Carver.

Shortly after the gang's escape, Special Agent Joe Lefors and five deputies gave chase. During the pursuit the lawmen and the desperados engaged in a spirited gun battle, resulting in the deaths of deputies Thomas Coryell and William Byler.

However, days later Lefors and posse did come upon and captured a wounded Bronco Bill Walters, said to be hiding in an abandoned ranch.

When asked about Butch Cassidy and the Wild Bunch, Charles Siringo was quoted saying, "Butch Cassidy is the shrewdest and most daring outlaw of the present day. Butch Cassidy's Wild Bunch keeps a system of blind post offices all the way from Hole-in-the-Wall in northern Wyoming to Alma in southern New Mexico Territory. These post offices being in rocky crevices or on top of round mounds on the desert.

"But, no matter how smart and clever Butch Cassidy is, the law will prevail; time is running out for the Wild Bunch."

"So News, was the story in the paper a pretty accurate description of the goings-on?" Sundance asked.

"Yeah, pretty much. That Siringo turned out to be a real lowdown dirty scoundrel. I'm glad we threw him from the train. But just wish it woulda kilt him." I said.

"But at least you got your name in the paper."

"Yeah, and they even spelled it right." I said gleefully.

Elzy happened on by while Sundance, and I was a jawing, so I asked, "Any word about Bronco Bill?"

"News, the last I heard is that he had broken out of the Santa Fe jail with the help of an old whore and he skedaddled outta town on Lefors's horse. No one has seen or heard from him in weeks."

I said, "I bet he's held up somewhere with that whore, Bronco has always had a way with womenfolk, lucky bastard."

It wasn't too long after we all got back to Hole-in-the-Wall that Butch had set his sights on robbing the Union Pacific Flyer.

We robbed the train near Folsom, in the New Mexico Territory. A shootout ensued with local law enforcement, during which Elzy shot and killed Sheriff Edward Farr and Henry Love. As we were making our escape Elzy was wounded and taken into custody. He was tried and convicted of murder and was sentenced to life imprisonment at the New Mexico State Penitentiary.

We were dogged by several posses all the way to our hideout at Hole-in-the-Wall; and there were several shootouts as posses attempted one after another to enter, all resulting in the being repulsed, and being forced to withdraw.

No lawman has ever successfully entered Hole-in-the-Wall to capture any outlaw, ever.

I was visiting my brother in Bozeman, Montana. His wife had just passed, and he was feeling mighty poorly, so I decided to go visit him. I hadn't seen him in eight years, ever since I took to the life of thieving and criminality. Billy, my brother, was a farmer, always was a farmer, but since his wife died, he told me he had little interest in continuing farming. He decided to give the farm to his two boys, both in their twenties and getting ready to leave.

"So, got any plans." I asked.

"Nothing definite." Says he.

"Well, if you want, you can ride with Butch and me."

"Become an outlaw? Ain't it dangerous?"

"Can be, but if you ride with a good gang, like with Butch and the Wild Bunch it can be a good life."

"But, I've never shot anyone, I don't know if I could."

"Billy, you do what you have to. Tell you what, let's go give it a try."

"What, we go rob a bank?"

"Yup, on our way down to Hole-in-the-Wall. What'd say?"

"Just you and me?"

"Just you and me."

The town of Bridger was named for the Indian scout Jim Bridger, seems that back in 1898 the good folks wanted to name the town "Town" after one of the original settlers George Town, but George wouldn't have it. He wanted the town to be named after his good friend Jim Bridger.

The town had one saloon, one general store, one blacksmith, one dry goods store, one bank, and no sheriff.

Billy and me tied our horses at the hitching post, strolled into the bank pulled our pistols and announced that this here was a stickup.

At the time, there was only one teller in the bank; he was seated behind the counter eating a sandwich when we entered the bank. He kept on eating his lunch even after we alerted him to our intentions.

"Get a move on boy and fill this here sack with cash!" I roared as I cocked my pistol.

"We don't keep much money at this here bank, all the big money is kept in the bank at Absarokee, cause of the Stillwater Mine."

"Well, how much money you got?" I asked.

The boy reluctantly put down his sandwich and counted the money in the till it totaled out at forty-two dollars and eighty-seven cents.

"What about the vault?" Billy asked.

"Ain't got one, we only have on average, maybe one hundred dollars. But this here is everything we got, honest mister."

"Okay, hand it over." I said.

As me and Billy was leaving the back, the cashier pulled out a shotgun and let loose of both barrels, killing Billy and wounding me. I turned around and fired off all six rounds, striking and killing that no-good snake.

Killing a fella is one thing, but shooting someone in the back, makes you just a lowdown cowardly bushwhacker, and that goes against the code of the west.

I walked outside the bank carrying my brother's dead body, put him over his saddle, mounted my horse and shouted, "My name is News Carver and I just done robbed your bank and killed that there bank teller who shot my brother in the back. You folks should be ashamed of what that yellowbelly poltroon did, if he's the kind of people that you all are, I don't want your dirty money!"

As I rode off, leading my brother draped over his saddle, I emptied the sack of money on the ground. I could not believe that a town that was named after such a brave man as Jim Bridger could be so craven.

Butch and Sundance knew that it could take weeks for everyone to get back to Hole-in-the-Wall, and after a week or so, they got bored just sitting around. So, they decided to take the Wells Fargo & Co stagecoach south towards Santa Fe from Denver.

The roads, if you could call them that were dusty, bumpy, and slow; only about 5 miles an hour and 70 miles a day. The trip took six days of rough and tumble, kidney gouging torture, when they stepped off the stage, they both walked over to the Plaza Hotel and slept for two days.

They hung around Santa Fe for a couple of days drinking and gambling. It was when they were playing stud poker at the Long Branch Saloon that they first heard the rumors of a large payroll coming in on the stagecoach in two weeks time to supply the prodigious railroad worker's wages.

They traded in their stagecoach return tickets and bought horses, saddles, and gear, then headed north towards Arroyo Hondo along the Rio Grande River, twenty-five miles from the Taos Pueblo.

They planned to hit the stage after the scheduled stop at the Questa Stagecoach Station in the foothills of Flag Mountain north of Taos.

They arrived at Arroyo Hondo, that sits on a small tributary of the Rio Grande. The only thing there was the burnt-out remains of an early settler's adobe house. It looked to be abandoned for many years, probably the sodbuster was either killed or run off by the Indians of the Pueblo.

Sundance went off hunting while Butch set up camp within what was left of the roofless structure. Off in the distance, Butch heard the sound of a single rifle shot.

"Sundance," Butch said out loud.

About twenty minutes later, Sundance rode in with a six-point buck draped over his saddle.

"Hope you're hungry." Sundance said as he took the deer off of his saddle and hung it over what was left of the door jam so he could start to butcher it.

While Sundance was dressing the deer, he went off to collect firewood for the night. As he was returning to the campsite, that when they encountered four renegade Indians from the Taos Pueblo. I assumed that they had heard the shot and decided to investigate. They didn't seem threatening, nor did they seem friendly.

As they followed me into camp, I let Sundance know we had company.

"Sundance, we have guests."

Sundance smiled, so as to seem inviting, "Welcome, come, we will share our deer if you are hungry."

He was smiling, but he was ready to draw down on them if it came to that.

The leader stepped forward, held up his hand in peace and said, "I am Barking Crow, this is Two Bears, Running Elk, and there is Standing Bull, we will accept your offer."

"You speak very good English. Where did you learn to speak so well?" Butch asked.

"I speak Spanish, English, and a little Latin, I learned from the priests at the Pueblo, and of course, I still speak my native tongue."

Sundance approached them, "Come sit, what brings you out from the Pueblo, hunting for game?"

"We have been cast out, at least for the time being for going rogue. The elders say that we brought shame to the tribe."

"What did you do, to be cast out?"

"We refused to accept the white man's latest treaty. They want to take our scared mountains and control the waters of the Red Willow Creek from the Blue Lake that flows thru our Pueblo village. So, we are on the warpath against the bluecoats and any settlers that try and possess any of our scared lands."

"Well, we are not settlers nor are we blue coats. I guess you could say that we too are on the warpath against our government and big companies." Sundance said.

"I do not understand." Barking Crow said.

"You see, we take money from the government to protest the uneven distribution of wealth in the country. When we take the money sometimes, we give some of it away to needy people." Butch explained.

"So, you're thieves?"

"Basically, yes. Tomorrow, we're going to rob the Wells Fargo stagecoach, we believe that they will be carrying a lot of money. If you help us, we will share the money with you, half for you and half for us. You will be able to buy a lot of guns and bullets with that money, or you could buy food, blankets, and tools for the tribe."

"But, won't the blue coats come after us and our village?"

"Tell you what, how about if you stay hidden while Butch and I rob the stage and you be on the lookout to see if anyone is coming. If there is, then warn us with a shot into the air."

"Whadda say?" Butch asked.

"Let us talk amongst ourselves." Barking Crow said.

The four went off into the darkness to decide if they were interested in helping these two white men or possibly killing them, they chose the former.

Barking Crow said to the others, "If they try to double-cross us, we'll kill them."

Standing Bull said, "Let's eat!"

The next morning both Butch and Sundance were a little stiff from sleeping on the cold hard ground. Barking Crow and the others had a good laugh at that.

"White man too soft." Barking Crow laughed.

Butch shot back at them, "I'd like to see you boys spring up from a night on the ground when you're our ages; we're old enough to be your fathers."

Sundance looked at his pocket watch, "Butch, they should be heading our way soon."

"Okay, now if you see anybody heading our way, fire off a couple of rounds. You got that?" Butch asked Barking Crow.

"Understood. Then we meet back here to divide the money."

"Right."

"Butch, as I do not know you and Dances with the Sun, do not take offense at what I am going to say, but…"

"Listen, Barking Crow, we aren't going to cheat you. We'll meet you right here after the holdup. Lessen we are kilt."

Butch and Sundance rode down to the trail where the stage will be passing. They found good cover behind a small grove of towering pine trees and waited. They could see Barking Crow and his men up on the top of one of the foothills that would give them excellent viewing in all directions.

Butch noted that Standing Bear was waving and pointing in the direction of where the stage would be coming, he acknowledged by waving back.

"Sundance, here it comes, you ready?"

"Ready."

They pulled their bandanas up to cover their faces, pulled down their hats, and drew their guns. When the stage was almost on them, they spurred their horses Butch rode out on the driver's side so as not to give the cowboy riding "shotgun" a clear shot. Sundance circled around to get the drop on the man with the scattergun.

"Whoa! Whoa! Whoa!" Butch yelled as he grabbed the reins of the coach.

Sundance pulled up alongside the man riding shotgun and shouted, "Stand and deliver. Now drop that gun, pardner. Easy."

Once the man dropped the gun, Sundance got off his horse and bellowed to the people inside the coach, "Come out with your hands up, you will not be harmed if you do so."

Butch said to the two men up in the driver's box, "Come down nice and easy and bring the strongbox with you."

Meanwhile, Sundance had the five passengers stand in a line away from the coach. There were three men dressed in business attire and two women, looked to be an elderly mother and daughter.

"Folks we are not going to harm you if you do as you're told. So, just stand there quietly, and this will be over soon. Men deposit your firearms on the ground… slowly."

Sundance picked up each of their weapons, including the shotgun and emptied the out the shells and bullets on to the ground, tossing the guns off into the bushes, he then checked inside for weapons, finding none he mounted his horse and waited for Butch to give the all-clear signal.

Butch had the men lay the strongbox down on the ground and fired one shot that blew the lock off. He quickly opened it and there, were dozens of stacks of hundred dollar bills. He started grabbing the loot out of the box and began stuffing them into canvas bags that he had brought.

Once finished, Butch jumped on his horse and gave a whistle, which was the signal to Sundance that it was time to go, and said to the driver, "You wait here for an hour, we may or may be nearby, you wouldn't know. We might have an accomplice in those trees watching over yonder. If you leave before an hour, we'll come back and kill you, understand?"

The slightly overweight doughy driver nodded, "Understood."

Butch and Sundance rode back from the way the stagecoach had come, then doubled back and up the foothills to where Barking Crow and the others were waiting.

"Is there anyone coming?" Butch asked Barking Crow.

"No one."

Butch and Sundance began counting out and dividing the money into two piles. The split was three thousand dollars cash for Barking Crow and his band and three thousand for Butch and the Kid. There were also two small bags of gold, which Barking Crow said, "You take. Yellow rocks are bad medicine for my people, it drives the white man crazy. You take."

Butch and Sundance switched out two of Barking Crows horses for theirs since the folks at the stagecoach robbery could identify them, and they then changed their clothes.

"Barking Crow, Two Bears, Running Elk, and Standing Bull, thank you, and we wish you well." Butch said as he held up his hand in peace.

Barking Crow held up his hand, "t'ónya."

"Peace, to you as well." Sundance said.

I had been on the road for nearly three weeks after burying my brother Billy under a grove of Aspen trees next to Little Goose Creek. Little Goose Creek was the campsite of General Crook after the Battle of the Rosebud against the Sioux and Cheyenne, months after Custer lost the Battle of the Little Big Horn.

So, not far from where Billy lies in the town of Big Horn, although I was not far from Hole-in-the-Wall, I was weary and thought I would indulge in a hot bath and shave, afterward maybe I would partake in a couple hands of stud poker.

Feeling refreshed after my bath, I wandered over to the Big Horn Saloon for a beer and a sandwich. As I was enjoying my beer, I spied none other than Three-Fingered Jack McDowell, Jefferson "Soapy" Smith, and John Wesley Hardin sitting playing stud poker.

I could not resist, I walked over to the table and said, "Howdy fellas, might I join in?"

Soapy Smith looked up from his cards and said, "Well, I'll be God Damned if it ain't News Carver, hoe the Hell are you? Grab that chair and sit down. Boys, ya'll know News Carver?"

Three-fingered Jack and John Wesley both said that they had heard of me, but never had the pleasure, as did I.

John Wesley said, "News Carver, funny but I was just reading about your exploits in the small town of Bridger. It says that you and your brother robbed the bank and your brother got bushwhacked by the bank teller, who you upped and killed. Be that the truth?"

"That was the case."

"It also said that you threw the money in the street that you stole. That be accurate, too?"

"I told them that I couldn't cotton to stealing any money that was associated with such a dastardly deed as bushwhacking. It's just not Christian"

"I must say you did the right thing, News. I woulda done the same thing myself." Three-fingered Jack said.

We proceeded to engage in several hours of pleasantries, congenial conversation, consuming mass quantities of alcoholic libations, and stimulating gamesmanship.

"John, is it true that you killed six or seven men for snoring?" Asked Soapy Smith.

"They tell lots of lies about me. Well, it ain't true. I only killed one man for snoring." Hardin complained.

Three-fingered Jack said, "John Wesley, I notice that you wear your guns like nobody I've ever seen."

"I got my holsters sewn right into my vest, so the butts point inward across my chest, I find it the fastest way to draw. Let me show you." Hardin said as he stood to demonstrate.

I have never seen anyone so quick on the draw, he was lighting fast, but what was even more surprising was his pinpoint accuracy. There were two Mexican pistoleros standing at the bar facing each other. As they went to raise their shot glasses of whiskey, John Wesley Hardin drew both pistols and in a blink of an eye, he had shot both glasses from their hands.

The younger of the pistoleros drew his gun and shouted, "¡Oye! Qué demonios quién hizo eso?"

"It was me, Pancho. No disrespect, barkeep give my two amigos another couple more rounds on me." Hardin said coolly, still having both of his pistols drawn.

"My name is not Pancho, and I am not your amigo."

"Just take it easy now. We don't want this to get out of hand. Here have a drink." The bartender said, trying to diffuse the situation.

"I don't want no stinking drink, I want an apology." The young gunfighter said, sliding his pistol back into his holster and taking a stance of aggression.

The bartender leaned towards the pistolero and whispered, "Best leave it, son. That's John Wesley Hardin."

The young pistoleros thundered, "I'm waiting for my apology, John Wesley Hardin."

The other pistolero held up his hands and slowly walked away from his friend wanting no part of the fracas.

Hardin replaced his guns into his holsters, looked the kid in the eye, and said, "Do you need a count?"

"No."

KA-Pow! Pow!

The young pistolero lay dead on the bar room floor, shot once in the chest and once in the head. His compadre still holding his hands in the air backed out of the saloon, got on his horse, and casually rode out of town.

Moments later the Sheriff, Sheriff Tom Duncan waltzed into the saloon, sized up the situation and asked Hardin for his guns.

It was the first and only time I ever did see anyone use the "road agent spin" also known as the "Curly Bill spin." It's a gunfighter's maneuver that's a ruse used when you're forced to surrender your weapon to an unfriendly party.

Hardin reached down, picked his revolvers up from the holsters, and handed the guns to Duncan butts first, then swiftly rolled them over in his hands and suddenly Duncan was staring right into the barrels.

"Sorry, Sheriff, but if you don't mind, I'll just be on my way." He said as he eased towards the swinging doors. Before exiting the saloon, he peered over to us and said, "Boys, it was a pleasure, hope we can do it again real soon."

And with that, he was gone. That was the last time I ever saw any of those hombres again. John Wesley Hardin claimed to have killed 42 men. He went to prison for seventeen years. While in prison he became a lawyer and wrote his autobiography. He was killed one year after he was released from prison, shot in the back in an El Paso saloon.

Three-finger Jack and Soapy Smith were both gunned down after a bank robbery gone wrong, one of the robbery gang betrayed them for the reward.

Butch and Sundance were heading back up to Hole-in-the Wall from their adventure in Denver, when they decided to stop in Chugwater, Wyoming.

Feeling a bit gritty after the day's affairs, both Butch and Sundance felt that they needed a bath and a shave since they had been on the trail for several days.

They checked into the Chugwater Hotel and Emporium got two rooms, after getting gussied up they headed over to the Stampede Saloon & Eatery. The Stampede was your typical saloon. As you walk in your nose is assaulted with the smell of stale beer, cigarettes & cigar smoke, and breath-taking cheap perfume. Your eyes tear up from the cloud of smoke, that's thick as a foggy day in ole London town. Then there's the inevitable sound of the tinkling of an out of tune piano, loud boasts of drunkenness, the complaining of losing gamblers and the propositioning from the ladies of the night.

Butch and Sundance felt right at home as they made their way to the backroom where the food was being served.

"What can I get you, boys?" The waitress asked.

Butch figured that at one time she was a prime hooker. Whoring is a brutal business, and it wears on you hard. She was probably no older than forty, but she looked sixty. She had a pleasant disposition and a sweet smile.

"I'll have the steak." Butch said.

"How's the chili?" Sundance asked.

"You'd be wanting the steak, cowboy."

"Because?"

"We had an old tom cat that was always pissing on the cook's boots, well ain't seen that cat since cookie's made the chili."

"In that case, I'll have the steak, too."

There was only a hand full of people eating in the back, a couple of cowboys, what looked to be a few farmers and three or four town's folks. Everyone was quietly enjoying their meals when three men burst into the dining room and began acting rowdy and obnoxious.

"Hey, how about some service!" The youngest of the three shouted, banging his fist upon the table.

"Keep your pants on!" The waitress snapped back as she entered the room, carrying Butch and Sundance's meals. She placed their steaks down in front of them, then turned to the three big mouths.

"Yeah?" She barked.

The young man, slightly inebriated, asked, "How's the chili, sweet-cheeks?"

"Freshly made this morning, chock full of beans and meat."

"Beef?" He inquired.

"Okay." She smirked and gave a glance to Butch and the Kid.

"Ill have the Chili. Jack?"

Jack was Nathaniel "Texas Jack" Reed, not to be confused with Texas Jack Vermillion, Texas Jack Omohundro, Texas Tom Miles or even Tulsa Jack Blake. Nope, while all of them other Texas Jacks and what-have-you'd were for dirty, mean low-down mean hombres for sure, but old Texas Jack Reed, he was a real vile loathsome desperado.

Jack was known for his prowess as a robber of many a banks, stagecoaches and the occasional train. He usually would act on his own but was known to occasionally work with a gang. He operated primarily in the Rocky Mountains and in the Indian Territory, but sometimes he'd stray out on to the plains.

His two compadres were Buz Luckey, and the snot-nosed upstart was Tom Root. Tom was a full-blooded Cherokee who was reputed to be a natural born killer, cold-blooded and ruthless, he was rumored to have killed eleven people by the time he was eighteen.

Buz was a friend of Billy the Kid, and together they were involved in the infamous Gunfight at Brewer's Mill where there were a dispute with a ruffian by the name of Shotgun Roberts. It's not clear what the variance was all about, but as it turned out Billy and Buz had cornered Roberts in the mill where he barricaded himself. It was reported that during the three-hour gunfight Roberts sustained a stomach wound and took refuge inside the mill to tend to his wounds. Buz sneaked up to one of the windows in the mill, where he spotted Shotgun lying prone on the floor and shot him dead.

As Buz would later retell the story, it was that he and Shotgun shot it out face-to-face and his killing Roberts was due to his superior skills as a gunfighter.

Jack looked over to where Butch and Sundance were sitting and said to the waitress, "I'll have what those two are having."

Buz said, "Chili."

As the waitress started to walk away, Tom reached out and pinched her on the ass. She swung around and clocked him upside the head, knocking him out of his seat and onto the floor.

Root rose off the floor and drew his pistol and sneered, "You're dead bitch."

Both Sundance and Butch sprung up revolvers drawn, as did Texas Jack and Buz. They were in a virtual Mexican standoff pointing their guns at each other.

Texas Jack holding up one hand as to slow things down, yelled, "This don't concern you two."

"Whatta ya think, Sundance?"

Sundance ready to go at it replied, "They're discommoding my supper."

Texas Jack's eyes widened, "You're the Sundance Kid?"

"Yup. We doing this?" Sundance asked.

"Tom, stand down, boy. Ya hear me, put the piece away." Jack said as he took hold of the boy's arm.

"But she slapped me."

"Let it go boy." Jack said.

Butch and the Kid waited until the others holstered their guns before they put their weapons away. The waitress left the room to place the order. When she came back, she brought two pieces of apple pie to Butch and Sundance as a thank you, she smiled and mouthed "thank you."

Tom Root, Texas Jack, and Buz Luckey all got their order, with a little something extra. After dragging the steak on the floor and spitting in the chili, the cook found a couple of rat turds on the floor and added it to the kid's chili.

As Sundance and Butch were leaving to go out to the saloon and have a couple of whiskeys, they stopped at Texas Jack's table.

Sundance looked down at the three men, "We'll be leaving now, you leave the lady be."

"There won't be any problem." Jack said.

After they walked out, Tom mumbled, "I'm gonna get that bitch."

Texas Jack leaned in real close to Root and said, "Well, if'n you do, you're dealing with Butch and the Kid on your own. I don't fancy me getting in a shoot out with them two over some whore."

Sundance and Butch had just polished off their second shot of whiskey when Texas Jack and company came out from the dining room. The three of them sauntered up to the bar. Jack was getting ready to order three whiskeys when he turned and said to Butch, "Sorry 'bout the fracas; buy you and Sundance a drink?"

Butch glanced at Sundance and said, "That's mighty neighborly of ya, pardner."

Jack called over to the bartender, "Hey, barkeep, whiskeys for my friends."

When the drinks were all poured, Butch held up his glass towards Jack and said, "Here's mud in your eye."

Jack reciprocated, "And to you."

"So, how was your dinner?"

"Mine was a bit gritty, but Tom and Buz said that the chili 'bout the best they ever had."

Butch smiled, "I'm glad."

While Butch and Texas Jack were engaged in small talk, Sundance had his back to the bar leaning against it with one foot resting on the floor railing, keeping an eye on Tom Root. He could see that the kid was still stewing about being reprimanded by the waitress, he just wasn't going to let it go.

It wasn't too long after Jack, and his crew had left the dining room when the waitress came out and placed a "closed" sign on the doorknob. She walked passed everyone without giving the hothead eye contact. She did give a wink to Sundance as headed towards the swinging doors out to the street.

Tom Root finished his whiskey, then headed out to the street, Sundance did the same. Jack finished his drink, looked at Butch, and said, "I told him, I'm not dying for some whore."

Then he held up his glass and said, "Bartender, another please, this time make it a boilermaker."

Out on the street, Sundance could see that Tom Root was holding a large knife and gaining ground on the waitress, he grabbed her, forcing her up against the brick wall of the general store. Holding the blade to her throat, he said, "Now bitch, I'm going to carve you up."

Sundance shouted, "Hey, Root, let her go."

Without looking away from the woman and still holding the knife to her throat, Root shouted, "This don't concern you, Kid."

"I'm afraid it does, see she forgot to give me my change."

"Well, how about a pound of flesh." He said as he ever so slightly cut her neck.

"Tom, you go ahead, do the deed, and then I'll kill ya where ya stand."

Tom was in a bit of a jam, he was holding the knife up to the woman's throat, and his pistol was still down in his holster. He knew he couldn't slit the bitch's throat and get to his gun before Sundance killed him.

"If I let her go, you're going to kill me."

"No, if you let her go, I'll let you go for your gun, fair and square."

"Okay, kid. I'm gonna let her go."

Root took hold of the woman and turned her, so she was standing between him and Sundance, she was a shield for him.

Sundance knew that this wasn't going to end well for the girl, he felt he had to act, and quick. He calculated the odds of getting off a shot, hitting Root and not harming the woman. Time was running out he could see in Tom's eyes that he was ready to kill the girl, still using her body as a shield, and go for his gun.

Sundance drew and without taking aim, fired a shot from the hip, striking Tom Root in the right eye, killing him instantly. The woman stood there like a statue as her assailant melted away down from her towards the ground.

It was only then that she allowed herself to cry, Sundance walked over to her and held her as she broke down.

"You're alright now, Miss."

"I thought I was dead."

"Shall I take you to see the doctor?"

"No, I just want to go home."

"Very well, allow me to escort you home. You know I don't every know your name, I'm Sundance."

"Nancy, Nancy Richards. I'm sorry that I was so surly earlier to you and your friend."

"That's quite alright, I'm sure that after having to deal with rowdy cowpokes all day, you'd have to grow a bit of bark on you to deal with folks."

"Thank you."

"Now, let's get you home."

Butch, Buz Luckey, and Texas Jack were on their second round of drinks when they heard the shot. They waited to see if there would be return fire, but alas no. Looking at each other curiously, Butch said, "I'm afraid gentlemen, that that was Sundance's revolver, I fear the young Tom Root has met his demise.

"Oh, bartender, another round in remembrance of our dear friend."

"I shall accept your condolences as a sign of friendliness, Butch, but to be honest Tom Root was a real pain in the arse. He shall not be missed." Texas Jack said, holding up his glass to Butch.

"That's the truth." Buz added.

Moments later, Sundance walked thru the saloon's swinging doors, showing no sign of accomplishment or pleasure. Sundance never drew joy from taking another man's life. For him it was a matter of last resort.

"Can I get you a drink, Sundance?" Butch asked.

"That would be kind of you Butch. Texas Jack, young Tom Root is dead, I'm afraid he left me no choice. Folks nearby stated that it be a fair fight."

"I never had any doubt, Kid." Texas Jack said.

"His body is currently at the sheriff's office, if at some time you care to take him with you."

"I think not. Even though he rode with us, we do not feel a kinship towards him. I'm fine with folks of this fair city laying poor Tom to rest."

"And what of the woman?" Butch asked.

"Nancy Richards. She is fine, a little shaken up after her ordeal, but she seems quit resilient. I saw her home safely and proceeded to see the sheriff before returning back here."

After finishing his drink, Sundance announced that he was going back to the hotel and retire for the night.

The next morning as Sundance was getting ready to go downstairs for breakfast, he heard a light knock on his door. He quick, strapped on his holster, stood on the left of the door and asked, "Who is it?"

A small mousey voice said, "Mr. Sundance, my name is Perkins, Tony Perkins and I'm from the Chugwater Gazette. I was wondering if I might have a moment of your time?"

Sundance opened the door, to reveal a short, balding, overweight man, holding a pencil and pad of paper, the voice matched the man.

"Come in, Mr. Perkins."

"I hope I haven't come at an inopportune time?"

"Not at all, have a seat." Sundance said gesturing to the only chair in the room.

Perkins walked across the room and sat in the straight back chair located by the window.

"What can I do for you, Mr. Perkins?"

"Well, I have spoken to several of the people who had witnessed the unfortunate incident, and I wondered if there was anything you'd like to say?"

"There's not much to say. The man appeared to have evil intentions on the young woman. He held a long knife against her neck and from what I could surmise he intended to slit her throat. So, I stopped him from doing so."

"People say that Mr. Root was hiding behind Miss Richards, leaving very little room for error and yet you took the shot."

"It was a lucky shot."

"People say that you're a cracker jack-shot."

"Like I said, I was lucky. Is there anything else I can help you with?"

"What if you'd have missed?"

"Well, I guess you'd be writing a whole different story. Is there anything else, Mr. Perkins?"

Perkins stood and said, "No, Mr. Sundance, I believe that is everything. Again, thank you for your time."

"Its just Sundance and I'm glad I could be of some assistance."

The chubby old man walked out the door, then turned around and said, "People say you're a hero."

"Just a lucky shot."

It was back round July of 1933, Butch and the gang went down to Missouri, with our ladies in tow to kick up our heels and enjoy life for a change.

We drove down in 3 Ford Model "C" automobiles. Butch, Sundance and Kid Curry each bought one after a particularly good score making off with the payroll of the Idaho Panhandle Silver Valley Mine.

Things were getting hot, and it felt like they were closing in on us. We barely escaped the long arm of the law. They hounded us for over two weeks until we finally gave them the slip. It was a wild and wooly time all across the country. We was in a depression, which gave way to a lot of folks turning to crime.

We stopped one night in Platte City, Missouri, on our way to St. Louie at the Hotel Phillips downtown. After we checked in, we all decided to head on over to Stroud's Restaurant & Bar for some home-style pan-fried chicken and ice-cold beers. We was eating good, having a great time when all of a sudden, a group of people come sashaying into the diner. There were four men and two women, and they was acting loud and obnoxious.

They commenced to placing an order to take away and being real rowdy. Several people just got up and left. Sundance noticed that two of the men were carrying concealed firearms, as were we.

He leaned into the table so as not to be heard by outsiders and said, "You boys be at the ready, I do believe that those folks are looking to rob the place."

As we continued to eat, we had our weapons ready. They ordered six meals and six beers to go, while they was waiting, one of the men looked over to our table and nudged one of the others and whispered something. Suddenly they got real quite. The short man with greasy black hair grabbed a chair from another table and slowly dragged it over to our table, placed the chair facing away from us, swung his leg over the seat and sat down facing us, arms crossed over the back of the chair.

"You folks from around here?" He asked.

Butch looked him in the eye and said, "Who wants to know?"

"I'm Clyde Barrow, you might have heard of me."

"We heard of you." Butch answered as he continued to eat.

"That there is my brother Buck, his wife Blanche. Those fella's are W.D. Jones and Raymond Hamilton, and that's my sweetie Bonnie Parker."

"And?"

"And, so we was wondering if you might be Butch Cassidy?"

"I'm sorry to disappoint you."

"That's a shame," Clyde said straightening upright.

At this point, we were all expecting something terrible to happen. Our guns were halfway out of their holsters.

"Why?"

"If'n you were Butch Cassidy, I'd be right proud to team up with you and the Wild Bunch. I truly would. I'd dare say we would do some real earth shaking, and groundbreaking."

"I bet." Sundance said sarcastically.

"You know, I'm getting the feeling that you all don't like us."

Sundance said, "You're smarter than you look."

With that, Clyde sprung up from his seat and drew his gun from behind his back, but by the time he had cleared his holster, we had four guns pointed at him and his friends.

It was a Mexican standoff to be sure, we had our guns pointed at them, and they had their guns pointed at us.

Sundance stood up and said, "Listen here, squirt, you're nothing but low-life gutter-trash, and that goes for the rest of you, too. We don't work with the likes of you, sure we've killed, but we don't kill for pleasure, and we sure as shit don't execute people.

"Now, if'n you want a shootout, just say the word or make the first move, and we'll be happy to oblige ya, ain't that right Butch?"

Butch had his Colt 'Peacemaker' revolver pointing right at Clyde's crotch when he said, "That's right Sundance. Now, Clyde why don't you all just take your guns, and your food and leave, nice and easy. Cause we don't want these nice diner folks to have to clean up a lot of blood and guts, and your testicles up off the floor, now do we?"

Clyde glanced down and saw where Butch's Peacemaker was pointing. He looked back at his gang and quipped, "Come on, we don't need these old geezers, Wild Bunch, my ass. They'd probably end up getting us killed anyways."

We followed them outside, making sure that they didn't try any shenanigans. As they were driving away, the one named Raymond Hamilton began to fire at us. Sundance returned fire, striking him in the arm, forcing him to drop his pistol on to the road.

A couple of days later while we were listening to the radio, we had heard that the Barrow gang was involved in a gun battle at the Red Crown Tourist Court, just south of Platte City.

Apparently, someone got suspicious when one of the women went to buy food, beer, and bandages. The druggist contacted the local sheriff who put the cabin under surveillance. After seeing that the occupants had placed newspaper over the windows, he called for reinforcements, including and an armored car.

At around midnight a group of officers armed with Thompson submachine guns attacked. A ragging gun battle ensued. They did manage to escape but not before Buck sustained a massive head wound that blasted a large hole in his head exposing his brain. And Blanche, his wife, was blinded by shattering glass during the skirmish.

It was only days later in Dexter, Iowa, that Buck was killed after being shot in the back and his wife, Blanche was captured during a shootout with local police officers. Clyde, Bonnie, and Jones escaped on foot. Raymond Hamilton had left the gang the day before; three months later he was apprehended in Texas, charged with the murder of Deputy John Bucher, tried, convicted and executed in the electric chair at the Texas State Penitentiary, Huntsville.

Bonnie and Clyde went on for almost another year before they betrayed by W.D. Jones and were gunned down on a rural road in Bienville Parish, Louisiana.

When word came of their demise, Butch commented, "Good riddance to bad trash."

Sundance said, "Those two gave outlaws everywhere, a bad name."

By 1940, most of the original members of the Wild Bunch were either in prison or dead. Recently, Black Jack Ketchum had been convicted and sentenced to death by hanging in Clayton, New Mexico Territory. Unfortunately for Black Jack, nobody had any experience in conducting hangings; it turned out that the death rope was too long, and since Black Jack had gained a significant amount of weight during his time in jail, he was decapitated when he dropped through the trap door.

It was shortly after Black Jack's gruesome death that Butch approached Governor Heber Wells of Utah with the possibility of him granting an amnesty for Butch and the remaining Wild Bunch.

While Governor Wells was attempting to broker a deal with the Union Pacific Railroad to drop their criminal complaints against us, Butch just couldn't resist, so we robbed the Union Pacific train No.3 near Tipton, Wyoming, thereby ending any chance for amnesty.

That's when Sundance had the idea that we should maybe flee the country. With the FBI and law enforcement becoming more and more sophisticated and most all of the headline criminals like John Dillinger, Baby Face Nelson, Ma Barker, Al Capone, Bugsy Siegel, Bonnie and Clyde, and Machine Gun Kelly all dead or in prison it would be just a matter of time before we were number one on the FBI's most wanted. Besides, the world looked more and more to be on the brink of another World War, what better time to leave.

We had heard stories that the President of the Union Pacific Railroad, Mr. E.H. Harriman had assembled a private army of bounty hunters to track down Butch, Sundance and what was left of the Wild Bunch and either bring us to justice or kill us. It was said that he hired the best of the best, Lord Baltimore, Joe Lefors, G.H. Theil, William J. Burns, our old nemesis Charles Siringo.

After many hours of discussions, it was decided that we would leave. The only question was where we decided that one of the only safe places would be South America. It didn't look like they would be getting too involved in the war if and when it came.

Having done a bit of research we picked Argentina, as their country seemed to be the closest fit to our culture, with their Gauchos and cattle ranches, plus we all spoke enough Spanish to get by.

So, it was Butch, Sundance, Kid Curry, and me who took the Union Pacific train from Boulder to New York City. Butch said it was the first time that he was ever on a train that he didn't rob.

We spent five days in New York City. I didn't like it; it was too big and crazy for me. Up until that point, the biggest city that we had ever been to was Denver, and Denver looked like a dinky little town compared to New York City.

The four of us stayed at the Westchester Hotel on Broome Street, down in the Bowery and traveled under assumed names. Butch was Brad Thomas, Sundance was Tommy St. John, Kid Curry went by the name John Hanson, and I was Roger Everhart. The Westchester was a really deluxe hotel, it even had an elevated train outside, I could see it pass right outside my window; what will they think of next?

It wasn't too long before Butch received a knock on his door. Standing there were two men stone-faced, wearing overcoats and fedoras, with their hands in their pockets.

The taller of the two asked, "You Brad Thomas?"

"Depends."

"Depends on what?"

"Depends on who you are?"

"It don't matter who we are; my boss wants to see you."

"And he would be?"

"Charles Luciano."

"Never heard of him."

"Don't matter, he's heard of you, and he wants to see you."

"You go tell Mr. Luciano if he wants to see me, he knows where I am."

And with that, Butch slammed the door. He took three steps back and waited. Seconds later, the door came crashing open from the force of them kicking it in.

Butch stood there with his Smith & Wesson .38 pointing directly at them.

"Do you want me to blow your head off, or are you going to go tell your boss if he wants to see me, he has to come here?"

"You're a dead man."

Butch cocked the gun and said, "Oh, yeah, you owe me five dollars for the door, leave it on the table."

The man reached into his pants pocket and threw a five-dollar bill on the floor.

"I said the table dip shit, now bend down and pick it up and put it on the table."

The man begrudgingly did as he was told, all the while sneering at Butch.

"Thank you, now you may go."

As the two of them walked towards the elevator, people were starting to peek out from their rooms to see what all the commotion was about.

Butch picked up the phone and dialed zero for the operator.

"Hello, this is Mr. Thomas in room 308, could you send someone up to repair my door, it seems that some bit of trash knocked it open. Thank you."

Butch relayed the story to us. Neither Sundance nor myself had ever heard of this Luciano character. Butch asked if I would nose around and see what I could come up with.

Meanwhile, Sundance was adamant that he was going to stay with Butch until we sorted this out.

Well, it didn't take me more than ten minutes to get the scoop on this Charles Luciano mug. It seems that he was the top dog of this large Italian gang known as the "Commission."

The Commission was made up of the five major crime families in New York and this guy Luciano was appointed the chairman. This Luciano was nicknamed "Lucky." The buzz on the streets was that it was because of all the escapes from murderous attacks, like one back in '29 that gave him his scarred chin and drooping right eye.

I reported back to Butch and Sundance what I had found out.

"This is one tough mutt, and the goons he has working for him would just as soon slit your throat as look at you."

"We've dealt with worse." Sundance said.

The phone in Butch's room rang and Butch walked over and answered it.

"Hello, yes, sure send him right up."

Butch hung up the phone, "It's a Mr. Luciano and friends."

Moments later there was a knock on the door, Butch answered it with Sundance and Kid Curry standing off to one side each holding a .38 Smith & Wesson in both hands behind their backs. Butch also had a revolver in his right hand.

Standing there was a middle-aged, well dressed Italian man with a large scar on the left side of his face holding his hat in his hand. Behind him was the thug who kicked in the door, with his hat also in his hands looking very sheepish.

"Mr. Cassidy, my name is Charles Luciano, I've come to apologize to you personally for the actions of my men. Vinnie, don't you have something to say?"

The fireplug of a man stepped forward and said, "Yo, like da boss says, I am very sorry to bring you any incontinence."

"Thank you, Vinnie, I know that you sincerely meant it." Butch said with a hint of sarcasm that went right over the big jamoke's head.

"Mr. Luciano, I'm afraid you have mistaken me for somebody else. I'm Brad Thomas."

"Sure, sure. It's my business to know everyone who comes into my city and everyone who goes out, Mr. Butch Cassidy. And those two handsome cowboys holding two pistols behind their backs must be Kid Curry and the Sundance Kid. It's a pleasure to meet you both. Oh, and you all can put your pieces away, we're not packing any heat, if you know what I mean."

Sundance and Curry both laid their guns down, far enough away to appear innocent, yet close enough to get if something terrible should happen.

"Your city?" Butch asked.

"Hey, it's just a figure of speech, you know whadda mean."

"So, Mr. Luciano, what can Sundance and I do for you."

"Nuttin, I've admired your work, you know what I mean. You guys got class, not like some of these mutts running around today, going in half crazy, shooting up the joint, killing innocent people. You know what I mean, no class."

"Thank you, won't you come in?"

Luciano turned to Vinnie, "Not you, you go tell Mario to come up armed, and stay outside."

Lucky took a step inside and said, "Hey, I hope you'd guys don't mind, but I have lots of enemies, and I need a show of muscle everywhere I go. They don't call me Lucky for nuttin. They'll stay outside, my word."

"Come in, Mr. Luciano, and please have a seat."

"Call me Lucky."

"Come in… Lucky."

Luciano walked in, sat down in the chair by the window and as the train roared by, was briefly distracted.

Butch brought him back by saying, "I'm sorry Lucky, but we aren't sophisticated in the New York crime scene, coming from out west and all."

"Hey, that's okay, I mean with all these gavones going around trying to prove how tough they are, trying to get their names in the papers, thinking that their big shots. You know what I mean? But it's the wise guys that know, the ones that you don't hear about, the ones you don't even know their names. They're the ones that have the real juice.

"So, whadda you boys doing in town?"

"We're just here for a few days before we head off to South America."

"South America, what the fuck you going to South America for?"

"We're beginning to top the charts on the FBI's most wanted, so we thought we'd lay low way down south."

"Hey, if you guys want, yous can come work for me; we don't worry about no stinking Feds, or police. They leave us alone as long as we don't kill any civilians. I'm into drugs, prostitution, gambling, loan sharking, extortion, and the occasional whack job. We could use a couple of old pros like yourselves, whadda say?"

"Lucky, we're just humble bank robbers, and although we appreciate your offer, I think we'll have to pass."

"Ah, fugget about it. How's about I take yous all out for a night on the town, Lucky Luciano style? I know there's three of you's, where's your amico, News?"

"He out running some errands."

"So, how's about me picking you all up at eight, out front. You all got tuxedos?"

"Fraid not."

"Not a problem, I'll have my guy, Luigi come by and fix you up. So, it's all settled, I'll see yous at eight."

Lucky got up and walked towards the door, he shook both Butch's and Sundance's hand and was just about out the door when Butch asked, "Lucky, I'm curious, how did you know who we were?"

"Like my father once told me, knowledge is power. It's what you don't know that'll kill ya."

We were down in the lobby at eight o'clock when we noticed three big black limousines pull up to the hotel. Two goons get out of each car and start looking around like they were going to be attacked. We haven't seen such protection since that time we saw General Nelson Miles attend a pow-wow with Red Cloud at the Taos Pueblo in New Mexico.

It was Butch, Sundance, Kid Curry and myself. We had just robbed the National Bank of Arizona in Phoenix, and we was hightailing it out of Arizona because a large posse was on our trail. Butch figured we'd sneak thru the Indian reservation and give them the slip, which we did. And that's how we came to be at the Taos Pueblo.

Butch and Sundance had been there before and had made a friendship with several of the warriors: Barking Crow, Two Bears, Running Elk, and Standing Bull. The plan was to give them a small cache of weapons in exchange for their help.

We figured we had about a six-hour lead on the posse. When we got there, we were taken aback by all the U.S. Cavalry that was at the Pueblo. There must have been close to a hundred. It looked like the whole tribe was standing out in the center of the Pueblo surrounded by soldiers by the edge of Red Willow Creek that runs down the middle of the village.

As we approached, one of the sentries stopped us; "Halt! You men can't come in here."

"What's going on, soldier?" Butch asked.

"Official army business. I'm sorry, but you'll have to leave."

"Why, don't want witnesses?" Sundance asked sarcastically.

"If you men don't leave right now, I'll have to arrest you."

"Come on, boys, we'll come back after they kill everyone." Butch said.

We rode along the Rio Pueblo de Taos downstream for about a half a mile and rested under a grove of Honey Locust's trees and waited for the shooting to start.

We had some idea why General Miles was at the Pueblo, the Ghost Dance.

You see, Old Red Cloud was one of the prominent chiefs of the Tiwa tribe that believed in the growing religious movement known as the Ghost Dance ceremony.

The movement began soon after the Wounded Knee Massacre, or as the white folks called, it the Battle of Wounded Knee.

There wasn't any battle at Wounded Knee Creek. It all happened back in the winter of 1890 on the Lakota Pine Ridge Indian Reservation in South Dakota. It started when gold was found in the Black Hills, which was sacred land to the Lakotas. It was given to them as part of a peace treaty, that is until gold was found there. Then Uncle Sam decided they wanted it back. We couldn't have them stinking Indians be sitting on a mountain of gold; no, gold was a white man's privilege.

So, on the morning of December 29th, the brave men of Custer's 7th Cavalry began to disarm the Lakotas. What happened next is a matter of dispute. The soldier's version is that while disarming the natives, one of the warriors fired a shot and the army's appropriate response was to kill over 300 men, women and of course all the children, too. Sadly, twenty-five courageous soldiers were also killed that day.

The dead Lakotas were buried in an unmarked mass grave, while over twenty gallant soldiers of the 7th Cavalry were awarded the Medal of Honor for their bravery and courage in defeating such a ferocious adversary.

A short time later, a Paiute medicine-man, Wovoka had a vision in which God came to him and spoke to him, telling him that by practicing the Ghost Dance ceremony, the white man would leave their lands and their ancestors would come back to live in peace for eternity.

The religion spread like wildfire throughout the entire west, and this scared the bejesus out of the white settlers. So what did the U.S. government do? You guessed it, they sent in the army to kill any Indian that they even suspected of being a member of this radical movement, or participated in the dance; be it man, woman or child.

The General wanted assurances from Red Cloud that no one at the Pueblo was a member of the Ghost Dance cult. He warned the chief what the consequences would be death.

Red Cloud told Miles that none of his warriors were participating in the Ghost War, even though they were. With that, the cavalry saddled up and rode out. They headed south, heading right towards us. As they rode past, Sundance shouted out to the sentry who we had encountered, "Kill any Indians, today?"

To which he replied, "The only good Indian is a dead Indian."

There came a thunderous roar and cheers from his fellow soldiers.

Anyway, Luciano's "soldiers" reminded me a lot of the Cavalry of General Miles. They both were looking for someone to kill and would enjoy the experience.

From the middle limo, the back window rolled down, and we heard Luciano shout out, "Come on, boys get in."

The four of us all climbed into the back of the stretch limo, sitting in the back seat Lucky sat with two beautiful women, one on either side. We sat on the seats opposite them.

"Champagne?"

"You got anything stronger?" Sundance asked.

Lucky said, "Sure, push down on that panel next to you."

Sundance did, and two Waterford Crystal carafes of whiskey with four crystal glasses popped up.

"Gentlemen, help yourselves."

"Thank ya kindly, Mr. Luciano."

"Lucky, call me Lucky, please."

Sundance poured the four of us a glassful of rye, I held up my glass and said to our host, "Here's mud in your eye."

"What does that mean? It sounds a bit insulting." Luciano asked.

"No, it's a good thing, you see it's from the Bible. It's when Jesus spat in the dirt and rubbed the wet dirt or mud into the eye of a blind man, and then the man was healed." I explained.

"Ah, very good, I will start saying that, if you don't mind?"

"Feel free, I didn't come up with it."

Luciano lifted his champagne glass up, "Here's mud in your eyes."

After finishing off his drink, he said, "You boys are in for a real treat. We're going to the Copacabana, the most exclusive joint in all of New York City. Yeah, you see a good friend of mine's the owner, Frankie Costello, so we're going have the best seat in da house."

When the three limos pulled up to 10 East 60th Street, there were dozens of people standing out front, some trying to get in and even more, people waiting around to see what famous celebrities are going in.

There was a gaggle of press with their photographers in tow hoping to get pictures and bits of gossip for their papers. Right before we arrived, Bing Crosby, Gary Cooper, and Betty Grable got there. They signed autographs for their fans and posing for pictures, which was quite a contrast from when we arrived. Lucky's goons made sure nobody got close, and they went after anybody taking photos. If someone was foolish to snap a picture, one of his thugs would grab the camera and smash it on the ground, while another would rough up the offender with a couple strategic blows to the gut.

One gutsy young photographer wanting to make a name for himself did manage to get a photograph and made it off safely. It was in the society pages of the Daily News. There was the picture of our host with those beautiful ladies, one on each arm, and there was Butch, Sundance, Kid Curry, and even me. The caption under the photo read "Lucky Luciano and friends taking in the show at the Copa."

I have to admit that of all the bars, dance halls and casinos that I had ever been to, this place was the classiest. Everyone was dressed to the nines. The women were all beautiful, the food and drink was the best that I ever had, and the entertainment was great. We saw the comedian Bob Hope and singer Peggy Lee. It was a night I won't ever forget.

The other thing I won't forget was the gunfight we encountered in Little Italy on the way back to the hotel. We stopped for drinks at Scungilli Bar – Sea Food restaurant. We just left the Copa and were driving back to the hotel when Lucky said, "Hey, you boys hungry? Me, I could use a little something to eat, maybe some clams casino, whadda say?"

Butch not wanting to be rude, after the night out on the town, said, "Well, maybe something light, after all, it is one in the morning."

"Sure, sure light. For you, I think a little Pasta Fazool."

When we got there before we got out of the car, Lucky's Boys went in to make sure everything was secure. A few minutes later they gave the all-clear.

Scungilli was a small mom and pop restaurant with ten tables, a bar with eight stools, and two waiters. We sat at a table that was always reserved for Lucky and his Boys. There were four other tables where different size groups eating huge portions of food.

The four of us sat down at the table, with Lucky facing the door, while two of his gunsels stood behind him keeping watch. An old man dressed in black pants, a long-sleeve white shirt, and suspenders carrying menus approached the table.

"Yo, Vinnie!"

"So good to see you again, Mr. Luciano." The old man said with reverence.

"Vinnie, these are my special friends. I want you should treat them right." Luciano said as he handed the old man a hundred dollar bill.

"I shall treat them as if they were my own family, Mr. Luciano.

We all ordered our meals and were enjoying a couple glasses of Chianti when one of Luciano's men stuck his head in the door and said, "Hey, Boss Bugsy just pulled up."

Lucky smiled and said, "Molto bene! My old friend Bugsy Siegel, you boys will like Bugsy he's a funny guy."

A few minutes later, a tall, sharp, good-looking man walked in with two of his henchmen right behind him. He came over to our table, and he and Lucky greeted each other with a fake kiss on both cheeks, I guess that must be some sort of Italian thing, but I can tell you that out on the range that kind of thing just wouldn't be abided.

"Bugsy, I want to introduce you to a couple of my new friends, this fella here is Butch Cassidy, this is the Sundance Kid, and those fellas over are Kid Curry and News Carver. Boys this is my goombah and associate, Bugsy Siegel."

Bugsy snapped his fingers, and his two goons stood next to Lucky's goons behind them. He sat down next to Lucky, lit a cigarette and called Vinnie the waiter over to the table and said, "Yo Vinnie I'll have some spaghetti alla carbonara and bring us a couple bottles of Masciarelli Montepulciano for the table."

"Si, right away, Mr. Siegel. Right away." Vinnie said, and off he ran.

"So, you boys are the Wild Bunch, huh? I've read about you guys, I like your style, fabulous stuff."

"Thank you, Mr. Siegel." I said.

"Bugsy, my friends call me Bugsy and any friends of Lucky's are friends of mine." He said, smiling a big toothy smile.

He leaned into the table, looked around to see if anybody was listening and asked, "Sundance, are you as fast and as good a shot as people say? How many people you killed?"

Sundance hated when people tried testing him, he said, "I never kept count, and as far as my marksmanship, I'm still standing."

Lucky elbowed Bugsy and said, "I like this guy, he's modest, not like that these trigger happy gavones we got running around here, am I right?"

"When you're right, you're right." Bugsy replied.

"Hey Sundance, hows about you show Bugsy how good a shot you are?"

"Here? I couldn't fire a gun off in here, all the noise, and the people, too dangerous."

"Are you kidding? Yo, Vinnie, is it okay if my friend here pops one-off, just for fun?"

Vinnie looking nervous said, "Yeah, sure, Mr. Luciano."

Lucky looked at us, smiling and said, "See, no problem."

He then stood up and said, "Ladies and Gentlemen, may I have your attention. Now there's no need for any of yous to be scared, but my friend here is going to give us a quick demonstration of his marksmanship, and I will buy all of yous dinners as my way of saying thank you. Whadda ya say?"

The people at the other tables and bar were all nervous, but not wanting to upset two of New York's most notorious gangsters, they all looked at each other and started to clap.

"See, what did I tell you, no problem." Lucky said.

"What's my target?" Sundance asked, knowing he was boxed in a corner.

Bugsy got up, walked over to the bar, and placed three bottles of Chianti spaced about two feet apart on the bar. He walked over to Vinnie and took out a wad of hundred dollar bills and counted out two thousand dollars and said, "Here, this should cover any damage. Sundance hit the bottles."

Sundance got up from his chair and walked to the other side of the room opposite the bar, about forty feet away. He took his Colt 45 pistol that he had tucked in his belt behind his back and held it down by his side.

"Anytime you're ready, Sundance." Lucky said.

In a blink of an eye, Sundance brought the pistol up and fanned the hammer back on the Colt three times, *KAPOW! KAPOW! KAPOW!*

The noise was deafening inside the small restaurant. After the smoke clears, the three bottles were still standing.

Bugsy laughed and said, "Marksman my ass, he missed all three."

Sundance tucked the pistol back into his belt behind his back and sat down.

Butch said, "Go check the corks."

Bugsy and Lucky slowly walked over to the bar to investigate, they discovered that all three corks had been blown out of the bottle, with no damage to the glass bottles.

They both turned around with their mouths open aghast.

"I would have hated to waste three good bottles of wine." Sundance said with a grin.

"Jesus Christ! That was incredible." Lucky said.

"My God, that was amazing. That was the best shooting I've ever seen. I apologize for my remarks earlier, please forgive me." Bugsy pleaded.

Sundance smiled, "That's quite alright."

The people in the restaurant started to applaud and laugh, they too were skeptical when they saw the three bottles still standing, but soon were awed when it was revealed that the corks had been shot out.

Sundance turned to the people and gave a quick wave of gratitude.

Bugsy said, "What will it take for you boys to work for me? Name your price."

"Fugget about it, Bugsy. I already asked they're not interested."

"I'm planning on opening up a casino out in Las Vegas, and I could use a couple of good men like yous out there." Bugsy said.

"Las Vegas? There's nothing out there but sand and scorpions." Butch said.

"Now, but give me five years, that joint is going to be hot, baby, hot!"

I said, "Hot is right, it's a thousand degrees in the sun."

"But people aren't going to be in the sun; they're going to be inside the air-conditioned casino losing all their money, their houses, their kid's college funds, everything. Cause people love to gamble, and they're suckers.

"Ya see, I'm not going to have any windows or clocks, so they won't know what time it is, and I'll give them free drinks. The more they drink, the more they'll lose. It's going to be like printing money. Are you sure you boys don't want in?"

"We appreciate your offer, Bugsy, but no." Butch said.

The rest of the evening, we just made small talk and every now, and then the topic of Las Vegas kept popping up. As the evening was winding down, Sundance had been noticing that a group of three men at a table near the door were acting oddly. He nonchalantly brought his pistol from behind him to place it on his lap, leaned over to Butch and whispered, "Keep your eye on the three hombres to your right."

Just as we were preparing to leave, the three men jumped up and began to fire in our direction. Two of Bugsy and Lucky's men were hit. Kid Curry, Sundance, and Butch started to return fire, while I leaped over toward Bugsy and Lucky knocking them both down out of their chairs and onto the ground.

The commotion was over in seconds; Kid Curry and Butch hit one of the gunmen, while Sundance killed the other two.

Bugsy and Lucky got up off the floor and walked over to the three dead assassins. Their bodyguards followed close behind.

Lucky looking down on the bodies asked the henchmen, "You recognize any of these mugs?"

Bugsy man answered, "Yeah, they work for Bugs Moran."

"He's strictly, Chicago." Lucky said.

"Maybe he's looking to expand." Bugsy quipped.

"You boys saved our lives, we owe you guys. Whatever you want. It's yours, anything." Lucky said.

"That's right, that goes for me, too. You boys are goombahs for life. If ever yous should need anything, you got it." Bugsy said.

Sundance smiled and said, "Fuhgeddaboudit."

Lucky and Bugsy both laughed and gave us all fake kisses on our cheeks and big hugs.

"I'm serious, anything you need." Lucky said.

"Well, there is one thing we could use." Butch said.

"What's that?" Lucky inquired.

"A cache of weapons and boxed to pass thru customs. Think that's possible? Butch asked.

"You got it."

Just then we began to hear the sound of police sirens.

Lucky said, "We better take it on the lam, come on."

As we were leaving, I asked, "What about your two men?"

"Fuhgeddaboudit 'em. Their families will be taken care of, but we gotta run." Lucky answered as we got into the limos and sped away.

FIVE RUBBED OUT AT RESTAURANT IN A HAIL OF BULLETS DOWN IN LITTLE ITALY.

NEW YORK, N.Y., July 18.–Three known Chicago gangsters from the Bugs Moran Gang along with two noted members the "Lucky" Luciano and Bugsy Siegel's gang, Murder Inc. were shot to death in an apparent shootout at Scungilli's Restaurant, Little Italy.

Earlier that evening, Luciano was seen in the company of two women and four unknown men entering the Copacabana. (See photo above).

This newspaper wonders if this could be the beginning of an intercity gang war? When asked for a comment, Bugs Moran said, and we quote, "I don't know nuttin 'bout no killing, I ain't never seen this mugs before."

"Lucky" Luciano said, "I was home visiting my mother."

New York City Police Chief John Mahoney said that the investigation is ongoing, and arrests are imminent.

The next morning, as I was making my way to have breakfast in the hotel coffee shop, I stopped by the lobby newsstand and picked up a copy of the New York Tribune, where I saw on the front page, a large photo of us going into the Copa with Lucky.

"Hey, Butch did you fellas see this?" I said as showed them the front page.

"Well, that's not good." Sundance said.

"Yeah, we better be careful and not be seen together. We'll split up and just meet on board the ship on Friday." Butch whispered.

Both Sundance and I got up from the table and left from different doors. I ended up having breakfast at a Horn & Hardart Automat. It was like nothing that I had ever seen before.

It was a huge boxy room with shiny, lacquered tables with women with rubber tips on their fingers in a glass-enclosed booth giving customers these special five-cent coins to be used in these food machines. You'd drop the coins into slots and turn a chrome-plated knob, a little glass door would pop open, and you would take out the food or drink.

Then in a few seconds, someone from behind the doors would replace the item that you just took out with another. You would slide your tray down on a chrome counter and pick and chose whatever dishes you liked. You had your choice of either hot or cold meals. I liked it, it was fun, although I did miss having a waitress you could flirt with.

Over the next three days, I didn't see Butch or Sundance, although we did talk to each other on the hotel phones in our rooms.

Butch did tell us of his meeting with Lucky and Bugsy in regards about the cache of weapons that they had promised to gift us for saving their lives.

Lucky had sent a car to pick Butch up at the hotel on Thursday morning. He was driven to the Capricorn Lounge, a "Social Club" located on Flatbush Avenue in Brooklyn.

When they got there, there were two of Lucky's men standing guard outside. They looked to be loitering, but they were very much on duty. As Butch passed by, he could see their gun bulges under their BanLon shirts.

Butch was surprised how modest the place was; a half dozen wooden tables with chairs, a bar with dozens of bottles of assorted liquors and whiskeys, a coffee machine at one end of the bar, and a jukebox in the corner playing Frank Sinatra tunes.

The place was dark, and coming in from the sunny outside, it took Butch a few minutes to get his eyes adjusted. He heard Lucky before he could see him.

"Butch, come in, come in." Lucky said as he stood up from a table in the back.

As Butch started to walk toward Lucky, one of his goons approached to frisk him, Butch held up his left hand and had his right hand on the handle of his Colt, when Lucky shouted, "It's okay, he's my goombah. Butch come, come."

The thug backed down and went back to his station and assumed his position.

"Butch, you have to forgive me, it's just that one can never be too careful, you understand."

"Sure. It's just that I don't abide someone laying hands on me, you understand."

"Scusa, scusa. Butch, I meant no disrespect."

"It's okay, Lucky."

"Bugsy should be here any minute. Can I offer you something to drink?"

"A whiskey would be nice."

"Tony, un whiskey per il mio amico e prenderó un espresso."

Tony, the bartender, was a twenty-something overweight, slightly mentally challenged Italian boy that had a clubfoot; he seemed to be the club's mascot.

When Tony brought over their drinks, Lucky slipped him a fifty-dollar bill.

"Thanks, company." Lucky said.

"Grazie. Anything else I can bring yous?"

"Naw, we're good."

Tony hobbled back to the bar and stood behind waiting for another order.

It wasn't too long after Tony brought the drinks that Bugsy walked in from the rear exit.

"Saluti a tutti." Bugsy said in a singsong manner.

He slapped Lucky on the shoulder and shook Butch's hand, "Greetings my friend, good to see you again."

"Good seeing you, too."

Bugsy gave a wave to Tony, the bartender and said, "Yo, Tony. My usual per favore."

"Yes sir, Mr. Siegel."

"So, Butch the reason we had you come down here is to show you what all we was able to put together for yous." Lucky said with a big smile on his face.

"Yeah, you guys could start a war with this stuff." Bugsy added.

"Come on back to my office." Lucky said as he rose from the table.

The three of them walked to the back of the club to a metal door with a wire mesh window about the size of your fist. Lucky knocked three times, and the little window slid open, and all Butch saw was a pair of bloodshot eye peering out at us.

"Open up Louie." Lucky said.

The little window slammed shut, and the door opened. Inside was the usual office equipment, an old wooden desk stacked with papers, a wooden matching chair, a couple of filing cabinets, a bookshelf with no books, and a floor lamp. Opposite the desk, there was an enormous wooden crate filled with armaments, stolen recently from the New York State National Guard Armory in Manhattan.

Lucky walked over to the crate and lifted the lid, "In here yous got your Thompson Submachine guns, three of them babies, four BAR's, eight Colt .45 automatic pistols, eighteen grenades, and of course over two thousand rounds of ammunition for each and every one of da guns. So, whaddya think about that?"

"Is there anything that you think you might need, tell us now, and we'll make sure you have it before you sail." Bugsy said.

"Gentlemen, I'm speechless."

"And don't worry about customs or any that shit, cause we own the docks, so badda bing badda boom, it's all good, capish?" Bugsy said.

Lucky leaned into Butch and whispered, "If anybody gives you shit, you call me, and we'll take care of everything. And don't worry about those jamokes down in Buenos Aires, we got friends down there, too."

"What time's your ship leave?" Bugsy asked.

"Tomorrow at five."

"Viaggi sicuri amico mio." Lucky said as he gave Butch the traditional kiss on the cheek.

Bugsy gave Butch the same goodbye kiss on the cheek, "Safe travels my friend, arrivederci."

"Thanks for everything, adios, amigos."

Lucky smiled and said, "God Damn it, I love it when yous talk cowboy."

We boarded the SS Argentina on the next day and set sail that night. The journey would take twenty-six days, with stops in Havana, Cuba, Rio de Janeiro, and finally Buenos Aires.

We planned to spend several weeks in Buenos Aires, looking things over and seeing if we could get a grubstake and buy a ranch with a couple hundred head of cattle. Once we were settled and established, we would send for the ladies.

The SS Argentina was 613 feet long, over 80 feet wide. It was a US turbo-electric ocean liner, that hit speeds up to 18 knots, and she held 184 first-class & 365 tourist passengers. She had a black hull with white trim. The upper decks were white with a golden yellow and black striped smokestack with a big white circle with red M in the center. She was a beaut.

We were traveling first class, so we were on the Promenade Deck on the port side of the ship, that's the left side for all you landlubbers.

We checked in with the purser at the top of the gangplank. He showed us to our staterooms and gave us a general review of what we could expect during the voyage as well as a list of the activities that we could take advantages of. He mentioned to Butch that his large wooden crate was safely on board and is being kept in the hold.

We decided to each go to our rooms, unpack, relax for a couple hours and then meet for lunch. Our rooms were like a small apartment with round windows, known as portholes. We had a living room, which they called a sitting room that had two chairs, coffee table, and a couch, nice size bathroom with shower and a big bedroom.

My living room had a large wooly white area rug with what looked to me to be blue wave-type graphics all along its border. Against the wall opposite the porthole, which had full-length drapes, was a long leather sofa with two armchairs on either side. In front of the couch was a large coffee table and painted on the wall behind the sofa was a mural of a seascape of the SS Argentina majestically sailing off into the sunset. All the walls in my stateroom was painted a soft baby blue with white trim. There were brass accent lights in the four corners of the room that had dimming switches.

In the bedroom, they had the queen-sized bed against the wall with the portholes, covered with sheer cream-colored curtains. At the foot of the bed was this couch like chair that had an adjustable back with an arm on one side. I never did get the hang of the dern thing. There were two armless chairs opposite the bed, a black chest of drawers, and a full-length mirror. It had a deep blue diamond-patterned wall-to-wall carpeting, and it even had a fake fireplace, that when you turned it on gave off heat and pretend flames. Crazy.

After unpacking my duds, I plopped down onto the bed and fell fast asleep. The bed was so comfortable that I didn't wake up until Butch came knocking on my door.

"News! Wake up we're all going down to the bar to get something to drink. News!"

I opened the door all bleary-eyed, "Hey, Butch, gimme two minutes." I said as I scurried around getting my shoes on.

When I opened the door there stood Butch, Sundance and Kid Curry all giving me the stink-eye.

"Hey, I fell asleep, so shoot me."

Sundance put his arm around me as we headed to the bar, "Come on News, what you need is a stiff eye-opener."

The Dunn Brothers were a group of five brothers that hailed from Pawnee, Oklahoma. They were old school bounty hunters, but recently they had fallen out grace with the good folks of Pawnee. There had been several complaints that they had started getting involved in rustling and bank robbery.

The brothers Dunn – Bee, Calvin, Dal, George, and Bill found themselves on the other side of the law. Sheriff Frank Canton, an ex-gunfighter who settled in Oklahoma from Chicago, arrested Bill Dunn for rustling and began to investigate the other brothers. They could see the writing on the wall, so they too decided to skip out of the country, leaving poor Bill holding the bag.

When he found out that his brothers had left and were going to leave him to take the fall, he had his younger sister, Rose sneak him in a pistol, which he used to break out of jail. Sheriff Canton arrested Rose for aiding her brother to escape from jail.

He rode back to the family ranch to gather his belongings and try and join his siblings in New York, on their way to Brazil on the SS Argentina.

The Dunn Brothers had initially thought about hiding out in Mexico, but from the parts they had seen of Mexico, it looked pretty much like Oklahoma, and they were sick and tired of Oklahoma. They wanted different. Calvin had heard about a recent gold rush going on down in Brazil. So, without any real investigation or research Calvin had convinced his brothers that anywhere that you planted your shovel you'd strike Gold.

Bill decided that before catching the 11:40 to Tulsa, he'd go into Pawnee, free Rose and Kill Sheriff Canton. Canton finished eating at the local greasy spoon, and as he walked out of the restaurant, Bill was standing in the middle of the street, when he saw the Sheriff he shouted out, "Canton, I'm a calling you out!"

Canton slowly walked out into the street and took his stance. He looked around at all the bystanders, "You people get out of the way. Go on now, get!"

"Canton, you're a lowdown dirty Yankee."

"Bill, you don't want to do this."

"You arrested my little sister, Rose. You let her go, and we can forget all about this."

"I'm afraid I can't do that."

"Then, I have no choice, Sheriff."

"Bill, you need a count?"

"Naw."

Bill started out the quicker, but his gun had a problem clearing the holster, Canton drew his revolver and fired two shots, killing Dunn.

We were sitting at a table in the back of the Gallipot Bar when I noticed Calvin Dunn stroll into the bar, moments later the other Dunn Brothers, minus Bill, waltz in and sit at the bar.

"Hey fellas, take a look over there at the bar, I swear them's the Dunn Brothers." I said.

"Can't be, what the Hell ate the Dunn Brothers doing on this ship?" Butch asked.

Sundance said without looking, "Maybe they're after us, after all, they are bounty hunters."

"Nope, I read that they had got caught robbing the Stillwater National Bank and they're on the run." I said.

Butch leaned into the table towards me and said, "News, I'm so glad at least one of us reads the newspaper."

"Well, I got to know." Sundance said as he got up from the table and walked over to the bar.

"Howdy, boys." Sundance said.

Calvin almost choked on the peanut he was eating. "The Sundance Kid? What the Hell are you doing here?" Calvin asked.

"I'm wondering, what the Hell you and your brothers are doing here?"

"Hey, look, it's Sundance. Are you here by yourself?"

Sundance turned and pointed to us sitting at the table, "Nope, there's Butch, Curry, and News. I heard a rumor that you boys are on the run?"

"Like you, Sundance."

"Yeah, except that we was always on the run. What happened with you boys, bounty hunting not as profitable as it used to be?"

"Ever since the FBI started in collecting and arresting, they simply put us out of business."

"So, where you headed?"

"Going down to Brazil, there's a gold rush going on. You?"

"We're headed to Argentina, try ranching."

"Somehow, I can't see the Sundance Kid as a cowpoke, punching cattle."

"Yeah, well it beats digging a hole looking for flecks of gold. Any of you boys speak Portuguese?"

"And why would we need to speak Portuguese?"

"Cause they don't speak Spanish in Brazil, they speak Portuguese."

"You're joshing us."

Sundance waved the bartender over, "Say, barkeep, what language do they speak in Brazil?"

"Portuguese." The bartender responded.

"Do me a favor, the next round for these gents is on me, just put it on my tab, room 4A."

"Calvin, what the Hell have you gotten us in to, we don't know no Portuguese!" Brother George cursed.

"Hey! I didn't see any of you doing anything, you left it all on me."

"Well, I'll let you boys sort out your problems. I'll be seeing ya'll." Sundance said as he walked back to the table with a big grin on his face.

When he got back to the table, he relayed the story, which brought a round of laughter to us all.

I said, "You know those Dunn boys are all a bunch of bushwhackers. They're the ones who killed Charley and Bittercreek Newcomb."

George "Bittercreek" Newcomb and Charley Pierce, both rode with the infamous Dalton Gang. They were among the three-gang members, out of the twelve who survived the failed bank robbery in Coffeyville, Kansas.

The gang had been trying to rob two banks across the street from each other, the First National and the Condon banks. Things turned bad when the good citizens of the town recognized the gang members wearing their disguises of fake beards, they attacked as they fled the banks.

U.S. Marshal Charles T. Connelly and three citizens died defending their town. Nine members of the Dalton Gang were either captured or killed. Emmett Dalton survived with 23-gunshot wounds, stood trial, was convicted, served 14 years, was pardoned, and became an author, real estate agent and a movie actor in Hollywood.

With the official demise of the Dalton Gang, Bob Dalton and Bill Doolin got together to form the Dalton-Doolin Gang. Besides Bittercreek Newcomb and Charley Pierce, the gang consisted of some of the meanest and violent hombres in the west. Men like George "Red Buck" Waightman, Richard "Little Dick" West, William "Little Bill" Raidler, Tulsa Jack Blake, and Oliver "Ol" Yantis.

Six months after the Coffeyville disaster the gang got caught up in, what was later known as the "Battle of Ingalls". It was a bloody gunfight between members of the Dalton-Doolin Gang and U.S. Marshals, ending in the deaths of three Deputy Marshals, two civilians, with one gang member captured and four wounded, including Bittercreek Newcomb and Charley Pierce, who managed to escape.

After the gun battle, Newcomb and Pierce hid out with friends until their wounds had healed. Once they were well enough to travel, the two of them rode to Pawnee, Oklahoma to visit Rose Dunn, Newcomb's girlfriend. Her brothers got wind of their coming and ambushed them to collect the 5000 dollar reward. As Newcomb and Pierce dismounted from their horses in front of Rose Dunn's house, the Dunn Brothers shot them down.

I never found out where Bittercreek was buried, but I do know that Pierce was buried in Guthrie, Oklahoma, where the Dunn's took his body to collect the reward.

Now, the story goes that many years after Charley's death, someone places flowers on his grave every year on the anniversary of his death and throws hog guts on the graves of the Dunn Brothers who killed him.

Butch decided that the Dunn Brothers weren't to be trusted, especially now that they realized their dreams of striking it rich in the goldfields of Brazil had some major kinks in their plans.

He feared that they might want to take the easy way out and cash in by collecting the rewards on us. I estimated that the total reward for the four of us would bring close to 80,000 dollars.

It happened when we were three days out to sea, it was late at night, close to 2am. The four of us had just left a private poker game in the Captain' stateroom, and we decided to take a stroll around the decks to get some fresh air, Kid Curry had a bit too much to drink, so after a while we all sat down on four deck chairs to wait for Curry's head to clear before going to bed.

The wind was a tad brisk, so we placed the blankets provided for such an occasion over us. I was starting to doze off when Butch whispered, "Heads up, here comes the Brothers Dunn."

It was all four brothers walking towards us. They were wearing full-length overcoats with their hands in their pockets.

"Howdy, Butch. Fellas, how's everyone doing?" Calvin Dunn inquired.

"We're fine. What brings you, boys, wandering about on such a brisk morning?" Butch asked.

"Couldn't sleep." Brother Dal said.

"Having bad dreams about not being able to speak Portuguese?" Sundance asked sarcastically.

"Not funny, Sundance." Bee Dunn said.

"Sorry, Bee. No offensive given." Sundance replied.

"None taken, but that did get us to thinking. Why travel all the way to Brazil to get rich, when we can strike gold right here on board this ship." George said, revealing his pistol from his overcoat.

His brothers all did the same, they all took out their guns and pointed them at us.

"You know George, it was you thinking that got you boys into this mess in the first place. Now, why don't you put your guns away and we'll forget all about this? What do you say?" Sundance said.

"I'll be asking you boys to put your hands in the air, and don't try anything funny." George demanded.

"Butch?" I asked.

Butch sighed and said, "Now."

From under the blankets that were covering us, came a volley of bullets, from us our 45 Colts automatic pistols that we had drawn the moment we saw the Dunns approaching.

K-POW POW. POW. POW. POW. POW. POW. POW. POW. POW. POW. POW. POW.

Seconds later, there lay all four brothers in a bloody heap at the foot of our deck chairs. We got up and disposed of the bodies, tossing them overboard. We took out blankets and wiped up the blood best we could and tossed them overboard as well.

We then went inside and went to bed. I don't know about the others, but I slept better than I had in weeks, knowing that it could have gone the other way and we could be sleeping with the fishes.

The SS Argentina steamed into Havana, Cuba the next morning for a two-day layover. It was reported later that day that four passengers were missing. A complete search of the ship from stem to stern proved fruitless. It was reported to authorities that the Brothers Dunn were presumed to be possible victims of foul play after a search of their rooms revealed several varieties of firearms.

The disappearance of the Dunn Brothers was the topic of conversation at every dinner table for days to come.

We were strolling the streets of Old Havana in the afternoon enjoying looking at the architecture, the culture, the women, when we spotted a young man sitting at a street café reading a copy of Karl Marx's The Communist Manifesto.

"Is that all you can do on such a beautiful day is sit here and read?" Butch asked.

"Perdóneme?"

"Why are you sitting here all alone reading and not with a beautiful young lady?"

"I guess I'm just shy, senor."

"Nonsense, a good looking kid like you. You should be beating the girls off with a stick."

I said, "Maybe if you were sitting here reading some poetry rather than books on revolution, they might find you more approachable. Try someone like Keats or Whitman or Pablo Neruda."

The others looked at me like I had a third head.

"What! I read more than just newspapers." I retorted.

"Mind if we join you?" Sundance asked.

"No, please. My name is Ernesto." The young man said.

"Ernesto, I'm Butch, this is Sundance, that's Curry, and over there is News. Pleased to meet you. Can we buy you a drink?"

"You're very kind."

We all grabbed some seats and sat down. The waiter came by to take out orders. We all had Cuba Libres, in fact, we all had several Cuba Libres. Sitting a couple hundred feet from the ocean, with that pleasant breeze and the sun shining down on us, we were getting quite mellow.

"You are all from America?"

"Yes we're all from America. We're sailing on the SS Argentina, going down to Buenos Aires." Kid Curry said.

"Business or pleasure?" The young man asked.

"A little of both, I guess." Butch answered.

"I'm from Rosario, a small town in the Santa Fe province. It is largely farms and cattle ranches, and it is quite beautiful."

"Are you planning to go into politics?" I asked.

"No, medicine."

"I just thought that since you're reading Karl Marx, that you just might be interested in politics."

"You are correct, I am very much interested in politics. But I feel that I might best serve the people by going into medicine."

"That's very noble." I said.

Butch said, "There are too many politicians in the world already, and not enough doctors. Good for you Ernesto."

"Say, would you gentlemen like me to give you a tour of Havana?"

"Aw, that's very kind, but you don't want to spend your day hanging around with a bunch old guys." Butch said.

"No, I don't mind, really."

Sundance said, "Ernesto, I think what Butch is trying to tell you is that we're not really interested in exploring the sights of Havana. We're interested in exploring the women of Havana if you know what I mean, and I think you do."

"Oh, I see, you're looking for Jineteras. Then you will want to walk along the Malecón. It's the broad promenade by the seawall, and there that you will find the companionship that you are looking for."

The sun was going down, the breeze coming in from the Havana Harbor was cool. Somewhere off in the distance musicians were playing a jazz rumba fusion, and after having four Cuba Libres each, me and the boys were feeling frisky.

"Ernesto, it has been a pleasure. We wish you good luck with your studies, who knows, perhaps we will meet again." Butch said.

"Buena suerte, good luck to you all. I truly enjoyed our time together, adiós."

As we were leaving, I turned to see Ernesto continuing to read his Communist Manifesto, totally oblivious to three beautiful young women sitting at the table next to him.

"Butch, I'll catch up with you guys." I said as I went back to where Ernesto was reading.

I walked up to the three young women and said, "Ladies, I'd like you to meet my friend Ernesto. He's a little shy, but I think you will find him quite interesting."

The three girls started to giggle, and I called the waiter over, "Would you please give these ladies whatever they would like, my treat."

I handed the waiter a U.S. ten-dollar bill, which was a lot of money. Then. I gestured that they come and sit at Ernesto's table, which they did.

I leaned down close to Ernesto's ear and whispered, "You're on your own now, kid."

As I was leaving, I heard the three girls giggling and Ernesto fumbling to make any semblance of coherent conversation.

I caught up to Butch and the boys as they started the quest to get laid. We didn't have to walk too far to encounter ladies of the evening. All along the promenade, there were tall women, short women, big, skinny, old, young, dark-skinned, light-skinned, blondes, brunettes, and redheads.

One by one, they each found a lady of their liking until there was just me, I was almost to the end of the promenade when I saw a tall redhead who had legs from here to there. She said her name was Camila. I don't know if it was the Cuba Libres, the cool ocean breeze, her intoxicating perfume, or a combination of all of them, but for that moment in time, I was in love.

We spent the evening at the Hotel Inglaterra. The Hotel Inglaterra is the oldest hotel in Havana, built-in 1875.

We had dinner at the sidewalk café, the Gran Café el Louvre. Then we went up to the roof for drinks at the rooftop bar, where the view of the city was spectacular. Afterward, we went to our suite and made passionate love until sunrise.

When I woke up, late morning Camila was gone; my money and wallet were still laying on the nightstand beside me. She had only taken the amount we had agreed on.

I ran into Sundance on my way to the ship walking on the promenade. Sundance looked like Hell. He told me that his evening didn't turn out as well as mine. Turns out that his escort turned out to a man dressed as woman, which didn't turn out too pleasant for either of them, Sundance didn't get laid and the poor fella who tried to fool him ended up with a broken nose. Sundance had to scoot outta there before the police arrived. Poor Sundance, he spent the night at another hotel all by himself, not wanting to try procuring another "date" for the evening.

"News, don't say nothing to Butch or the Kid about this. Promise?"

"You have my word."

Butch and Kid Curry were already on board the ship when me and Sundance arrived. We found them having breakfast, laughing, and having a good old time.

"I'm going to go get cleaned up, then come back for some breakfast." Sundance announced.

"Me too, we'll be back." I said.

On the way back to our rooms, I said, "You'll feel a lot better once you get cleaned up."

"Yeah, I guess. The sooner we get away from Cuba, the better as far as I'm concerned."

The Cuban police were called once the ship had docked and the Dunn Brothers were reported missing. Their investigation consisted of going thru the rooms and possessions of the deceased, conducting several interviews of passengers, who including Sundance that they had contacted within the two days sailing from New York to Havana.

The police had set up a small headquarters for interviews in one of the first-class staterooms.

"What is your name, senor." The police sergeant asked.

"St. John, Tommy St. John." Sundance answered.

"Now, Mr. St. John, did you know the deceased?"

"Yes, I knew them from back home."

"And where might that be?"

"Oklahoma."

"Were you friends?"

"More like acquaintances."

"You were seen buying the four Dunn Brothers a drink, is that so?"

"Yes."

"Yet, they were not your friends."

"Right, well I heard that they had just received some bad news and I thought that I would try to cheer them up."

"Can you tell me about the nature of their bad news?"

"Sure. They were going down to Brazil to pan for gold. But they hadn't planned it out too well, since they didn't realize that in Brazil, they speak Portuguese, not Spanish. And none of them spoke or understood Portuguese. When they found out, they all seemed depressed, so I bought them a drink."

"Was that the last time you saw them?"

"No, I think I may have seen them at dinner."

"Where were you between the hours of 1 and 4am two nights ago?"

"Part of that time, I was playing poker with some other passengers and crew members until one or two, and then I was back in my room sleeping."

"Can anyone vouch for you after you left the poker game?"

"Unfortunately, no. Sorry."

"Do you have any firearms?"

"I have a .38 Smith & Wesson revolver. Would you like to see it?"

Sundance reached behind his back and pulled the gun out from being tucked in his belt. The sergeant was taken back.

"Do you always carry a pistol with you Mr. St. John?"

"No, but I figured that at that point you'd want to see it. It is unloaded," Sundance said as he handed the weapon to the officer.

The sergeant examined it and handed it back to Sundance.

"Mr. St. John, do you know of anyone who might want to do harm to the victims?"

"I do not, sir. They were bounty hunters, and that is a profession that usually makes more enemies than it does friends. So, you think it was foul play?"

"I doubt that it was suicide. No notes and there was blood on the deck. No, I'm afraid it was murder, I'm sure of it."

"That's going to make passengers paranoid."

"I see that you are going to Buenos Aires, is that correct?"

"Yes."

"Business or pleasure?"

"Both, I'm looking into the possibility of starting a cattle ranch."

"Hablas Español?"

"Si, bastante bien."

"Not bad, Mr. St. John. At least you won't have the same problem that was facing the Dunn Brothers."

"Well, I must say your English is excellent, where did you learn to speak it?"

"My parents were divorced when I was a boy, my father moved to New York, I spent a lot of time with him during the summers."

"Well, sergeant I must say you speak it very well."

"Thank you, senor. Here is your pistol back, you may go."

"Thank you, sergeant."

"Goodbye, Mr. St. John, thank you for your time."

"Good luck with your investigation." Sundance said as he left the room.

Sundance walked down to his room, where we were all waiting to hear how it went.

"So, how'd it go?" Butch asked.

"It went well.

"They're going to have to wrap this up, we're scheduled to set sail by midnight, it's eight o'clock already." I said.

Butch stood up and said, "Let's go grab some dinner."

"Sounds good, I'm starving." Kid Curry uttered.

"You are not starving, Kid. Look at you; we've only been on board this ship for three days, and you look like you've gained thirty pounds." Butch stated.

The Kid shot back, "Very funny. Well, none of you look like you're wasting away either, except for maybe News."

"Yeah, News has always been lanky. What's your secret, News?" Sundance asked.

I smiled and said, "Clean living and a clean conscience."

'What a load of horse pucky!" Butch said.

During dinner, all anyone talked about was the police investigation. It was announced that the ship would indeed set sail as scheduled for midnight and there was a thunderous round of applause and laughter of relief from the dinners.

During dinner, seated at our table was a couple from Great Britain, the Lord and Lady Rupert Bickford-Smyth the third. They were traveling down to Brazil to visit their rubber tree plantation. They had spent several weeks in New York visiting with the Rockefellers, who are in their book, really top-drawer people, even if they are from the colonies.

"I say, old man, I find all this talk about murder quite disturbing and distasteful, don't you?" Lord Rupert asked of Butch.

Butch figured we'd have some fun with these Limey snobs, "Why, heck no pardner. Where we come from murder and death is just a way of living. Back home in Tombstone, Hell how do you think it got its name?"

"Good heavens!" Lady Bickford-Smyth gasped.

"I'm sure that might have been quite rough and tumble back in earlier times, but surely things have become more civilized, now." The Lord said.

Sundance reached behind his back and produced his .38 Smith & Wesson and laid it on the table, "They don't call it the Wild West for nothing, ma'am!"

"My word, Rupert, I'm frightened."

"Now, now ma'am, don't go fretting yourself none, not as long as we're around. We're pretty tough hombres, but we are God-fearing folk. Just so you know that if any ruffians try anything, you just let Mr. St. John or myself know." Butch said.

"I say, that's quite sporting of you chaps." Rupert said.

I asked, "Is it true that the sun never sets on the British Empire?"

"Sadly, not as much today as in the past, changing times and all that."

"How are you folks holding up against that lunatic, Hitler?"

"It's been a tough slog, but we're keeping a stiff upper lip and carrying on. Just wish you damn Yanks would come and join the fight."

"All in good time, I'm sure. We yanks like nothing better than a good war, it gives us an excuse to kill." I said.

The look on the Lord and Lady's face was one of sheer shock and amazement.

Butch smiled and gestured for them to come closer, while he looked around as if to make sure no one was listening in, "You folks shouldn't look so surprised, just look at our history; we're a gun culture. It all started when we landed on Plymouth Rock with our Blunderbuss and flintlock rifles, it made it so easy killing all the native Indians that got in our way.

"But, we weren't satisfied with just the original thirteen colonies, we wanted more, more land, more natural resources, just more of everything. So, we started pushing west and God help anyone or anything that stood in our way. And all along we were developing bigger and deadlier guns to kill more people faster and more efficiently.

"We took away people's land and made them settle on land that we didn't want. Occasionally we decided that we did want their land, after all, so we either killed them or made them move to an even more worthless land. If they resisted…BANG!

Back East, people became more civilized, they stopped carrying guns because all the Indians were either dead or on reservations. But out west, everyone strapped on a shooting iron. Soon, we had killed all of the evil redskins, but we still had our guns, so we started killing each other, over land, gold, cattle, cards, and even women. Hell, we even killed each other to see who was fastest on the draw. Eventually, carrying a gun on your hip became obsolete as the wild west became tamed.

"Now, only police, and criminals carry guns in America. People do still have guns to hunt and for personal protection that they usually keep in their homes. So you see, the history of the gun is the history of America."

"My word." Lady Bickford-Smyth uttered.

"I say jolly good, old man, jolly good. May I offer you, gentlemen, a brandy?" Rupert said.

"You're too kind, yes, thank you." Butch said.

"Very good. Gentlemen, let us retire to the bar to partake in brandy and cigars. Victoria, my dear if you'll excuse us." Lord Bickford-Smyth said as he rose from his seat.

We went to the same bar where we encountered the Dunn Brothers and sat at the same table. Lord Bickford-Smyth called over the waiter, "Five snifters of your finest brandy, my good man."

"So, tell me Mr. St. John, after such an elegant dissertation of guns and America from your friend, Mr. Thomas, how is it that you're in possession of such a fine firearm? I don't quite see you and your companions as police officers, would you by chance be, and please don't take offense, criminals?"

Sundance smiled and said, "In a past life."

We are scheduled for two days in Rio de Janeiro, I don't know about the others, but I'm a little nervous going ashore since none of us speaks Portuguese. I had heard from some of the crewmembers that once you go outside the tourist area, things can go south pretty quick.

On our first day in Rio, Lord and Lady Bickford-Smyth were kind enough to postpone their trip to their rubber plantation to show us around.

The first stop was to the giant statue Cristo Redentor, Christ the Redeemer that overlooks the city of Rio, sitting high atop Sugarloaf Mountain. The mountain's nickname is Corcovado, which means the hunchback. The statute is a towering 125 feet tall, it is considered to be one of the "new" seven wonders of the world. We took a cable car to the top and I didn't like it, cause seems un-natural. The darn thing started to sway back and forth due to high winds. Once we got to the top, I was looking for a different way down, but unless I was willing to spend the whole day climbing down, the cable car was it. Thank goodness the ride down was a lot smoother.

Lord and Lady Bickford-Smyth were keen on showing us several of the art museums.

"I say, old man, I really think you fellas would find it quite smashing." Rupert said.

"Thanks, old man, but what say you, me and the boys treat you and the misses to a really nice lunch. Then me and the fellas think we'd like to do a little exploring on our own." Butch countered.

"That's very sporting of you, Butch."

"Great."

Once we got back down off the mountain, we caught a taxi to Restaurante Rio Minho e Cabaça do, a historical seafood joint. Opened in 1884, Restaurante Rio Minho e Cabaça do is one of the oldest restaurants in all of Rio.

When you walk into Rio Minho the space is long and narrow, the walls are mahogany, decorated with prints of many varieties of fish and large conch shells mounted above the prints. The dozen or so tables are covered with a blue and white tablecloth, and the plates are white with an ocean green stripe. The waiters are all dressed in black pants, white shirt, black bow tie, topped off with a white dinner jacket.

Lord and Lady Bickford-Smyth ordered the grilled octopus served with rice and broccoli. Me and the others weren't as adventitious. So we ordered the grilled shrimp casserole. I have to admit everything was delicious and a good time was had by all.

We said our goodbyes to Lord and Lady Bickford-Smyth as they were heading back to the ship to collect their luggage and hook up with their plantation manager. Butch noticed a couple of shady characters lurking around while we were chatting with the Lord and Lady. They then jumped into a car and followed them.

"I got a bad feeling about those guys." Butch said.

"Let's go and alert Rupert." Sundance suggested.

We called for a taxi and made our way back to the ship. Kid Curry noticed that the car with the two men was parked down the street from where the SS Argentina was docked.

"There's the car with those two jokers sitting and, trying to look inconspicuous. Who do you think they are?" Curry asked.

"I bet they're Nazis." I said.

"Nazis. Why would Nazis be interested in Lord Bickford-Smyth." Curry asked.

"I guess it's their rubber plantation. England needs rubber for the war effort, and Germany is interested in preventing them from getting any." Butch surmised.

"How do you think we should handle this, Butch? Sundance asked.

"Well, we could try and tip-off Rupert, or we can see what happens and see if we need to intervene. We don't know if these guys are Nazis, we just might be jumping to conclusions."

"What the Hell, I say let's see where this takes us. We can always get laid; besides I hate Nazis. Whadda say, boys, you in?" Sundance asked.

"Let 'er rip." Curry said.

"Count me in." I agreed.

We saw Lord and Lady Bickford-Smyth coming down the gangplank with a man all dressed in khaki, wearing a pith helmet. They got into a large Land Rover that was loaded down with the Lord and Lady's luggage.

The suspect's car waited a few seconds before following.

Butch looked in his Portuguese to English translation book, handed the cabbie 500 Brazilian Real and pointed to the car with the suspected Nazis in it and said, "Siga aqueie carro."

We made our way out of the city and onto Highway 116 towards São Paulo. Soon we were passing thru the Itatiaia National Park, the oldest national park in Brazil. It's a South American rainforest in every sense of the word.

We weren't following too closely, we didn't want to give ourselves away. The roads were winding and at times mountainous. We would lose sight of them, but since there weren't any turnoffs, we were confident that they wouldn't give us the slip.

It just goes to show you, you should never get over confidant. Butch, sitting in the front seat turned to us and said, "I don't see them, they must have stopped!"

I said, "I haven't seen any roads where they could have turned off."

Sundance and Kid Curry agreed, they hadn't seen any roads either. Butch quickly gave our driver the signal to turn around and go back the way we came.

"Let's keep a sharp lookout for roads, trails, turn-offs, anything." Butch said.

We went about ten miles when Sundance pointed to our left, "There! That dirt road."

The driver slowly turned left and stopped. He started babbling, we couldn't understand him, but he was indicating that he didn't want to go down that dirt road.

Butch handed him $500 U. S. Dollars and pointed down the road. The driver hesitated for a minute, but the temptation of earning more money on this one ride than he would make in a year persuaded him.

We slowly crept along until we saw the chase car with its doors open. We stopped and we all got out of the taxi. As Butch got out, he took the keys from the cabbie, smiled, and said, "Esperar."

The driver wasn't too happy about being told he had to wait, but when he saw that we had pistols, he sat quietly and waited.

The four of us walked along the dirt path hugging the foliage along the road. Butch and Sundance led with me third, and Kid Curry watched the rear. As we got closer to the suspect's car, we could hear a heated exchange between, what sounded to us to be Germans and the Lord and Lady Bickford-Smyth's manager.

"What exactly is it that you want from us?" Lord Bickford-Smyth asked.

The older of the two men said, "Herr Bickford-Smyth, Brazil is not safe for you and Lady Bickford-Smyth."

"And why is that, might I ask?" Lord Bickford-Smyth demanded.

The two German agents were an odd pair. The older of the two was short, balding and wore thick bifocals. His partner was tall, skinny with long blonde hair, the poster boy for Hitler's Aryan race. The younger one didn't speak. He was nervous, twitchy, inpatient, and seemed frightened by the sounds of the jungle, whereas the older man was cool, calm, and did all the talking.

"It is no secret that our two countries are at odds with one and another. We're here to see that your rubber never reaches England."

"And how pray tell are you planning to do that? By shooting us?"

"Come, come Lord Bickford-Smyth, we're not some sort of American gangsters, who are going to rub you out, as the saying goes. No, but you must know that life is cheap here in Brazil and of course accidents can happen."

"I can't help but think that that does sound like a threat, old man."

The younger Nazi pulled out his Luger, pointed it at Lord and Lady Bickford-Smyth and said, "Enough! Listen, old man, no rubber is leaving Brazil, understand? Now, either you turn around and get back on the SS Argentina, or I'll shoot the lot of you right here and now. What's is going to be?"

At that moment, we stepped out from the jungle, all pointing our Colt .45's at the two gunmen. Sundance took the lead and fired once, striking the barrel of the Luger, knocking it out of the young man's hands.

"Hold it right there, Fritz. Don't nobody move." Sundance said as we all emerged from the bushes.

"Lord and Lady Bickford-Smyth, are you alright?" Butch asked.

"Yes, we're fine. These men were threatening and trying to intimidate us."

"Well, why don't you all be on your way, we'll take care of these two."

"You're not going to do anything drastic are you?"

"Oh no, we're just going to have a little talk with them and try and come to some sort of mutual understanding."

"You all run along, we'll straighten everything out with these fellows." I said.

Butch asked, "Will you be alright, Lord and Lady Bickford-Smyth?"

"Quite alright, old man. The British government was posted armed soldiers around the plantation."

"Good luck with everything." Butch said.

"Gentlemen, we can't thank you enough. Thank you all again."

Lord and Lady Bickford-Smyth got back into their car, turned around and continued on to their plantation. Once they were safely out of sight, Butch said to Kid Curry, "Frisk 'em."

The Kid patted down the older man first, he found a pistol in a shoulder holster and a German diplomatic passport.

The man said, "You have no right detaining us. We are German diplomats and as such have complete immunity."

"That's right Butch, he has a diplomatic passport. His name is Reinhart Müller." The Kid acknowledged.

"I suggest you let us go before you get in trouble with your government."

Butch started laughing, "Listen, Fritz, we don't have no government."

"Was meinst du? Aren't you Americans?"

"We was, but now we're not."

"I do not understand."

The younger man tried to resist getting frisked, Kid Curry cracked him upside his head with his pistol.

"Stand still you lousy Kraut!"

"Schweinehund!" The young Nazi said as he spit on the ground.

Kid tossed me the man's wallet, I was going thru his credentials and found his Gestapo ID card. I held it up, "Hey, this guy's Gestapo!"

All four of us pointed our guns at the man and fired at the same time.

K-Pow. Pow. Pow. Pow.

"Kinda makes you homesick doesn't, Fritz. You Nazis like going around shooting Jews and gypsies in the head for sport, isn't that right Fritz?" Sundance prodded Müller.

"Those are all lies, and besides I am not Gestapo." Müller said nervously.

"But you are a card-carrying Nazi?" I asked.

"Under the Fuhrer, we all are Nazis, but we all don't hate the Jews or go around killing people. I am a diplomat."

"Maybe, maybe not, but by not speaking up you allow others to go around killing innocent people, rounding up Jews, gypsies, and anyone else that disagrees with you and putting them in concentration camps. Besides, I thought all you Nazis want to lay down your lives for da Fuhrer and for the Fatherland?" Sundance challenged Müller.

Müller got defiant, "I am a German diplomat, and I demand that you release me at once!"

"Fucking Nazi." Butch said as he raised his pistol and shot Müller in the heart.

Butch stood motionless for a minute looking down at Müller the diplomat and the Gestapo agent then said, "Come on."

We placed both bodies into their car, took their guns and IDs, and set the vehicle on fire. Our cabbie was standing by the side of his cab and he looked scared, I guess he thought we were going to kill him too. Butch just indicated that we wanted him to take us back to Rio.

The ride back was eerily quiet, when we got back to the dock, Butch gave the poor man another hundred U.S. Dollars. When Sundance got out of the car, he went to the driver's window and put his index finger up to his lips as a sign to keep silent and made a shhh sound.

The man nodded sheepishly and repeated the silence gesture back to Sundance, and quickly drove away without looking back.

The next morning before the SS Argentina was to set sail, I went ashore and bought a copy of Rio de newspaper, O Globo. The headline was *Dois Nacionais Alemães Encontrados Assassinados*, Two German Nationals Found Murdered. There was a large color photograph of the burnt car with two bodies inside. The car was surrounded by police

The story went on to say that police found the charred remains of two German nationals, who had been shot and their bodies were set on fire in their car. The men were burnt beyond all recognition. The police hoped that they may be identified by the use of dental records.

Meanwhile, the police said that they found several shell casings at the scene, along with multiple tire tracks and footprints.

The automobile was registered to the German consultant, who had no comment at this time.

A police spokesperson said that arrests are imminent.

I had one of the ship's crew translate the story for me. Further in the paper, there was a small blurb about the return of the Lord and Lady Bickford-Smyth to their plantation and all the extra British troop protection.

I found Butch and the boys eating breakfast at one of the six restaurants that serve breakfast. I brought in the newspaper and showed it to them.

"I didn't know you read Portuguese, News." Butch said.

"I don't Butch, I had one of the stewards translate it for me, along with several other articles, just I didn't seem too curious about this particular one."

"You're such a clever boy." Quipped Kid Curry.

"Got to know what the opposition is up to, right Sundance?"

"Right, News. The Kid is just jealous that he hadn't thought of it."

"Ah, bullshit." The Kid shot back.

Butch looked at his watch and asked, "Say, what time do you think we set sail?"

"I believe we set sail at 5pm, Butch, why?" I said.

"News, do you still have the German's ID cards?"

"Yeah."

"Are they photo IDs?"

"No, just the passports have photos."

Butch sat back in his chair and clapped his hands, "Whadda say we have some fun."

Butch decided to portray Reinhart Müller, and I was to act as the Gestapo agent, Siegfried Krüger. Butch picked me to play the Gestapo agent because I was blonde and because I was the only one who had a trench coat.

We left the ship wearing out regular clothes and carrying our costumes under our arms, Sundance and Kid Curry followed as a backup, in case we needed any.

Butch asked me if I spoke any German.

"I only know a couple of phrases, like, do you speak German, thank you, how much is that, and goodbye."

"That should be just enough to get the job done."

The four of us took a taxi to the Bar Copinha on Rua Leopoldo Miguez about two blocks away from Banco do Brasil. The bar is a small local hang out, sitting on the corner, there are four bar stools that you can use outside. People mostly just buy beer by the bottle and either stand on the corner under a large shade tree drinking or they buy a bottle and continue on their way.

They had a bathroom that you access from outside. So you didn't have to go into the bar to take care of business. We drank our beers while standing out on the corner under the tree and when we were done, Butch went into the bathroom first to change, I followed suit a few minutes later.

We walked down Rua Bolivar towards Copacabana Beach, then turned left on Rua Barão de Ipanema for a block and there on the corner was Banco do Brasil.

Sundance went in to scope out the lay of the land. He came out minutes later.

"Looks pretty straight forward: one guard, an old guy, who shouldn't give you too much trouble. Me and the Kid will be outside if things get hairy."

Me and Butch put on sunglasses and went inside, and just like Sundance said, it was a cakewalk. Butch walked up to the guard as if to ask a question, he pulled his piece and stuck it in his ribs.

I went up to the youngest teller and asked in my most German accent, "Sprechen Sie Deutsch?"

"Não." She answered timidly.

"Do you speak English?" I asked with my phony German accent.

She smiled and nodded, "Sim."

I put a canvas bag on the counter and showed her the Luger that we had taken from the German diplomat, I said, "Place all the money from ze cash drawer into this bag. Do not do anything foolish, and no one will get hurt."

The young lady proceeded to fill the canvas bag, and when she was finished, I said, "Do not try any zing foolish, do you understand?"

She nodded again and said, "Sim."

I smiled, "Danke und auf Wiedersehen."

As I walked towards the door, I intentionally dropped Herr Krüger's ID card on the floor. Butch waited until I got out of the bank before taking the guards gun and casually walking out behind me. Once we were outside, the four of us began to walk separately toward Copacabana Beach. As Butch and I were walking, we were discarding our outer garments into trashcans on the corners of the streets.

By the time we got to the beach, Butch and I looked totally different than when we entered the bank. When we got to a stoplight, we huddled close together and quickly divvied up the loot into four small shopping bags.

There were so many people on the beach that we just blended into the massive crowd. We all separated and meandered along the beach walk and eventually took separate taxis back to the SS Argentina.

Back on board, we totaled up our haul to be over 8000 dollars, that night, while out to sea, we toasted our German friends who made this score possible-diplomat Müller and the Gestapo swine Krüger.

Later that night while standing by the railing looking out to sea, I threw Müller's gun and ID overboard. Both had the Nazi swastika insignia printed on them, they made me feel disgusted even to have them in my possession. Little did any of us realize that we would someday tangle with Nazis again.

By the time we docked in Buenos Aires, we had heard some buzz that Brazil and Germany were having diplomatic issues. A couple of high-ranking members of the Third Reich had allegedly been involved in a robbery of a Rio de Janeiro branch of the Banco do Brasil.

The SS Argentina docked at Puerto de Buenos Aires, she was surrounded by dozens of freighters and cargo ships loading and unloading cargo from all around the world. Try as you may, you couldn't stay asleep with all that noise, so we went down for our last breakfast onboard ship before we departed.

Me and Kid Curry headed over to our hotel, the Alvear Palace, while Butch and Sundance stayed behind to make sure our luggage and crate of weapons made it safely thru customs. Just as Lucky Luciano promised, his man got the crate thru without any hitches.

The city of Buenos Aires was different from New York, more open and airy. New York seemed to me to be all scrunched together and stacked up on top of each other, whereas Buenos Aires feels more spread out, someone said it looks and feels like Paris, France. Since I never been to Paris, I guess I'll just have to take their word on that.

As I walked around the city, I got a sense of real pro-German sentiment. It seemed to me that Argentina's government was leaning towards the Axis while trying to give the appearance of neutrality. As America was yet to join in the war, we had been treated nicely. For the most part, the Argentinean people have been really friendly and fair to us.

Most days Butch and Sundance have been meeting with bankers and real estate folks to see about obtaining us a cattle ranch. We have been on several outings looking at ranches in different provinces. Most have been overnight trips, finding a ranch for the four of us was like that story of Goldilocks and the three bears.

A couple of the ranches were way too big, a few were just too small, but after six weeks of traveling all around, we found one that was just right. And none too soon to suit me, I'm just not a city boy, I like being out in the country.

We met with a Mr. Gonzalez with the Banco de la Nacion Argentina to sign the papers to take ownership of our cattle ranch.

"Congratulations Señors Thomas, Hanson, Everhart and St, John. I wish you la major de las suertes, the best of luck."

"Gracias, Señor Gonzalez, for all your help." Butch said.

And with that, we were now legitimate cattle ranchers.

We discovered that the province of Santa Fe had an area named 'the Pampas' which is perfect for cattle ranching, so we pooled our money an bought a spread along with two hundred head of Argentine Criollo cattle, not far from the tiny village of Los Nogales.

The ranch came with a house, which was quite spacious was a five-bedroom log home with living/dining room and verandas. It also had a manager's house, three sets of cattle handling facilities, an irrigation system with eight windmills, two water storage tanks, and six drinking troughs. There was also four-grain silos, two machinery sheds and two back up generators.

It was official, we were "los rancheros yanquis."

The attitude throughout Argentina at the time, was pro-Germany. Being that America was still remaining neutral meant we weren't involved in any of the local political squabbles, we just went about our business of ranching.

We were actually surprising ourselves how successful we were. In fact, we had to hire several cowboys to help tend to the cattle and help maintain the ranch; they refer to themselves as gauchos. They're very much like us

American cowboys, rough and tough. They're excellent horsemen, but they don't carry pistols. They used something called a bolas, that's three leather-bound rocks tied together with approximately three feet long straps. They twirl the darn thing over their heads and release it at the feet of a running steer, and wham. That doggie goes down, quicker than you can say, Jack Robinson. They seem to prefer it to the use of lariats.

Their getups are different than the cowboy. They wear a poncho, which doubles as a saddle blanket, carry a facón (a large knife), a rebenque (leather whip), and loose-fitting trousers called bombachas, cinched with a tirador belt, while we would be wearing our blue jeans, shirt, vest, and chaps. About the only thing we both agreed on was our hats and our boots.

The cowboy and gaucho's tasks are the same, to basically move the herd between grazing fields, branding the livestock, drive the herd to the market sites, and the taming of ranch animals.

Things were going well for us, due to the war going on in Europe, Argentina was split between the main political parties. Newspapers and intellectuals supported the Allies and the military was very pro-Germany. At the time, we didn't give a hoot which side was which. All we cared about was selling our beef to the highest bidder.

We were riding high in 1940-1943, until the revolution of 1943. A military coup d'état headed by the United Officer's Group with the leadership of pro-Nazi General Arturo Rawson and the then Colonel Juan Perón helped lead the overthrow of the government of President Ramón Castillo.

Now that the fascists took power, things were changing, and not for the better. Since we were yanquis, and America looked like they would soon be entering the war, we were always under the constant watch of the GOU,

Argentina's secret police. They would watch us all the time, and we would be followed wherever we went.

It happened in January of 1944. Argentina, under pressure from the Allies, broke off diplomatic relations with the Axis powers. We had driven our herd to the city of Rosario to market when we ran into a group of Communist protesters demonstrating against the fascist's leadership that was suppressing the labor unions. They were singing songs and carrying signs, marching in a peaceful protest when all of a sudden, the police goons came charging into the crowd swinging batons and cracking heads.

They were smashing men, women, and kids, showing no discretion in who they bludgeoned. Soon we got caught up in the fracas, and at one point Butch sees an officer heading towards a young male teenager from behind, ready to bash his head in with his baton. Without thinking, Butch pulled his pistol and fired, wounding the officer and saving the young man's life. Me and Sundance grab the teenager and with Butch and Kid Curry, slipped into an alley to work our way to a safer part of the area.

"Muchas gracias señor. You saved my life." The young man said.

"Da nada." Butch replied.

"You are Americans, no?"

"Yes. Is it that obvious?

"Si, sorry señor, but aren't you the American's I met in Havana four years ago?"

"Ernesto?"

"Si, si, and you are Mr. Butch."

"What's a young fella like yourself doing out in the middle of this brawl?" Asked Sundance.

"We are protesting the fascist government, who don't give a damn about the people and workers."

"Damn good cause, kid. But, ending up dead ain't helping the cause. You need start using your head not getting it caved in." Butch said.

"Yes, I understand, Señor Butch."

"Are you a worker?"

"No, soon I am going off to medical school and then to become a doctor, so I can help people."

"That's great, kid." I said.

"What are you all doing here?" Che asked.

"We have a small cattle ranch not far from Los Nogales."

Sundance asked, "Do you think you'd like us to escort you home?"

"No, gracias, I just live around the corner."

Butch patted the boy on the shoulder and said, "You take care, Ernesto."

"I will Butch, please my friends call me Che." The young man said.

"You take care… Che."

"Adiós, señors."

Ernesto "Che" Guevara was an Argentine Marxist revolutionary, physician, author, guerilla leader, diplomat and military theorist.

He was the eldest of five children to a middle-class family. His father was an architect with of some Irish blood.

His father would later say of Che's restless nature, it's the blood of the Irish rebels flowing thru his veins. When Che turned twenty he and a friend, Alberto Granado took a year off from college to take a 5,000-mile motorcycle trek thru South America, with the final goal of volunteering for a few weeks at the San Pablo leper colony in Peru, on the banks of the Amazon River.

Throughout their trip he was struck by the crushing poverty and the deplorable working conditions of everyone from copper miners, peasant farmers to factory workers, people so pitiful that he described them as "the shivering flesh-and-blood victims of the capitalist."

His journey took him all through Argentina, Chile, Peru, Ecuador, Colombia, Venezuela, Panama, and even to Miami, Florida, before going home to Buenos Aires. At the end of his adventure, he came to the conclusion that Latin America isn't a collection of separate countries, but a single entity in need of a continent-wide liberation, hence the revolutionary was born.

After returning home to Argentina, Che did go on to receive his medical degree. He spent the next couple of years practicing medicine in Bolivia, Peru, Costa Rica, Nicaragua, and El Salvador, among others. By 1954, Che was working in Guatemala City, and it was during this time that he really became radicalized into communism and the teaching of Lenin and Mao. It's where he also came into contact with a young Cuban freedom fighter named Fidel Castro.

After the attack on Pearl Harbor and the pressure that the United States was putting on all the Latin American countries to join the Allies, governmental attitudes towards us American's was changing in Argentina, and not for the better.

We were having our cattle rustled, our fences destroyed, one of our wells tainted, and when we filed a police report, the local police did little to nothing to investigate. All we got from the police captain was a shrug and a "Sorry señor, these things happen."

"Well, if you can't help us, we'll just have to help ourselves." Sundance stated.

"Señor, I would not advise you to take matters into your own hands."

"Nobody steals from us and gets away with it, el Capitan." Kid Curry said curtly.

"You will only get yourselves into trouble, señor."

"Captain, we know trouble, Hell, we come from trouble. Now, here's how it's going to be, if we catch anybody on our land trying to steal our cattle, we'll kill 'em, understand?" Butch said.

"That would be a big mistake."

Butch shrugged and said, "These things happen."

When we got back to the ranch, all of our gauchos were gathered at the main house, horses saddled, and their bedrolls packed. They had been warned that if they did anything to assist us and someone got killed, they too would be held as an accessory to murder or at least manslaughter.

Our ranch foreman, Pablo Ramirez, a man in his fifties, stood by his horse with the six gauchos mounted behind him. He approached us, hat in hand, his head slightly bowed and said, "Señor Butch, we have been warned by the police that we could all face criminal charges if we stay and somebody gets hurt or killed.

"We have families and are poor, we can not afford to get mixed up in such things, I hope you understand. Sorry."

Butch held out his hand and shook Pablo's, "You all have nothing to feel sorry for, we understand. This is not your fight. Vaya con diaos."

We stood there and watched the men who helped us grow our ranch into one of the more successful ranches in the Los Nogales Valley leave. As for us, we saw that the writing was on the wall. The pro-Germany sentiment was against us, it would be just a matter of time before we would be forced out. It was ironic; yes, we were American, but we had no loyalty to America, we were, after all, wanted outlaws and would soon be again.

Knowing the criminal mind as we do, we knew that nighttime would be the best time that these cattle rustlers would make their move. So, we moved the cattle into an area that would be difficult for anyone to round them up quickly. It was a grassy area where the typography was filled with dozens of crevasses, that would prove to be time-consuming, which would work to our advantage.

It was almost a full moon, and the four of us had positioned ourselves strategically so as to have a clear shot to the rustlers and yet not be in direct fire of each other.

Sure enough, it was about 2am when we heard the first of six semi-trucks pull up. It was the last semi that unloaded the twelve riders on horseback that would try and collect the herd, round them up, drive them to the trucks where they would be loaded and then, vamos.

We had pre-arranged that we would all hold our fire until Butch fired the first shot. I had taking cover-up in the branches of a large oak tree. I was equipped with a BAR, Browning Automatic Rifle, two 45mm Colt semi-automatic pistols, and a Remington sawed-off 12 gauge shout gun, just in case things got personal.

Butch and the others each had either a BAR or a Thompson submachine gun, assorted handguns and Kid Curry had procured a dozen hand grenades, we were, as they say in the US of A, loaded for bear.

At approximately 3:10am, the shit hit the proverbial fan, as the rustlers had fanned out to try and engulf the scattered herd. Two of the riders practically stepped on Butch they were so close. After they passed him by, he stood up and opened fire with his Tommy Gun, killing both of them instantly.

I shot and killed two men with my BAR, as they were driving directly at me with what looked to be about fifteen head of cattle. I then climbed down from the tree to encounter gunfire from a rider charging at me full speed, I waited until he was almost upon me then I stepped out from behind the tree, using my sawed-off Remington and shot him in the face, forcing him to fall from his horse. He was not killed, but severely wounded. He crawled along the ground, screaming, "Ayudame por favor, soy ciego!"

I couldn't stand to watch him suffer any longer, so I walked up to him holding both of my 45 Colts and put a single bullet in his brain. As they say, no good deed goes unpunished, because that's when I took a bullet in the back of my thigh from a gaucho who had snuck up from behind, trying to bushwhack me. I spun around and fired both my Colts simultaneously, striking him no less than eight times in the torso, killing the 'perro sucio,' that he was. I have kilt many a man, but I have never shot a man from behind. Only a low-down dirty villain, that has no honor would do something like that.

Meanwhile, Butch and Sundance had pinned down five of the rustlers in a small ravine, they were engaged in a fierce fire-fight. It wasn't until Kid Curry appeared with some grenades that turned the tide, and the two surviving varmints declared their willingness to surrender. They climbed out of the ravine, with their hands raised above their heads surrendering, yelling, "No dispares, nos rendimos!"

Off in the distance far from the shooting, a lone rider began to drive a couple dozen head of cattle towards the trucks. It was Kid Curry who took aim with his Winchester

Model 70. The rider was positioned low hanging on to the opposite side of the saddle so not to give anyone a clear target. The gaucho was hidden entirely from Kid Curry's view, except for his right hand that was holding on to the horn of the saddle. This was a display of horsemanship that I had only seen rivaled by Apache warriors in battle.

But, it was all the Kid needed, he fired a fantastic shot hitting the saddle horn, thereby causing the rider to lose his only hold on the saddle, except for his foot being trapped in the stirrup.

When the rider fell, with his foot stuck in the stirrup, his horse dragged him over a mile. The horse slowed to a slow gallop and finally to a complete stop; by then the poor fellow was dead.

Sundance stood in awe, saying, "Kid, that was one Hell of a shot."

Kid Curry, still looking off into the distance, said, "No, it wasn't, that was a terrible shot."

"Whadda ya mean, it was amazing." I said.

"I missed." The Kid said disappointedly.

"Whadda ya talking about!"

"I was aiming at the horse." The Kid replied, and then walked away.

We hog-tied the prisoners and lined up the bodies of the fallen side-by-side under the big oak tree that I had taken refuge in. As we were gathering all of their weapons, we could see that all the semi-trucks had left.

After we rounded up the rustler's horses, we just left their saddles scattered on the ground where we found them and drove the ponies back to the corral at the main house.

Before we had left for the skirmish, we had pre-packed all of our belongings and stowed them in the pickup trucks, hitched up the horse trailers, so when we returned we could quickly leave Argentina. As to put a fine point to our leaving, we set fire to all the buildings on the ranch, and we then made our way north towards Bolivia, except for one stop along the way.

SS Hauptsturmführer Klaus Barbie sat quietly at his desk, caressing a small grey kitten on his lap when there was a knock on his office door.

"Eingeben!"

The door opened, a German Gestapo officer, wearing the traditional black leather trench coats shoved a thirteen-year-old girl inside.

"Simone Lasevre, Jude." The Gestapo agent said as he closed the door and went down to the basement to one of the interrogation rooms.

Barbie placed the kitten down, stood up, smiled and in French said, "Venez ici, Simone."

The child, having seen the man gently petting the kitten when she entered the office, felt no fear. She couldn't imagine someone who loved animals to be evil. She was wrong, when she got close to him, she smiled, "Oui monsieur?"

Barbie picked up a leather-bound copy of Victor Hugo's Les Misérables from his desk and smashed her in the side of the head, knocking her down. He leaned down and grabbed her by the hair and dragged her to the center of the office where he began punching her in the face and stomach, all the while asking her questions, trying to obtain information on the whereabouts of other Jewish families.

Every time he knocked her down, he would grab her by the hair to have her stand up. This went on for over a week; finally, he grew bored of her and had her sent to Auschwitz, death camp.

The Butcher of Lyon earned his moniker thru horror, cruelty, terror, torture, and murder. He personally tortured men, women, and children with joy.

He tortured Lilly Vauquelin, a woman he believed to be a member of the Resistance, for nine days, by beating her with a rubber hose while she hung naked from her wrists by handcuffs. He then would immerse her in freezing water and hold her underwater. During her last interrogation, he had her lie flat on her stomach while he whipped her on her back with a spiked ball attached to a chain, which broke several of her vertebrae.

One summer evening in June while taking a stroll with his wife Regine, they stopped at an ice cream parlor to get a couple of sundaes. Klaus observed that the two ice-cream peddlers were acting suspicious, Barbie accused the two men of being Jews. Instead of arresting them, he beat one man to death with an ashtray and shot the other in the head. While both men lay dead on the parlor floor, he and his wife continued to sit and to eat their ice-cream sundaes.

Regine leaned over to Klaus and said, "Pity, those kikes made an excellent sundae."

The first stop on our journey to Bolivia was a place called Termas de Rio Hondo, the Hot springs of the Deep River, a quiet, sleepy little town. We parked in front of El Camino Torcido, a local restaurant for lunch. It was after 1:30 in the afternoon. The host, an elderly man welcomed us at the door, Sundance asks, "Sigues sirviendo el almuerzo?"

"Si, señor."

"They're still serving lunch." Sundance translated.

We've been living in Argentina now for a little over five years, and me and Kid Curry are still a little slow on the uptake as far as learning the lingo.

The old man took us to a table in the corner away from the locals, which is fine by us. We have some serious things to discuss. After we ordered, Butch looks at us, and asks, "So?"

"What now?" Sundance asked gazing at us all.

"Well, we tried going straight, and that didn't exactly work out, did it? I said.

Kid Curry whispers, "Maybe we should just go back to the States."

But, Butch always the calm one said, "I think going back to the States would be tempting fate.

"So, we failed at ranching, Hell, let's go back to what we know we're good at, bank robbing. You know these local cops aren't as sophisticated as they are up north, and more importantly, they don't have the FBI.

"Whadda think, Sundance?"

"I think I see the Banco de la Naicón Argentina right across the street, Butch."

Butch turned around in his seat and looked out the plate glass window, and sure enough, there larger than life, sitting across the street sat our salvation.

Butch's plan was simple, we would drive the trucks and trailers north for about twenty miles, park well off the road in some secluded area hidden from the main highway, unload the horses, then ride back far enough to enter the town from the south. Then proceed to hold up the bank, ride south and at some point, split up, then circle back north to the trucks and continue onward to Bolivia.

Butch, Sundance and Kid Curry entered the bank with bandanas pulled up covering their faces, while I stood outside tending to the horses and acting as a lookout. The bank looked to me like the banks of Wyoming back in the 1800s, not very modern.

The first thing Butch did was to walk up to the bank guard and pull his revolver and disarm the man forcing him to lie down on the floor. Butch emptied the guard's pistol and tossed it across the room. There were three customers, two bank tellers, and three bank officers that Sundance and Kid Curry held at gunpoint.

Butch slowly walked towards the tellers and announced, "Esto es un asalto! Dame todo to Dinero."

The tellers began to do as they were told, emptying out their cash drawers into the canvas bag that Butch held out. After they had finished, they were made to lie down on the floor with the customers.

Butch walked into where the bank officers were seated next to the open vault, pointed his 45 Colt at the eldest of the men and calmly said, "Por favor, pon todo el dinero en esta bolsa."

The man took the canvas bag and placed all the cash from the vault in with the money from the tellers. When he had finished, he handed the bag full of cash back to Butch and said, "Por favor señor, no nos hagas daño."

Butch nodded an acknowledgment that he didn't intend to harm anyone. Once Butch had the bag, he walked back thru the bank ripping the phone lines out of the walls. When he reached the door he turned and said, "Nadie se mueva por diez minutos, tenemos un hombre afuera."

Then we were off. We headed south for about three miles, then split up into two's, me and Kid Curry and Sundance and Butch. We circled around the town on either side and met back where the trucks were hidden. As we were loading the horses onto the trailers, Kid asked, "What did you say when we were leaving the bank, Butch?"

"I said, don't anyone move for ten minutes, we have a man outside."

In less than four hours, we were in Bolivia.

The article from the Buenos Aires Times read:
DEATH ON THE PAMPAS
Police in Los Nogales have reported that the bodies of ten gauchos were found on the cattle ranch of American rancher, George Cassidy. The ranch is known locally as los rancheros yanquis because the four owners are all Americans.

The two-surviving gauchos, Jose Castillo, and Juan Franco tell this reporter that they were simply cutting across Cassidy's ranch when they were viciously set upon. They have repeatedly denied any wrongdoing.

However, police claimed that they found evidence of cattle branding manipulating tools, which calls into question the nature of the attack. If cattle rustling was indeed the intent of these men, then that may mean Cassidy and his partners may have been justified in defending their property.

There are still the charges of excessive force, none of the slain gauchos seemed armed with anything other than the traditional facón, rebenque and bolas.

The police are currently looking for George Cassidy, Harry Longabaugh, Harvey Logan, and William "News" Carver to get their side of the story. As to date, their whereabouts are still unknown.

After crossing into Bolivia, we checked into a small hotel, Las Tres Lunitas, The Three Moons in the border town of Aguas Blancas. When we were checking in we discovered something we hadn't thought of, we stole a lot of Argentine Peso's, but we were now in Bolivia, and their currency is the Boliviano, not the peso.

Luckily, the hotel owner said he'd accept the pesos, since he could trade them over the border in Argentina. Of course, he'd have to charge us more for his troubles.

The hotel owner, Alvaro Carrieri, appeared to be in his late fifties, salt, and pepper bushy hair, with a large unkempt mustache. He was built like a fireplug with several prison tattoos on his muscular forearms. His face looked like an old leather baseball mitt from having spent way too many years in the sun. His nose had been broken many times, probably from getting into one too many bar brawls.

He was a dubious character, one who seems to have the knowledge of how to navigate the murky underground world of crime. He told us that he had heard on the radio of four men who robbed a bank in Argentina. They had reported that the men were thought to be Americans, a sizeable reward was being offered for information leading to the arrest and conviction of the banditos.

"You speak very good English, Alvaro." Butch noted.

"I spent 10 years in Huntsville prison up in Texas."

"Oh, for what?"

"Armed robbery."

"How did you end up in this shithole."

"I got deported after I got out, and since this was where my mother lives, here I am."

"You clean?" Kid Curry asked.

"Not squeaky, what do you need?"

"Can you launder money, or do you know someone who can?"

"How much?"

"Sixty thousand pesos." Butch said.

"That would be ninety-four hundred Bolivialos, but that's a legit swap, you're looking at getting around four grand."

"Can you do it?"

"It will take a couple of days."

"Okay, do it." Butch said.

"Oh and Alvaro, don't go pulling any funny business, ya dig?" Sundance said revealing his 45 Colt in his shoulder holster.

I leaned over the counter and whispered, "This here is Butch Cassidy, and we're the Wild Bunch."

Alvaro's eyes got as wide as saucers.

"¡Caramba!" He said with a big grin on his face.

In 1953 while Butch and we were slipping in and out of Argentina and Paraguay robbing banks and building a notorious reputation as the "Banditos Yanquis" Che had become radicalized by the writings of Karl Marx, Lenin, and Stalin. He moved to Guatemala to help in the workers struggle against the American tyrannical, evil capitalistic overlords, better known as the United Fruit Company; the largest landowner in all of the country.

The newly elected president, Juan Jacobo Árbenz Guzmán was beginning to enact major agrarian reforms that would aggressively affect the UFC. By confiscating large swaths of land and redistributing them to poverty-stricken Agricultural laborers and indigenous people, they lobbied the United States government to have him overthrown.

Once President Eisenhower felt that Guatemala was heading to becoming a communist country in the Americas', he authorized the CIA to go ahead with operation "PBSUCCESS." The CIA began saturating Guatemala with anti-Árbenz propaganda through radio and dropped leaflets. They also started bombing raids using unmarked airplanes. They even raised an army of mercenaries to try and remove Árbenz from office and topple the government.

Che joined the armed militia organized by the Communists but became frustrated by their inaction, so he returned to medical duties instead of combat. It wasn't long before the coup succeeded and Árbenz was forced to seek refuge in the Mexican Embassy. Árbenz told his foreign supporters to leave the country for fear of reprisals. It wasn't long before Che got word that he was marked for murder.

Che later would tell Butch that it was what happened in Guatemala that finally convinced him of the necessity for armed struggle and for taking the initiative against imperialism. Che left Guatemala and headed to Mexico City and worked at the Hospital Infantil de Mexico. It was in Mexico City that he met and married his first wife, Peruvian economist and Communist leader, Hilda Gadea.

Butch and the gang moved to our official permanent residences in La Paz, the capital of Bolivia. We would travel to rob banks in other countries near the Bolivian borders. Most recently we've been traveling into Peru and Chile to hit small-town banks that are more rural and with less sophisticated alarms systems and police. Sure the hauls are less but so are the dangers. Knockoff big city banks and you're just asking for trouble.

By summer of 1956, things were going so well, that we felt it was finally safe to move our ladies down to join us permanently. They had visited us over the years, but it never seemed to be stable enough to have them relocate.

We decided that it would be a good idea to live in different parts of town for safety purposes. Butch lived a house in the Miraflores Norte area across from the Jardín Botánico. Sundance lived in an apartment in Chichas near the abbot of San Antoni. He said he moved there for the peace and quiet. Kid Curry had a small flat in the Cristo Rey area over the night club, Club 501 because it wasn't peaceful or quiet. And me, I had a small house across from the Plaza Villarroel in the Alto Puerto Rico Miraflores part of town.

We all met at Butch's house to welcome the gal's arrival from the States. The taxi from the airport pulled up around 5pm so overloaded with luggage, it looked like a clown car. Ann and Josie Bassett had sold off their ranch last year and were living in Boulder. Ever since Elzy's conviction and imprisonment, Josie Bassett took up with Kid Curry, I don't know if she really did fancy him or was it just having someone to be with.

Etta Place, Sundance's lady, had just up and quit her school teaching job in Casper, Wyoming once she heard from the Kid.

For the special occasion, Butch had some food brought in from Siloancheria Elenita, a local restaurant that serves excellent Bolivian dishes, and of course plenty of beers. The celebration went on until the wee hours of the morning, Della Moore and I didn't get back to my place until 4am.

It had been agreed that we wouldn't pull another job for at least a month, so we could spend time with our ladies, and show them the city and settle in.

Butch and Sundance made it a standard policy that we would never hit the same bank twice, however, there was one exception, the Agente Banco de la Nacíon in Puno, Peru on the shores of Lake Titicaca. Once a year all the farmers and ranchers come to Puno for the annual livestock auction and fair, thousands of people attend. The banks are flush with cash to accommodate the sale of livestock, so we thought that we'd help by relieving them of heavy the burden of holding all that money.

It was one in the afternoon, the auction was in full swing, when Sundance, Butch, Kid Curry and myself entered the bank wearing our traditional cowboy bandanas. We each were carrying shotguns, and 45mm Colts stuck in our holsters.

"Esto es un asalo!" Butch yelled, pointing his shotgun at the two-dozen bank customers, announcing that this was a robbery.

Sundance kicked in the door to the bank manager's office and said, "Pon las manos arriba enel aire."

The manager did as he was told, he put his hands in the air. As he was standing up from his desk, he tapped an alarm that was hidden from view on the floor.

Meanwhile, Kid Curry and I jumped over the cashiers counter, shouting, "No toques las alarmas!" and started grabbing the money from the cash draws.

Outside, sitting in the getaway car was Della Moore who heard the sound of sirens off in the distance, she could tell that the police had been alerted. She calmly walked to the corner where there was a phone booth and placed a call to the bank.

When the phone rang, Butch had the foresight to answer it, "Hola."

"Butch, you guys better cheese it, fast. The cops are coming!"

Now, we all could hear the sirens, we knew we didn't have much time. We all looked to Butch who shouted, "Vamonos! Let's go!"

Kid Curry got behind the wheel, Sundance took the front shotgun seat, while Della, Butch and, me hopped in the back seat. Once we were all in, the Kid stomped on the gas, and we took off like a rocket with the police in hot pursuit. We were weaving in and out of traffic on the main drag, Simon Bolivar Avenue. The Kid was blasting thru red lights, clipping parked cars, driving up onto the curbs from time to time, scaring the Hell out of the pedestrians walking on the sidewalks. It was when we jumped on to Highway 35 that they started using their weapons; there were at least six patrol cars on our tails. The lead car tried to pull up alongside us on the right, but at the last minute, Kid Curry swerved smashing into their front left fender and forced them to careen off the highway and into a ditch.

After that happened, one of the policemen leaned out of the passenger window and started to fire at us with his revolver, striking and shattering the rear window. Butch and I turned around facing backward and fired off several volleys from our Remington pump shotguns, hitting their windshield, demolishing it, and wounding the driver, causing him to pull off to the side of the highway.

We continued to fire at the remaining four police vehicles, trying to keep them at bay. We were heading to the small village of Chucuito that sat on the shores of Lake Titicaca, where we had the Bassett sisters waiting for us in a speed boat, ready to whisk us off to a waiting getaway car across the lake in the Bolivian town of Carabuco.

The Kid pulled our car as close as he could to the small dock where Ann and Josie were waiting with the motor running. The police cars pulled up with officers firing their weapons, they seemed to be shooting at no one and anyone. Bullets were whizzing all around us; we were firing back as we started to make a break for the boat.

Sundance grabbed his Thompson submachine gun and yelled out, "I'll cover you all, go now!"

As Sundance stood straight up from behind the car blasting away at the constables, we made a mad dash for the dock and the safety of the boat.

You know, nothing stops return fire faster than a barrage of bullets from a Tommy gun. Man oh man, you should have seen those cops duck for cover. Sundance then started to head back to the boat, continuing to give short bursts of machine-gun fire until he too was on board.

"Hit it!" Butch shouted to Ann.

Ann trusted the levers forward, and the Riva speedboat's two Chris-Craft MCL 5.5-liter six-cylinder engines roared to life nearly sending Butch overboard. If it weren't for the cat-like reflexes of Sundance, Butch would have been treading water.

It wasn't until we were well out on to the lake that we discovered that Della had been shot from behind. The wound looked to be quite severe, so we decided that she and I would be dropped off at the hospital at Puerto Acosta claiming that she was accidentally shot while I was cleaning my gun.

I was holding Della in my arms, as she was slipping in and out of consciousness.

"Come on, baby, stay with me." I said softly."

She would open her eyes every so often trying to stay awake, but by the time we reached the Bolivian side of the lake, Della had passed away.

"Butch, she's gone!" I said, crying.

Butch and everyone was very comforting, but we had to make a hard decision, what to do with her body? We could take her and bury her someplace out in the woods; we could weigh her down and let her down in the middle of the lake, or we could leave her body at a hospital to let them deal with her. But a gunshot would possibly lead the police back to us. In the end, we took her out into the middle of the beautiful forest on Monte Suma, where we had a small private service, and afterwards, I said my final goodbyes to my love.

Ever since we ran into Che during that worker's march in Argentina, when Butch saved his life, I have been keeping tabs on his career. First, his medical career and then his transition into becoming a Marxist revolutionary. Whenever I read an article about him, I would read it out loud to Butch and Sundance.

On November 25, 1956, Che and eighty–one other revolutionaries set sail for Cuba from Mexico on a small leaky cabin cruiser to try and kick start the revolution by overthrowing the Cuban government of Batista.

It was a disaster, many of the eighty-two men were either killed in the attack by Batista's army soon after they landed, or they were captured and executed; only twenty-two managed to survive, Che and Fidel Castro being among them.

They worked their way deep into the Sierra Maestra Mountains, where they hid among the poor subsistence farmers. There were no schools, no electricity, hardly any medical care, and over 40% of the adults couldn't read or write. During their time in the mountains, Guevara set up homegrown factories for making grenades, built ovens for baking bread, helped organizes schools to teach the illiterate to read and write. He also established health clinics, and a newspaper to disseminate information.

He soon became second in command to Castro, and even though he took the Hippocratic oath swearing to do no harm, Che became a brutal disciplinarian who sometimes would shoot defectors and deserters himself. Castro once described Che as intelligent, daring, and an exemplary leader who had considerable moral authority over his troops.

On one occasion when a young lieutenant was wounded in battle, Che ran to the man, and defying bullets threw the man over his shoulder and brought the man to safety.

"So whaddya think, Butch?" I asked after reading some of Che's exploits in the newspapers.

"I guess our little Che is all grown up."

"Sieg Heil." Karl Rauff said as he snapped to attention.

"Now, now there will be none of that here. We must keep our traditions to ourselves or at least for select occasions, my dear Karl. You must realize that there are Judas' and Jews everywhere, who would be willing to turn you in for far less than thirty pieces of silver just to see you hang." Klaus Barbie whispered as he sat on the veranda of his favorite restaurant, Erdinger.

"Sorry, Herr Barbie, I just arrived and am unfamiliar with the protocol."

"It's Altmann, Klaus Altmann. Have you been given a new identity?"

"Ja, Josef Reinhardt."

"Well, Joespf, won't you please sit down and join me?"

As Rauff sat down opposite, the waiter came over to their table.

"May I get you something to drink, señor?" The waiter asked.

"I'll have an Erdinger Dunkel."

"Very good, señor."

"Now Joespf, you must never use your previous name again, if you ever let it slip, it may lead to having the hangman's noose slip over your head. Understand?" Barbie stressed.

"Jawohl."

SS Hauptsturmführer Klaus Barbie aka Klaus Altmann aka the Butcher of Lyon was a wanted Nazi war criminal by the French government for having personally tortured French prisoners of the Gestapo, while in Lyon, France.

After the war, Barbie was captured, escaped, and eventually made his way to Bolivia to avoid the French, who had sentenced him to death in absentia for his war crimes.

He finally settled in the city of Cochabamba, Bolivia where he got a job working for the department of the Interior as a Colonel and instructor for the Bolivian security forces, teaching them the art of torture and disappearance of political dissidents under the protection of fascist Bolivian dictators General Rogelio Miranda and Luis García Meza Tejada.

Colonel Barbie/Altmann was also popular with the Bolivian Army for his anti-communist stance, thru his connections with the members of the Odessa organization and the Ratlines, he was able to provide information on known communists around the world but most important, communists operating in Latin America, like Fidel Castro and Che Guevara.

SS Obertsturmführer Karl Albin Rauff aka Joespf Reinhardt aka the Beast of Auschwitz was in charge of operations at the death camp. He was brought in to manage the gassings of new transports.

After the war, he was captured in Italy, but escaped from the Allies with the help of Bishop Alois Hudal, a Nazi sympathizer who provided false identity papers, and helped put him in contact with the 'San Girolamo ratline.'

Catholic Bishops would hide Nazi war criminals in the San Girolamo degli Illirci Seminary College in Rome, where they would receive fake passports, travel documents and safe passage on ships bound for Argentina.

Once he arrived in Argentina, it was decided that he would be sent to Cochabamba, Bolivia to help Barbie work with the government of Generals Miranda and Tejada in their fight against the threat of communists and political dissidents.

"Let's see, my rank is colonel, I think we'll make you a Major. Is that satisfactory, Joespf?" Asked Barbie.

"More than satisfactory, sir. What will my duties be?"

Barbie thought for a few moments, smiled, and said, "I think I should like you to be in charge of prisoner interrogations. It's something I believe that you'll enjoy, and one should always take pleasure in one's work, don't you agree, Major Reinhardt?

"Oh, absolutely Colonel Altmann, absolutely."

"Excellent, once you're all settled in, report to me at my office at San Sebastian Penitentiary."

"Jawohl Colonel, I will be there first thing on Monday morning." Reinhardt said sharply, coming very close to giving the Nazi salute, but catching himself in time.

"Relax Major, just enjoy your beer."

Ever since Della was shot and killed during the commission of the bank robbery in Puno, Peru, we have kept a low profile.

The Peruvian Times, the Peruvian English newspaper has been running a series of articles, about the Bandidos Yanquis. They believe they are headquartered in either Bolivia or Chile and cross over the border to commit crimes then slip back over the border to the safety of their home base. The Peruvian government has announced that a bilateral commission is to be set up to try and co-ordinate police unity and extradition between Peru, Bolivia, and Chile.

"What do you make of it, Butch?" I asked after reading the latest article out loud to him, Sundance and Kid Curry.

"Bolivia borders five countries, and we've only pulled heists in two of them so far. I'm thinking maybe we expand our horizons." Butch replied.

Sundance was looking at a wall map of South America that he had pinned up on his living room wall. Sundance was never one to spend his money on fancy home décor. He liked to live the good life, fine wines, gourmet cuisine, and traveling first class.

"We'll hit a bunch of random border towns in Chile, Peru, Argentina, and Paraguay. There won't be any pattern to it, so they won't be able to figure where we'll strike next. One day it could be Colchane, Chile, two days later, La Quiaca, Argentina." He said, pointing to the cities on the map.

"Yeah, and then we go back to Chile and then over to some dink-ass town in Paraguay. It'll drive them crazy. Why Hell, they can't have large concentrations of cops everywhere." Kid Curry said gleefully.

Butch, looking at the large wall map, thought a moment before speaking, "They probably won't be big scores, but they should be easy pickings."

"I think we should travel in two different cars, two different makes, two different colors. We'll take one into the country that we commit the robbery in and the other one for the getaway waiting for us across the border in Bolivia, so they'll be looking for the robbery car that we ditched." Sundance said.

I said, "Then we can use the getaway car next time as the robbery car, we'll just keep switching and ditching cars, brilliant Sundance."

It was just like the old days back in the States, it was the Wild West once again. I don't know who said, you can't go back in time', but he was wrong. We were the Wild Bunch again. Hell, we even introduced ourselves, "We're Butch Cassidy and the Sundance Kid with Kid Curry and News Carver, el Grupo Salvaje!"

We pulled over twelve jobs in four countries, under two weeks. We each cleared the equivalent of fourteen thousand US Dollars, which in 1958, in Bolivia was considered to be a king's ransom.

We shoulda been set for a couple of years of living on easy street, but with Kid Curry, it was always easy come, easy go, living in the fast lane. He went thru his share in six months, gambling and whoring, Josie Bassett had had enough, and so did the other girls. It was decided that they would all go back to the States. We all realized that sooner or later we would all end up like Della, it was just a matter of time. I believe that Della's death played a large part in their decision; death can snap one back into reality, fast.

Kid Curry wanted to pull another series of jobs, but the rest of us still had plenty of money where we wanted to take a break and enjoy ourselves. So, the Kid figured he'd pull a solo job all by his self. He just happened to be driving thru the city of Cochabamba, when he spied the Banco Nacional de Bolivia off of Highway 4, the Kid thought he'd waltz in and make a quick withdrawal and be on his way, easy peasy.

The Kid was wrong, the one thing he hadn't figured on was the presence of Major Reinhardt who was armed and a crack shot. The Kid walked into the bank with his bandana covering his face, walked into the middle of the bank, fired one shot in the air and yelled in English, "This is a stickup, everyone get on the ground!"

Everyone did as they were told except for Reinhardt. Curry pointed his 45 at the Major and shouted, "Listen Poncho, get your ass on the ground or I'll..."

Before the Kid could finish, Reinhardt whipped out from behind his back his 9mm Luger pistol, a sentimental souvenir from his Nazi days, and fired off one shot hitting Kid Curry in the shoulder knocking his weapon out of his hand. The Kid had the presence of mind to try and escape, unfortunately Reinhardt fired a second shot striking him in the leg causing him to collapse on the bank floor.

When the local police and emergency medical services came, Reinhardt had them take Kid Curry to San Sebastian prison hospital after he was stabilized for interrogation. Major Reinhardt was looking forward to finally getting the opportunity to torture an American. Maybe if he were lucky, this American would be a Jew.

SS Obertsturmführer Karl Albin Rauff was one of Himmler's fair hair boys working at the Auschwitz death camp. Himmler liked his SS officers not to be just efficient but cruel, the crueler, the better.

Rauff was notorious for walking thru the lines of women and girls waiting to be judged whether they would live or whether they would die in the "showers", he would snatch babies from their mothers arms, hold them by the legs and smash their heads against brick walls, killing them so they wouldn't have to waste bullets.

Rauff personally enjoyed hanging women and children in front of assembled prisoners with piano wire for stealing food and other minor infractions, then sit and have lunch while watching them die.

It wasn't uncommon for him to walk amongst the newly arrived prisoners that had just arrived on the trains, to ask for volunteers. Those who raised their hands he had them gather in a group, strip naked, then would shoot them, saying, "Well, you volunteered didn't you."

Once before a group of Jewish women and their children were being loaded into the gas-chamber "showers', before he closed the door on them he announced, "I have some good news for you, after your shower, you are all going to the finest hotels in Berlin."

The women and children started cheering and laughing. Rauff then shouted, "As a bar of soap." Then he'd slam the door shut and personally run to the roof and dump in the Zyklon B pellets.

Sitting on the roof smoking a cigarette, he listened to the screaming and moaning, after twenty minutes the

Sonderkommando's wearing gas masks would go in and drag the bodies out and over to the ovens. There they would remove the victim's eyeglasses, artificial limbs, jewelry, shave their heads and remove any teeth that contained gold fillings, so it could be melted down.

After the bodies were burned in the ovens, the ashes were either buried, thrown in the river or used as fertilizer.

Rauff loved to taunt the newly arriving Jewish prisoners as they were standing in line. He'd go up to someone and ask, "Would you like to hear a good joke?"

The prisoner would, out of fear, say yes.

"What's the difference between a ton of coal and 1,000 Jews?"

"I don't know."

Rauff would point to the crematorium chimneys and say laughing, "Jews burn longer!"

I rushed over to Butch's house, where I found him and Sundance having lunch in the backyard.

"Butch, Sundance, I just heard that the Kid has been shot and captured trying to rob a bank in Cochabamba." I said excitedly.

"News, are you sure?" Sundance asked.

"Yeah, I was listening to music on the radio when they broke in with a news alert. They said that an American named Harvey Logan was shot and apprehended while trying to rob Banco Nacional de Bolivia. He was shot twice and taken to the San Sebastian prison hospital, that's all I know."

"Damn it, Curry!" Butch cursed.

"Where the Hell is Cochabamba anyway?" Sundance asked.

"I looked it up before I got here, it's about 250 miles southeast, close to a seven-hour drive." I said.

Butch sat quietly for a long time thinking, then said, "We can't go and see how he's doing, but we could have Josie go. They're not supposed to leave for another week, whatta think?"

"I'm sure she'll do it." Sundance said.

"News, go ask Josie to come over, would you?"

"Sure Butch, be right back."

Josie, Ann, and Etta were sharing a hotel suite at the Hotel Republica in a not far from Butch's place. I walked into the central plaza courtyard, walked up to the second floor, and knocked on the door, Etta answered.

"News, is everything alright?" She asked.

"The Kid Curry has been shot and arrested, is Josie here?"

"Come in, come in. Is he alright?"

"I don't know. All I know is that he was taken to the San Sebastian prison hospital."

Josie walked into the living room from one of the bedrooms, "What's happening, News?"

"The Kid's been shot and arrested trying to rob a bank in Cochabamba, about seven hours from here. Butch asked that you all would come over to his place."

"What for?" She asked.

"I don't know, everything's been happening so fast, I don't know."

The three women were standing looking at each other wanting someone to make a decision whether to go or not, finally, I said, "Just come and listen, if you want to come back I will personally bring you all back. I promise."

The drive to Butch's house was tense, I could see Josie crying in the rearview mirror as Ann was comforting her. Etta sat in front with me, trying to make small talk in an attempt to keep everyone from thinking about the Kid.

When we got there, Butch and Sundance were waiting for us in the living room.

"Can I get anyone anything, perhaps something to drink?" Butch asked.

There were no takers.

"Well, as News has told you, the Kid has been shot and arrested. At this point, we don't know too much more about his condition.

"But, I'm sure once they fingerprint him, there's an excellent possibility that they'll find out who he is, and that's not good.

"So here's my thought, Josie, if you would, I'd like you to go and try to visit him to check on his condition. What do you say?" Butch asked.

"Butch, we're supposed to leave the country next week." Josie said.

"I know, but if we act fast, you can go down and visit him and still be able to leave on time. All we want is to see if he's being treated alright. I have spoken to the US Consulate here in La Paz, a Mister William Ackley, to see if he can persuade the police to allow you to visit him. I told him had you were his sister. He said he'd let me know by tomorrow."

"Well, as long as we will still be able to leave as scheduled, okay." She said.

"Great, News will take you all back to the hotel. I'll contact you tomorrow once I hear from Ackley. Thanks again, Josie."

Ann took Butch aside and whispered, "This is why we're leaving, we don't want to see you and Sundance end up like the Kid or worse. Give it up Butch, times are changing, it's not like the old days, the police are getting more and more sophisticated, it's just a matter of time."

Butch took her hand, "I wish I could babe, it's just who I am."

"I know." She softly sighed, gave him a kiss, turned, and left.

"How much longer will he be unconscious, Herr Doctor?" Reinhardt asked the prison doctor.

"At least another hour, Major. He was severely wounded and had lost a lot of blood, but I expect that he shall make a full recovery.

"Good, I shall be back in an hour."

Kid Curry aka Harvey Logan was stabilized at the bank, then brought to the prison hospital for surgery. Reinhardt had assumed, and rightly so, that the prison surgeons weren't the top doctors of their class in med school, and that was just fine with him. If it were left up to him, this swine would only have a tourniquet and swift kick to the head.

SLAP!

"Wake up you pig!"

The Kid had been slowly starting to come around when he felt a sharp pain as Reinhardt slapped him hard across his face. He opened his eyes and saw standing next to his bed a tall man glaring down at him, the man was wearing some sort of military uniform.

"Can you hear me, Herr Logan?" Reinhardt snapped.

The Kid nodded as the spider webs were starting to leave his head slowly.

"Where am I?" He asked.

"You Herr Logan, are at San Sebastian prison hospital."

"Who are you, and why do you keep calling me Herr Logan?"

"I am Major Joespf Reinhardt, and you are my prisoner."

"A German in the Bolivian Army?"

"Were you in ze war, Herr Logan?"

"No, I was too old, besides I was down here."

"Robbing banks, no doubt."

"I'd like to speak to a lawyer, Major."

"I'm sure you would," Reinhardt said grinning.

"I'm not saying nothing without a lawyer."

"Is that so, Herr Logan."

Reinhardt leaned over the bed, got nose to nose with the Kid, and punched him hard in the shoulder where he had been shot.

The Kid screamed out in agony and saw a flash of white pain before passing out.

"These Americans are so weak, I can't believe they won." Reinhardt said to himself. He walked over to the other side of the bed, where on the tray table, sat a glass and a pitcher of water. He poured himself a glass of water, took a sip, and threw the rest into the Kids face to try and revive him, to no avail.

A nurse who had heard the Kids scream came running into the room and saw that his shoulder bandage was soaked with blood. She looked at the Major and ran down the hall to fetch the doctor.

The doctor and nurse brought another pressure bandage to redress the wound, the doctor looked at Reinhardt and said, "Major, I must ask you to leave."

"No." Reinhardt said defiantly.

"Major, you can do anything you want to with him after he leaves my care. But, in this hospital, I am God, now leave!"

Reinhardt drew his gun, no one had ever defied him like this before, if this were Germany, this scum would be on his way to the ovens. He pointed his Luger at the doctor, who didn't flinch, instead took a step towards him and said, "Major, I don't have time for this, either shoot me or leave. This man needs my attention."

Reinhardt holstered his weapon and stormed out and went to see Barbie. He told him about his encounter with the doctor, he was looking for affirmation to be able to go and kill the doctor, but to his surprise and disappointment, Barbie sided with the doctor.

Apparently, Barbie had received a call from the US Consulate. They were sending someone to come to check on Logan, plus his sister was also coming to look in on him.

"Be patient my dear Joespf, your time will come to interrogate Herr Logan. I know it's not like the old days, but you'll see, it's going to get better. "

In February 1958, Che created the clandestine radio station Radio Rebelde (Rebel Radio) broadcasting national and international music, news, sports, combat news, and propaganda to the Cuban people 24 hours a day.

The first rebel broadcast began one night with the announcement: "Aquí Radio Rebelde, the voice of the Sierra Maestra, transmitting for all Cuba, I'm station director Captain Luis Orlando Rodriguez, and it's my honor to welcome Major Che Guevara."

"Thank you, Captain. It is my honor."

"Major, if you would tell the Cuban people how the revolution going?"

"Our fight for the rights of the Cuban people is going better than expected. Every day we are gaining more and more victories over Batista's army and the American capitalistic imperial pigs."

"Tell me, comrade, we hear rumors that Cuban government troops are executing rebel prisoners on the spot, no trial, nothing."

"This is true, not only that, but they round up innocent civilians who they beat, rape, and torture then shoot them as a tactic of intimation. But let me tell you comrades that we will not be intimidated. The people will prevail!"

"I have heard that because of all the atrocities carried out by the army's death squads, that the United States has stopped selling arms to Batista's colonial despotic regime."

"That is true, the world now plainly sees the brutal, oppressive and cruel dictatorship that the Cuban people have to live under."

"Are countries coming to the aid of the people's struggle?"

"Si, many countries are coming to our aid, the People's Republic of China and the Soviet Union are two of our closest allies, and they are sending us much needed arms and military advisors."

"Thank you, comrade and good luck."

"Viva la revolución!"

Josie met the Charge d'Affaires William Ackley at his hotel, the La Colonia, on the corner of Mostajo and Kapac Yupanqui Street. La Colonia Hotel it is located in a residential part of the city, it is a non-assuming or pretentious looking hotel, a three-story, white stucco building with large arched windows and a bubbling fountain in the courtyard.

When Josie entered Mr. Ackley's room, she was greeted at the door with one of his aides, a Mister Lance B. Lester, who brought her into the living room of the Presidential suite. He asked her to please have a seat on the leather sofa next to the fireplace and said that Charge d'Affaires Ackley would be with her momentarily.

"Would you care for something to drink, perhaps some coffee?" Lance asked.

"No, thank you." She said.

Josie sat quietly on the sofa with the soft tick-tock of a large pendulum clock mounted on the wall opposite her; it was twelve twenty-two.

Suddenly, the door to one of the bedrooms swung open, and a silver-haired man with a pencil mustache entered the room wearing a white shirt, vest and bright red and white striped bowtie, she figured him to be a man in his seventies. He wore a pair of wire-rimmed spectacles atop his head that looked to give him the appearance of wearing a crown.

"Miss Josie Logan, I'm Charge d'Affaires William Ackley, it's a pleasure to meet you. I just wish it might have been under better circumstances." He said as he shook her hand.

She smiled and said, "Yes, thank you, Mr. Ackley."

He sat down next to her on the sofa, "I'm sorry to hear about your brother's situation, but you must understand there's not much I can do, other than make sure he is well treated and possibly aid in helping him obtain legal counsel. He was arrested for attempted robbery."

"I understand, I'm mainly concerned about his well-being, I read in the papers that he was wounded."

"Yes, I was informed that he suffered two gunshot wounds, one to the shoulder and one in the leg. It is my understanding that they are not life-threatening, however, we shall go see him this afternoon just to make sure he is being treated humanely.

"We will be allowed to visit him in the prison hospital at one o'clock, he should be leaving." He said as he gazed at the wall clock.

As he stood up offered her his hand, she took it and rose from the sofa, "Thank you, you're very kind."

Lance, his assistant, brought in Ackley's suit coat and announced, "The car is waiting downstairs, sir."

"Very good, thank you, Lance."

Downstairs, in the driveway, sat a large black Cadillac with two American flags mounted on the front fenders, and the windows were all blacked out so nobody could see inside. Standing next to the car was a man dressed in a black suit, wearing black sunglasses. As they approached the car the man opened the back passenger door; William Ackley got in first, then Josie followed by Lance.

The drive to San Sebastian prison was draped in silence, everyone deep in thought, at least Josie was. She was glad that no one was talking since the closer they got to the prison, the more nervous she got.

"I'm nervous." She uttered.

"There's nothing to be nervous about, Miss Logan. We're here to check on Harvey's condition, you'll have an opportunity to speak with the doctor and then spend a few minutes with your brother. I promise you; no one will bother or intimidate you."

"Thank you, Mr. Ackley."

As they pulled up to the main entrance of the prison, two uniformed guards approached the car, one on either side. The guard on the driver's side spoke to the driver in Spanish, asking what the purpose of the visit was, and who was in the car.

When told that it was the Charge d'Affaires William Ackley, the guard wasn't impressed, he walked to the guard station and made a phone call. The other guard on the passenger side indicated that he wanted us to lower all the windows so he could peer inside the vehicle.

The guard that had been on the phone stuck his head out of the guardhouse and shouted, "Conducir por delante!"

The driver did as he was told, he drove thru the prison gates to the main administration building, where he parked, got out of the car, walked around to the passenger's side and opened the car door. By the time everyone got out, the warden was exiting the building to greet the Charge d'Affaires.

"Bienvenido, welcome, Charge d'Affaires Ackley. I am Jose Gomez, I'm the warden here at San Sebastian."

"Thank you, Mr. Gomez, it's a pleasure to meet you. This is Mr. Lester, my assistant and this young lady is Josie Logan, sister of Harvey Logan."

Gomez pleasantly greeted Lance and Josie, then escorted them to his office. When they got to the warden's office two men were waiting for them. One looked to be a doctor dressed in a white lab coat, the other was a man in a uniform that resembled the uniform of a German SS officer.

"Everyone, this is Doctor Rivera, he has been looking after your brother Miss Logan, and this is Major Reinhardt head of prison security.

"This is the Charge d'Affaire William Ackley, his assistant Mr. Lester and Josie Logan, the prisoner's sister."

Doctor Rivera just nodded hello, whereas Reinhardt not only nodded, he clicked his boot heels as he snapped to a stance of attention and said, "Willkommen."

The Charge d'Affaires extended his hand to shake the doctor's hand. "Doctor, how is Mr. Logan doing?" He asked.

"He's doing as well as can be expected. He suffered two severe gunshot wounds, but they are not life-threatening, so in time he will make a full recovery."

Reinhardt smiled and proudly said, "I am afraid that I am the one responsible for Herr Logan's wounds. You see

I was in the bank when he tried to rob it. Bad timing on his part."

Ackley didn't attempt to shake the Major's hand, he smiled and asked, "I'm sorry Major, what is your name again?"

"Major Joespf Reinhardt, Herr Ackley."

"Welcome to Bolivia Mr. Reinhardt, how long have you been in here?"

Reinhardt knew that Ackley could find out easy enough, so he decided not to lie. "I have recently immigrated to Bolivia, I have been here a little over six months."

"I assume you were in the war, Major."

"Yes, I was an Oberluetnant in the infantry. I hope you won't hold it against me, but I fought the Americans in France and in what you called the Battle of the Bulge."

"And now you're a Major, well done."

Reinhardt just glared at the old man and thought to himself, 'Ackley, I bet he's a Jew.'

Josie asked Doctor Rivera, "May I see my brother now?"

Reinhardt stepped forward and curtly said, "For no more than fifteen minutes, Fräulein."

The doctor led Josie and Ackley, followed by Reinhardt and Warden Gomez thru the administration building to the hospital wing. When they arrived, Ackley said, "Miss Logan, why don't you go in first, I'll be in shortly."

"Thank you."

When she walked into the room, she saw that the Kid had a large bandage on his right shoulder, a cast on his left leg, and his right hand was handcuffed to the rail on the bed. He was asleep as she approached him. She looked around to make sure no one was listening, then she softly touched his arm and said, "Kid, it's me, Josie."

He opened his eyes and tried to recognize her, but it didn't register until she uttered, "Kid, it's really me."

"Josie?"

"Yeah, I'm here. How are you?"

"Come closer." He said it with as if he were scared of something.

She leaned close to him and gave him a sisterly kiss, "I had to tell them I was your sister, or they wouldn't let me visit you. What's wrong?"

"It's that Nazi."

"Reinhardt?"

"Yeah, he can't wait until I get discharged, cause he's really looking forward to interrogating me."

"Kid, I have the Charge d'Affaire William Ackley from the US Consulate, here to see that you'll be treated fairly."

"That's all well and good until he leaves. He can't watch over me forever. I don't know what he wants but tell Butch and the others to change their identities cause I don't know how long I'll be able to hold out. You too, you better leave, it's not safe."

Charge d'Affaire Ackley entered the room, "Mr. Logan, I'm Charge d'Affaire William Ackley with the US Consulate, and I'm here to make sure your rights are being protected. Are you being treated humanely?"

"Yes, sir."

"Do you have an attorney?"

"No, sir."

"Would you like for me to help you secure one?"

"I would appreciate it if you could, sir."

"Do you have any idea when you'll be released from the hospital?"

"Doctor Rivera thinks in a month or so."

Ackley looked around and could see Reinhardt peering thru the window of the door, "I will check back with you in a month to make sure you're doing okay, in the meantime is there anything I can do for you, Mr. Logan?"

"Can't think of anything. But thank you for coming by and for letting me see my sister."

"I will speak with the warden to make sure that you will be able to contact me if you need anything. I'm sure I don't have to mention it but, if possible stay clear of Reinhardt, he's pure evil."

"Time is up! You'll have to leave now." Reinhardt announced as he entered the room.

Josie squeezed his hand and leaned over to kiss the Kid on the lips, "Goodbye, Kid." she whispered.

Fidel sat across from Che on the other side of a small wooden table where they were looking over a map of the island of Cuba. Fidel was pointing to the Sierra Maestra mountain range, where Castro's forces defeated the Cuban army's Battalion 18, by surrounding the army and with the use of snipers forcing their surrender.

Cuban General Cantillo ordered Battalion 17 to go to the aid of the 18th, but Castro's troops were able to block the road and prevent any relief for the surrounded army, leaving Battalion 17 exposed.

Cantillo called for more troops from nearby towns, amassing some 1500 men; however, rebel forces under the command of Che Guevara stopped the soldiers, thereby turning the tide of the battle and the revolution.

"Che, I must say that your appreciation of the battle was brilliant." Fidel said.

"We were fortunate, comrade. God was with us."

"You've become a master of guerilla warfare my friend, using a hit-and-run strategy, attacking the enemy and then fading back into the jungle before they can muster a counterattack, magnifico."

"As you know Fidel, in war, either one learns and adapts, or one dies."

"I want to discuss your next mission. It will be very difficult. As we are going to make our final push to Havana. Your mission is to take Las Villas province; if we are successful, we will cut the island in half."

Looking at the map, Che estimated that traveling by foot and only at night to avoid ambush, it would probably take at least seven weeks. Knowing that he and his men would have limited supplies they would probably not have enough food to eat every day, but he also knew failure was not an option."

"You're asking a lot of my men." Che said.

"I know, but a revolution is a struggle to the death between the future and the past. Are you and your men up to the task?"

"We will not fail you."

"Che, remember, men do not shape destiny; destiny produces the man for the hour."

"Adios mi amigo."

"Ve con Dios."

Josie left the prison knowing that this would be the last time she would ever see the Kid again, alive. We were all waiting for her when she returned to the hotel after Charge d'Affaire Ackley dropped her off.

Ackley indicated that he or someone from his staff would check in on her brother from time to time and that he would arrange for an attorney to be assigned to his case. But, he told her that considering the circumstances, she shouldn't hold out too much hope for his getting a light sentence.

Up in her room, Josie explained the Kid's situation with the possible sentence he was facing, but more importantly, she relayed the Kid's concern about Major Reinhardt and what he thought what was in store for him. Being the torture and mistreatment from this sadistic ex-Nazi.

"The Kid told me to tell you all that he doesn't know how much torture he can withstand once Reinhardt starts working him over. That's why he says that you all have to move and change the names you're using now. He said that it won't be long before they find out who he really is and he's sure that Reinhardt will want to capture or kill you all."

"Maybe, we should take care of this Reinhardt first." Butch said.

"Yeah, he probably would never think that we would be out gunning for him." Sundance added.

"Fucking Nazi, I bet he'd never expect a bunch of old gangsters like us hitting him first." I chimed in.

"News, you like reading the papers, go to the library tomorrow and find out all you can about this Major Reinhardt. Let's show this Nazi bastard just who he's fucking with." Butch said.

"Right Butch."

"Ann, I think it best that you all plan on making your flights on Friday. Things here could get ugly, Josie thank you for helping, I know it wasn't easy for you."

"Are you sure you want to go thru with this, Butch? Wouldn't the smart thing to do is just to leave?" Ann asked.

"Yeah, but sometimes the smart thing isn't always the right thing." Butch said.

"I'm tired of running, Butch. We've been running all our lives, and I'll be damned if I'm going to let some Nazi run me out of my home." Growled Sundance.

It was late at night when Reinhardt silently opened the door to Kid Curry's hospital room. The dim light from the small table lamp alongside the bed gave off just enough light to let Reinhardt see that the prisoner was asleep. He stood at the foot of the bed and opened Logan's medical cart that had been attached to the bedpost.

It indicated that patient Harvey Logan was to be released into the general prison population in two days. Reinhardt looked down onto Logan sleeping and smiled a smile of pure evil. He had plans for this American, torturous, barbaric plans that he hadn't had perpetrated since his days at the Auschwitz death camp.

The Germans have a word, schadenfreude, which is the experience of pleasure and joy that one gets from witnessing or causing the troubles, humiliation, or pain of another. Karl Albin Rauff aka Joespf Reinhardt elated in inflicting suffering and pain onto others. He felt no remorse, no empathy to those he tortured. To him it was just exhilarating, pleasurable, almost orgasmic. The screams, the contorted, grimacing faces, the twisting of the body, and the straining against their restraints trying to find some kind of relief, but of course, there would be none. The Beast of Auschwitz would make sure of that.

Reinhardt left the room, smiling to himself, "Sleep well, Herr Logan, while you can."

The Battle of Santa Clara will go down as a remarkable tour de force in modern warfare. In spite of being outnumbered ten-to-one. Often times his men were completely surrounded, outgunned and even overrun. Che and his men somehow prevailed, and by his leading his "suicide squad" in the attack on Santa Clara, they won what was to be the decisive military victory of the revolution.

It was announced on Rebel Radio on New Year's Eve 1959 that victory was theirs. The next day when Che and his troops entered Havana to take final control of the capital, President Batista fled to the Dominican Republic with more than 300 million that he had amassed through graft and payoffs. Six days later Fidel Castro arrived victoriously into Havana.

I read the news to Butch and Sundance since we've been following the exploits of Che, and they seemed pleased with all the accomplishments that he had achieved.

Now that the revolution was over there came the ugly task of prosecuting people for war crimes. Castro named Che commander of the La Cabaña Fortress prison. It fell upon Che to purge Batista's army thru revolutionary justice against those considered to be traitors, informants or war criminals.

I have read many different accounts of Che's handling of the revolutionary retributions. But where some say he was quite lenient when it came to pardons others claim that he relished in the ritual of the firing squads. Under his jurisdiction, the death toll was 105 executions by firing squads.

Everyone, friends and foes alike all agreed that revolution had hardened the man who had no qualms about doling out the death penalty. He was quoted saying, "to defend the revolution was to execute its enemies. He wouldn't be swayed by humanitarian or political arguments. The executions are firing squads and are not only a necessity for the people of Cuba, but also an imposition of the people.

It was in 1960 when we met up with Che once again. He was speaking at a "Workers of the World Unite" rally in La Paz, to a crowd of several thousand. Butch, Sundance and me went to hear him speak and see if we could somehow reconnect. We wormed our way close to the podium where he was getting ready to address the crowd.

There just happened to be a moment of calm when we shouted out his name. He glanced down at us with skepticism at first, I guess thinking we were possible CIA agents, but then you could see that there was recognition. He smiled and asked one of his assistants to come get us and invite us back to meet with him behind the stage in a small tent.

"Butch, mi viejo amigo. How are you?"

"I'm doing fine, you remember my partners News Carver and the Sundance Kid?"

"Si, si, yes, of course. What are you doing in La Paz?"

"This is where we live now, things didn't work out in Argentina as we planned."

"What is it you do?"

"We rob banks."

Che looked at the three of us in shock, but then started to laugh, "You are very funny, Butch. Seriously, what sort of business do you do?"

"We rob banks. Have you ever heard of Banditos Yanquis?"

"Yes."

"Well, meet Banditos Yanquis. If there ever comes a time when you might need a little extra financing to help with the revolution come see us, we are big supporters of yours."

"You're serious, Banditos Yanquis?"

"Si mi amigo, we are the Yankee bandits."

"But why?

"Because we're good at it." Sundance said.

"And it beats working for a living." I added.

"In Cuba, if you were caught, we would execute you."

"Well, it's a good thing we aren't planning on robbing any banks in Cuba." Butch said with a grin.

His assistant stuck his head inside the tent flap and said, "Che, debemos irnos."

Che looked at his watch and said, "Lo siento mis amigos, sorry, but I have to go."

"We understand, it was so good to see you again." Butch said.

"You all take care and be careful."

"You too, and remember our offer, we're here if you need us. Adiós."

I spent several days at the Librería de la Biblioteca del Bicentenario de Bolivia trying to find anything I could on a Joespf Reinhardt, but everything I found only went back as far as a year ago. Nothing of his history in Germany during the war. But I just happened to stumble across an article about Nazis that had escaped from Germany and made their way to South American. It seems that a lot of the

Banana Republic dictators were cozying up to these Nazi goons and welcomed them into their loving embrace.

There were several articles about Nazi hunters scouring South America for these war criminals that had escaped justice. I found twelve potential candidates that fit Josie's description of this Major Reinhardt. If this guy was indeed a war criminal, then he unquestionably would have come under an alias to avoid detection.

I talked it over with Butch and Sundance, and we agreed that we would all take a trip to Cochabamba and San Sebastian prison to see if we could visit the Kid. Before we left Butch called the U.S. Consulate and spoke with Charge d'Affaire Ackley's assistant Lance Lester, to see if he could get us permission to see Harvey Logan. He said he wasn't optimistic, but would try, Lester told Butch he'd call back in a couple of hours to let him know if he was successful.

Five hours later, Lester called back telling Butch that he could accompany him and a Mr. Humana, Logan's appointed lawyer to visit Logan the following Monday. That was when they were scheduled to meet with the prisoner.

Being that this was Friday, we had the weekend to travel to Cochabamba and see if we could find this Major Reinhardt, scope him out and see if we could identify him as an escaped war criminal. We checked into the Hotel Moraine, about a ten-minute drive to the prison and began our search.

I went to El Rincon del Libro Cochabamba to see if I could locate Joespf Reinhardt's address in the local phone book, I found four. I also went through past issues of Los Tiempos newspaper articles to see if there were any mentions of a Joespf Reinhardt. And sure enough, there was an article about a Major Joespf Reinhardt being congratulated by a Colonel Karl Altmann and Warden Jose Gomez as the new head of prison security. The accompanying photograph gave a sharp image of Reinhardt, who looks amazingly like SS Obertsturmführer Karl Albin Rauff, better known as the Beast of Auschwitz.

I made photocopies of all my documental evidence to show Butch and Sundance who was waiting for me back at the hotel.

"Well, I found the bastard. He's a fucking war criminal. His real name is Karl Albin Rauff, he's a real piece of work, and his nickname was the Beast of Auschwitz. It seems that he is under the protection of the government and is working directly under Colonel Karl Altmann, another Nazi mucky-muck."

"Did you find out where he lives?" Butch asked.

"Yeah, he has an apartment at 2554 Tumusla Street, literally right around the corner from the prison."

"The man must love his work." Sundance said.

"Let's go and check it out; hopefully, he's at work." Butch said as he went over to his open suitcase. He removed and strapped on his shoulder holster that held his 45 Colt revolver, we both followed suit.

"Or not." Sundance quipped as we walked out the door.

"Herr Logan, I just stopped by to tell you that Monday you and I are going to have our first interrogation session." Reinhardt said, smiling standing at the foot of Logan's hospital bed.

"I'm looking forward to it." The Kid said sarcastically.

"You may think so now, but I can assure you that you won't feel that way afterward."

"What's your fucking problem? What do you have against me, did I do something to make you hate me?"

"You American's think you're so superior to the rest of the world."

"Hey, man we didn't go around calling ourselves the master race, that was you. We Americans know that we're just a bunch of mutts, not pure breeds like you Aryans."

"That is right."

"Yeah, but us, mutts sure kicked your kraut asses, didn't we Fritz."

"You will pay for that, Herr Logan."

"And knowing how you Nazis always like a good clean fight, I can't wait."

"Oh, how much I look forward to dealing with you, Herr Logan. To see you scream in pain and beg for mercy shall bring me much joy."

"I'll try my best not to disappoint you."

"You think that this is a joke? That I am making with the funny stuff?"

"No, I think you're the joke, Herr Schicklgruber."

"You will pay dearly for that."

"What say you get me out of this bed and we go to duking it out right here, right. Hell, even with my bum leg and shoulder, I'll still kick your ass."

Reinhardt stood silent, thinking about it for a moment then said, "No, I think I will enjoy dealing with you Monday."

"Just as I figured, you're just a lily-livered, chicken-shit coward, who hasn't got the guts to go man to man. And that's why you krauts lost the war. It's easy to think of yourself as the super race when you beat up on the weak and defenseless. Didn't work out so well against the Ruskies and the Yanks did it, Fritzy?"

"Swine!" Reinhardt said as he stormed out of the room.

Reinhardt went down into the bowels of the prison, where he had set up his personal torture chamber. There was an old man hanging from his wrists that were tied behind his back, the man was suspended two feet off the ground. He had passed out from agony hours ago. Reinhardt picked up a cattle prod and stuck the man in the ribs, hitting him with 5000 volts.

As the old man screamed out in pain, Reinhardt could sense that he was actually getting sexually aroused, so he jolted the old man again and again, each time getting harder and harder. He walked over and retrieved a Louisville Slugger baseball bat standing in the corner, strode over to the man, lifted his head up with the end of the bat and said, "As they say in America, Let's play ball."

He swung the bat with all his might, splattering the man's brains onto the cellar walls, as he did, he actually ejaculated and was overcome with such a wave of pleasure that he hadn't felt since Auschwitz, and thought to himself, 'Just you wait Herr Logan, we'll see how tough you Yankee mutts are.'

Colonel Karl Altmann and Generals Miranda and Tejada were incognito at the "Workers of the World Unite" rally in La Paz when Che was the guest speaker. They observed what a powerful speaker he was and how he quickly he stirred up the crowd into a frenzy.

"This man is dangerous, he should not be allowed back into the country, coming here spouting his communist ideology among the peasants. Just look what happened in

Cuba. Communism is a fascist's worse nightmare." Colonel Altmann stated categorically.

"We agree with you, Colonel, we can not have the likes of him meddling in our affairs." General Miranda said.

"He could destabilize our regime, there's no telling the damage he could do." General Tejada added.

"We'll leave it to you Colonel to deal with this communist agitator if he ever comes back." General Miranda said.

"You can count on me, General. I've dealt with this kind of scum before."

"Excellent."

Klaus Barbie was awarded the prestigious Iron Cross with swords medal personally by Adolf Hitler himself for the cruelty that Barbie showed to the enemies of the State, and especially for his handling of the Moulin case.

Jean Moulin was a leader of the French Resistance, who was betrayed by a traitor in the Resistance and was personally captured by Barbie.

Moulin was taken to Barbie's office at the Hotel Terminus in Lyon, Gestapo headquarters, where he was forced to kneel on a wooden floor covered with rice, with his hands placed behind his head.

"Good evening Monsieur Moulin, I have been looking forward to this, I am Hauptsturmführer Barbie. Let me be clear, you will tell me everything that I want to know and sign this confession, or you will suffer such unimaginable pain. Do you understand?"

"I have nothing to say."

"We'll see about that."

Barbie called for two Gestapo agents that were waiting out in the hall, "Take this piece of vermin down to the cellar, room B."

The two agents each grabbed Moulin by the arm and manhandled him down several flights of stairs. When they arrived at room B, they strapped his arms and legs to the chair with leather restraints.

By the time Barbie walked into room B, the two thugs had beaten Moulin about the head and face, breaking his nose, splitting his lip, and knocking out five of his teeth.

"Moulin, playtime is over, will you give me the names of the Resistance leaders?" Barbie asked.

"I have nothing to say." He mumbled.

"Good, I love a challenge," Barbie said as he walked over to a table where there were multiple implements of torture. He grabbed a pair of pliers and got hold of one of a dozen red-hot 6-inch needles, which was sitting in an iron pot of hot coals. He held it up to Moulin's face and jammed it under the fingernail of his right thumb.

"Yeeeahhhh!" Moulin screamed before passing out.

One of the Gestapo goons threw a bucket of water on the unconsciousness man, bringing him around.

"Now, now, don't go passing out on us so early; we're just getting started," Barbie said with a wolf's grin.

He proceeded to shove hot needles under all of Moulin's fingernails, again causing him to lose consciousness.

"Leave him, we'll return later. I have to let the Führer know that we've captured such a prize." Barbie said as he left to go back to his office.

"Heil Hitler!" The two hooligans said as they snapped to attention giving the Nazi salute.

Walking away with his back to the officers, Barbie gave a half-hearted salute and mumbled, "Yeah, Heil Hitler."

When Major Reinhardt entered Logan's hospital room at 7am, he found Doctor Rivera and Warden Gomez conferring off to one side.

"Has he been released?" Reinhardt asked.

"Not yet." Warden Gomez answered.

"Why not? I want this man!"

"He is meeting with two men from the U.S. Consulate and his attorney at ten this morning."

"When do I get him?" Reinhardt snapped.

"What's the matter, Fritzy, run out of victims to torture?" Logan said sarcastically.

"Schweinehund! I will kill you!" Reinhardt hollered as he charged the bed.

"Major!" Shouted Gomez.

Reinhardt stopped inches away from smashing the butt of his German Luger revolver down on to Kid Curry's skull. The Kid never flinched, he just looked at Reinhardt and smiled. Reinhardt had never come across anyone who was either so brave or so stupid. Didn't he know what sort of things that he would and could do to him? Maybe the Major thought that just because the prisoner was an American, he would be safe.

Actually, Kid Curry was deathly afraid of what this Nazi monster had in store for him, but he would rather die than give this lousy kraut any satisfaction in showing pain. The Kid had seen this sort of bully throughout the west growing up, especially against the American Indians. People thinking that they were so superior that they would try to degrade them, but all it did was show how dignified the

Indians were compared to the white man. Of course the racist never saw or would admit it.

"Major, why don't you go about your business, I will contact you when the U.S. Consulate and Logan's attorney leaves." Warden Gomez suggested.

Reinhardt stood glaring down at the Kid seething. Then stormed out of the room.

"See you later, Fritzy." Curry shouted.

Doctor Rivera walked over to Logan's bedside, "Mr. Logan, why do you provoke Major Reinhardt so? You do know that he is going to hurt you and make you suffer?"

"Yeah, Doc, but what should I do, act terrified? That's just what he wants, and I'm just not going to give him the satisfaction. Do people know what goes on here?"

"To a certain extent, but either they don't care, or they're too scared. Unfortunately, most people feel that prisoners are guilty and deserve what they get. People don't want rehabilitation, they want revenge."

"Do most of the people Reinhardt picks on end up dead?"

"Occasionally, but most of the time, he has his fun with a prisoner until he gets bored with them or until someone new comes along. I've never seen him be so obsessed anyone like he is with you."

"Yeah, lucky me."

Butch met Lance Lester and Mr. Dipierri, Curry's attorney at the same hotel that Josie had met U.S. Consulate William Ackley, the La Colonia.

They rode to San Sebastian Prison in the same black Cadillac with the American flags mounted on the front bumpers. Doctor Rivera and Warden Gomez again met them, but this time no Major Reinhardt, which made the whole experience less stressful.

"Warden Gomez, Doctor Rivera, so nice to see you again. I'd like to introduce Mr. Dipierri, Mr. Logan's attorney, and this is Mr. Cassidy, a friend of the prisoner." Lester announced.

"Gentlemen, please follow me." Warden Gomez said as he led the procession up to the prison hospital.

Kid Curry was pleasantly surprised to see Butch walk thru the door, it really lifted his spirits. Butch leaned over and gave the Kid a hug, he stayed close as to keep their conversation intimate while Lester, Dipierri, the Doc and Gomez were talking shop.

"Hey, Butch."

"Hey, Kid. How's tricks?"

"Been better, how you doing?"

"Well, we miss having you around. Josie told us about this Nazi creep, we'll be taking care of this snake, not to worry."

"Better do it sooner than later Butch, this goon has it out for me."

"We're on it Kid, by tomorrow your troubles with this kraut will be over. Then we can concentrate on busting you outta here."

"Excuse me, Mr. Cassidy, we'd like to have Mr. Logan to consult with his attorney, if you don't mind." Mr. Lester said.

"Sure thing. Kid, I'll be in touch soon and don't worry about Jerry, we'll take care of him just like he was our own."

"Jerry?" Asked Lance.

"Yeah, Harvey's German Shepherd, Jerry. Say, Lance, if it's okay, I'm just going to wait in the hall. See ya,

Kid." Butch said giving a wink to Curry, who gave a slight wave with his manacled hand.

Butch was staring out the hall window looking down at the hundreds of prisoners milling around the prison yard, thinking to himself how one prison looks like every other prison, only the faces change. He was starting to drift off into a daydream when he heard the distinctive clomping of military boot heels. He knew before he even turned around what he was about to see. A tall blond-haired, blue-eyed, trim and slim, good-looking little Nazi, all spit-shined with military cresses, one of Hitler's S.S. elite.

Butch slowly turned to gaze at the "Wunderkind" approaching. Reinhardt didn't stop, didn't hesitate, he just walked into Logan's room, and voices started to rise.

"Major, I must ask you to leave. As Mr. Logan is conferring with his attorney." Lance Lester firmly stated.

"He doesn't need an attorney, he is guilty, I captured him myself."

"That might have been the way things were done in Nazi Germany, but here in the civilized world of Bolivia, they do things differently, Herr Reinhardt." Lester countered.

Again, Reinhardt's first instinct was to go for his Luger and shoot this insolent dog in the head for daring to be so impertinent. How dare he question a high ranking officer of the Reich, but then he remembered that this was indeed Bolivia and not the fatherland.

Mr. Dipierri took a few steps forward and said, "Major, my name is Mr. Dipierri, I have been assigned to represent Mr. Logan, I will need to see copies of his arrest report and any evidence that you may have, immediately. Also, I'd like to know why this man is in prison, instead he should be held in the local jail. Mr. Logan has not been found guilty of any crime at the moment; therefore I am issuing you with a writ of habeas corpus, ordering you to have Mr.

Logan in Superior Court in front of Judge León tomorrow morning at 9am. Do you understand?"

Major Joespf Reinhardt's head was pounding, and it felt like it was about to explode. A violent rage was coursing thru his body, so much so that he started to tremble. All he wanted was for all of them to be shot, and to die a long slow lingering painful death. It was all he could do, to snatch the writ from Dipierri's hand and storm out of the room, stopping out in the hall seething. He glared at Butch who was casually leaning against the wall, Reinhardt composed himself, tugged at the sides of his uniform jacket to straighten it out and approached the stranger smiling.

"Excuse me, I am Major Reinhardt, are you to see Herr Logan?"

Butch decided to play nice, the rough stuff would come later. "Yes, sir." He said.

"Would you happen to know if Herr Logan is Jewish?"

Butch looked deep in thought before answering, "You know, I actually think he's a Capricorn

The Bay of Pigs Invasion and the "Cuban Missile Crisis" really pushed Che so far to the left that even the Russians were scared of him.

The failed U.S. backed Bay of Pig invasion did nothing but help cement Castro and Che's grip on power and catapulted them onto the world stage as leaders of communist revolutionary leaders.

It was Che, who was the chief architect of the Soviet-Cuban relationship and played a crucial role in bringing

Soviet nuclear-armed missiles to Cuba. That precipitated the Cuban Missile Crisis and brought the world to the edge of nuclear war.

Che never forgave the Russians for backing down to the U.S. He said that if the missiles had been under Cuban control, they would have fired them off, believing that the cause of socialist liberation against the global imperialist aggression would ultimately have been worth the possibility of millions of atomic war victims.

I believe that at this point in Che's career, his nickname should have been, "News" Guevara. He, like me, really liked to see his name in print, on television, and in newsreels. By 1964 Che had emerged as a revolutionary statesman of world stature. In December of that year, Che addressed the United Nations.

In his speech, he criticized their inability to stop the brutal policy of apartheid in South Africa and continued to denounce the United States policy towards our black population.

It was during this visit to New York City that there had been two failed attempts on his life from Cuban exiles. The first was from Molly Gonzales, who tried to storm the barricades surrounding the U.N. and stab him with a seven-inch blade. Later that same day when Guillermoe Novo fired a bazooka from a boat in the East River, that too failed. It seems that Mr. Novo was just a lousy shot; apparently, he literary couldn't the side of a building with a bazooka.

Upon hearing of the attempts on his life, Che said, "It would better to be killed by a woman with a knife than a man with a gun, but I have to admit the bazooka was a nice touch."

By 6 am, Monday morning, kid curry hadn't been in his new prison cell long enough to pace from one end to the other when two guards led him out his cell, and down the same corridor he had just came from. But instead of making a right at the dead-end that led to the stairs to the infirmary, they made a left to a doorway that led to a flight of stairs going down into the basement, where it was dark, cold and damp. It had the distinct smell of vomit, blood, and death.

As the two guards, one on either side, escorted him down the dank corridor, they passed mostly empty cells there were some cells where there were prisoners held in what looked to be medieval torture racks, men hanging from their wrists, their feet not touching the ground, and a man forced into a wire cage box lying in a fetal position, unable to move.

They came to a room at the end of the corridor, brightly lit with a rough-hewn wooden table in the center of the room. At either end of the table were leather restraints. The Kid could see that the table still had blood on it from Reinhardt's last victim. Along one wall was a variety of implements of torture, some ancient, some modern, some primitive, some innovative and some of a medical in nature. Against the opposite wall, there was a waterboarding apparatus and what looked to be a dental chair with straps. Everything in the room represented anguish, suffering, and agony. There was absolutely nothing that would give one a scintilla of hope.

The Kid didn't have to wait long before Reinhardt walked in wearing a white lab coat, a pair of paratrooper boots and leather gloves. He walked past the Kid and went straight to the wall where his "toys" were, with his back to Curry. He said, "Mesa!"

The two guards forcibly shoved Curry onto the table, on his back and placed his hands and ankles in restraints.

With his back still to the Kid, Reinhardt asked, "Comfortable. Herr Logan?"

"Not particularly." The Kid replied.

"Good." The Major said, laughing.

Reinhardt finally grabbed a rubber truncheon off the wall, it was 18" long with a leather strap that he slid over his wrist. He turned around and proceeded to walk over to the prisoner stretched out and tethered to the table, slapping the baton in his hand and said, "I understand that you are due in court today at 9am, is that correct, Herr Logan?"

"Yep."

"You Americans, have such a colorful way of speaking."

"Thanks."

"Well, since you will be going before the judge today, we won't be able to break your nose, fracture your jaw, or remove several of your teeth. We'll have to save that for another day. However, I just wanted to give you a taste of what you can look forward to while I have you."

Reinhardt jabbed the weapon with all his might into the Kid's left kidney, forcing the Kid to whence in pain.

"How was that, Herr Logan?"

The Kid gained his composure before speaking, "Not bad, but I've had worse."

"And you will, Herr Logan. I can promise you, you will." Reinhardt said just before slamming the billy club into his stomach, knocking the wind out of the Kid.

"And have you had worse? Take all the time you need to catch your breath."

The Kid kinda saw the shot to the stomach, so he had a millisecond to prepare, but still, it hurt like a son-of-a-bitch.

"You know Major, I once had a horse kick me in the gut on a cattle drive and that there club came pretty close to matching that horse kick, but I have to admit the horse kick was worse." The Kid answered.

The Kid figured the more they were talking, the less he would be hurting.

"So, Herr Logan, you were a cowboy?"

"Yup."

"Did you have six-shooter, and wear cowboy boots and a cowboy hat, partner?"

"That's pardner, not partner."

Reinhardt looked at his victim and two things held his fascination. When growing up in Nazi Germany, the first of course was Hitler and the Nazi party, the second was his secret enthrallment with America's wild west. The tall tales of the American cowboy, but even more was the allure of the outlaws and gunfighters, like Jesse James, Billy the Kid, and Wild Bill Hickok.

"So, Herr Logan, you grew up in the American west?"

"I did, in Montana, outside of Yellowstone," Logan replied, and he thought he saw a hint of interest from Reinhardt that he might be just able to play on. "I grew up and knew several of the legends of the Wild West."

"Did you know Jesse James?"

"No, not Jesse James, but I did know Wyatt Earp, Billy the Kid, and I rode with Johnny Ringo and his gang for a while."

"You're lying."

"I was just thirteen when I saw my first gunfight, down in old El Paso, it was called the "Four Dead in Five Seconds Gunfight.""

Reinhardt's eye grew as large as saucers, he was intrigued, since he had never met anyone who had first-hand knowledge of the Wild West, someone who had actually witnessed such events.

"What happened?"

"Well, there was Sheriff Stoudenmire, who was walking by the saloon when he heard a ruckus inside between Johnny Hale and this cattle rancher George Campbell. When he heard gunfire, the Sheriff drew his Colt .45 and burst in. He saw Hale holding a gun, so Stoudenmire fired and missed, hitting a Mexican bystander, killing him dead."

"A Mexican, no great loss."

"Stoudenmire's next shot hit this fella Johnny Hale square in the head, blew his brains all over the bartender. He then shot Campbell, who took a shot at Stoudenmire as he was trying to run out of the saloon. The Sheriff pumped three slugs into his guts, and one of the bullets ripped thru his body hitting one of the barmaids, killing her as well. Four dead in five seconds."

"And you were there?" Reinhardt asked.

"Yeah, I was a busboy; I swept the floors and washed dishes, I was only thirteen."

"When did you start to carry a gun?"

"Sixteen. Those were rough times so everyone wore a gun. Back then, in the west, there were two types of men, those who worked and put money into banks and those who robbed and took money out of banks."

"You robbed."

"I did, and until recently, when the U.S. was hot on my trail, that's when I decided to skip out of the country, and I ended up here in South America. I was on my way to Argentina and needed some money, so I tried to rob that bank. Unfortunately, I didn't count on you being there."

"Yes, Herr Logan it was indeed your misfortune that I was in that bank. However, in one respect, your background shall spare you some immediate pain, but only until I get bored with your colorful stories of the wild west. Then I'm afraid I shall inflict you with such pain and agony you'll wish that it was you that Sheriff Stoudenmire had shot in the head."

Reinhardt waved his hand at the guards, indicating that they could release the prisoner's restraints and return him to his cell.

"Have a good day in court, I shall see you again soon, Herr Logan." Reinhardt said as the Kid was being escorted back down the dark, dank corridor.

"Yeah, I can't wait."

"That's it Herr Logan, stay defiant." Shouted the Major.

Kid Curry was transported to the courthouse in his black and white striped prison uniform and in shackles. Waiting for him when he entered the courtroom was his attorney Mr. Dipierri and sitting right behind the defense counsel in the first row of the gallery, was Me, Butch and Sundance.

The Kid looked like Hell; he was pale, walked all hunched over, and kept squirming in his seat, like he couldn't get comfortable. We got the opportunity to speak to him; briefly and he relayed his encounter with Reinhardt this morning, the beating and Reinhardt's fascination about cowboys, outlaws and such. He said that after the truncheon to the kidney punch, about an hour later, he started passing blood in his urine. The Kid admitted that he didn't know how much more he could survive.

"We'll take care of him tonight," Butch whispered, so Dipierri couldn't hear.

"You just have to try and hang in there for a little while longer." Sundance said.

"I'll try and keep him talking about the Wild West."

"Did you tell him you're Kid Curry?" I asked.

"I thought about telling him, but it could go either way. He might be impressed, or he might think he'll be the one who killed Kid Curry and torture me to death."

Butch tried to reassure him, "Do what you think is best, by tomorrow, it will be over."

The bailiff called the court to order, "All rise, Superior Court fourteen is now in session, the Honorable Enquie T. Piedra presiding."

"You may be seated." Judge Piedra announced.

The judge sat rustling papers in front of him for several minutes getting organized. He looked at both counsels and asked, "Mr. Dipierri, I believe that you have a motion, is that correct?"

"Yes, your Honor. My client, Mr. Logan was arrested and placed in San Sebastian Prison and has been held there for over six weeks, admittedly in the prison hospital. But now that he has been deemed fit enough to be released, we request that Mr. Logan be transferred to the county jail during his trial."

"District Attorney Rodriguez, do you have any objections?" The judge asked.

"No your Honor."

"Mr. Dipierri, how does your client plead?"

"Not guilty, your Honor."

"Very well, Mr. Logan shall be transferred at 8am tomorrow morning from San Sebastian Prison to the Cochabamba County Jail. Is that all Mr. Dipierri?"

"Yes, your Honor."

"Mr. Rodriguez?"

"Nothing at this time, your Honor."

"Very well, I'm looking at my calendar, let's set the trial date for six weeks from today, July 25th, unless there's an objection?"

There were none.

"Court adjourned!" Judge Piedra said as he raised and then slammed his gavel.

"I'll stop by the prison tomorrow morning to make sure everything goes smoothly," Dipierri said.

"Thank you. I'd appreciate it if you could speak to the warden, I'm a little concerned about how Major Reinhardt will react."

"I understand, I'll have a word with him when we're done here."

As the Kid was being escorted out of the courtroom, we all gave him thumbs up, hoping to bolster his spirits.

It seems that love can be found in the strangest of places, even in Block 10 at the Auschwitz death camp. Obertsturmführer Rauff was observing the infamous Doctor Mengele performing a dissection of two seven-year-old twin girls that he had just killed, so he could examine the effects of extreme exposure to massive doses of x-rays when he first saw Obertsturmführer Maria Mandl, the commandant of the women's camp.

It was love at first sight, Mandl had requested help transporting 150 women to the Bayer facility for the experimenting and testing of a new anesthetic.

It seems that Bayer paid the kind folks at Auschwitz 150 Deutsche Marks per inmate for the test; unfortunately, the first batch of inmates all died before the could obtain conclusive results, Bayer sent a letter to the camp's commandant requesting 150 more for the same price.

Mandl and Rauff would be in charge of transporting the new group for experiments. Mandl walked into the dissection room where Rauff was listening to Mengele telling a joke, "Where were black Jews first discovered? At the back of the oven."

After the laughter subsided, Mandl held up the Nazi salute and said, "Heil Hitler! Obertsturmführer Rauff, I am Obertsturmführer Maria Mandl, I'm the commandant of the women's camp. We are to chose 150 female inmates to be shipped to the Bayer facility at the Mauthausen camp, first thing tomorrow morning."

"Thank you, Obertsturmführer Mandl, yes I am aware of the order. I was going to stop by and discuss the details later today."

"If you're not busy now, we could go to my office."

"Lead on, Obertsturmführer."

"Maria, please."

They walked from Block 10 thru the compound, the barracks, over the railroad tracks towards the women's camp. As they arrived at the train depot, there was a train from Poland unloading a fresh batch of Jews. During the chaos, an elderly Jewish man accidentally bumped into Mandl, scuffing her boot.

"Look what you did to my boot!" She shouted.

"I am terribly sorry." The old man said, bowing his head.

"Get down and lick my boot clean!"

The man got on his hands and knees and proceeded to lick her boot to try to get the scuff mark off. When he finished, he looked up at her, she looked down to inspect the boot, "Clean the other one."

The man did as he was ordered when he was done, he again looked up at her for approval. Mandl inspected her boots, removed a pistol from her holster, and shot the old man in the head. She turned to Rauff and asked, "Care for some coffee, Obertsturmführer?"

Rauff was in love. He felt that he had found his true soul mate, someone who could be a cold and heartless. Someone who enjoyed seeing others in pain and misery as much as he did, a match made in Hell.

They would spend most of their nights together, having dinner talking about all the cruel things they did that day. Rauff discovered that the more heinous and evil things they did, the more intense the lovemaking was. Their sexual relationship turned into a such a mutual sadomasochistic entanglement that they would appear the next day with bruises, contusions, cuts, abrasions, and the occasional broken bone.

As the war was coming to an end, Rauff and Mandl saw the writing on the wall. They thought it best to try and escape the Russian and American advance separately, agreeing to meet in Italy. Rauff waited almost two years until he heard that Maria had been captured in mountains of southern Bavaria.

Mundl was handed over to the Polish People's Republic, where she was tried and sentenced to death by hanging.

Maria Mundl was hanged on January 24th, 1948 at the age of 36.

Word had reached Rauff while he was waiting to be smuggled out of Italy for a new life in Bolivia.

It was a couple of weeks after his 1965 Algiers speeches in which Che made it very clear that he was leaning more towards the Chinese style of communism rather than that of the Soviets. He returned to Cuba but seemed to drop out of sight.

His whereabouts were a great mystery and he was regarded as the number two man, the second in power behind Castro. His disappearance was quite disconcerting to the people of Cuba. However, the root cause of his going underground was the riff between Castro and Che in regard to the number of Soviet viruses, Chinese economic, military, and political influence over the new regime.

It was in early October of '65 that Che decided that, although he affirmed his enduring commitment and solidarity with the Cuban people and the Cuban Revolution, he felt that there were other fights for revolutionary causes in the world. He, therefore, resigned all of his positions in the Cuban government, to Cuban communist party and renounced his honorary Cuban citizenship.

On his way to the Congo, Che held a covert meeting in La Paz, Bolivia with some old friends. We met up with Che at 127 Avenue Cd Del Niño in one of the poorer sections of La Paz. We met at a tiny shack attached to a small bodega sitting up on a hill overlooking a field of grazing sheep.

We were driven by two men, in a white Ford Econoline wearing green army fatigues, matching berets, and Ray-Ban sunglasses. The ride was over two hours long thru back streets, alleys ways and dirt roads. All the while, our escorts never said a word. Butch and Sundance got so bored they slept most of the way.

When we arrived, the man in the front passenger seat got out and indicated for us to stay put, which we did. He walked to the gate entrance of the house, rang the bell, and sliding peep door slid open, where a pair of women's eyes emerged. Our man let it be known that he had the goods in the van, meaning us.

The metal door opened, the woman who had answered waved to us to come in. We got out of the van and entered the two-room house where we saw Che sitting at a small kitchen table peering over a map of Bolivia. When he saw us, he stood and welcomed each of us with big bear hugs.

"Amigos! It is so good to see you all. I hope that you are all well." He looked past us and asked, "Where is Señor Curry?"

"The Kid got careless and is currently in San Sabastian Prison awaiting trial." Butch answered.

"I am sorry to hear that. What do you think will happen?"

"Well, currently he's having issues with an ex-Nazi that is torturing him, so, we will have to take care of that problem. Then, once that's done, if possible, we'll see if we can bust him out.

"I hate fascists and imperialists, that's what I'm fighting against. Communism is the one true people's government, where everyone shares in the wealth. Don't you agree, Butch?"

"Che, there's no such thing as a communist bank robber, if he says he is, he's a liar. Now, what can a couple of capitalist bank robbers do for the Marxist movement?"

"I'm off to fight in the Congo, to help support the Marxist Simba movement. I'll be leading twelve Cuban expeditionaries and a hundred Afro-Cuban guerrilla fighters to try and start a revolution."

"And?" Butch inquired.

"And, we are in desperate need of financing."

"So, why don't you ask Fidel or the Chinese for the money?"

"Because, if it ever got out that it was another government trying to overthrow the Congolese, all Hell would break out. It has to look like the Congolese people are throwing the revolution."

"Well, why don't you go and rob a couple banks? You got the men."

"Because we're revolutionaries, not common thieves. Sorry, Butch, that came out wrong."

"No, it's quite alright, I get it, You're in the business of revolution, and were in the business of robbing banks. So, how much do you need?"

"A quarter of a million dollars."

"Che, the size banks we typically knock over, don't have nearly that kind of cash." Sundance said.

"I know, that's why I'm thinking the Central Bank of Argentina."

"No way! The three of us could never pull off something that big, we'd need at least six, maybe eight more guys." Butch said.

"And you shall have them, and whatever else you need."

"I don't want to sound like the capitalist pig that I am, but what's in it for us?"

"The gratitude of the workers of the world."

"And?"

"A quarter of everything over the quarter of a million."

"Half."

"A third."

"Half."

"Okay, half. How soon can you do the job?"

"Che, give me a break, something this big takes planning. Give me at least a week."

"Agreed."

Kid Curry was brought to Warden Gomez's office when he returned from court. The warden was sitting at his desk talking to Major Reinhardt sitting across from him as the two guards escorted the Kid into the office.

"Ah, Mr. Logan, please have a seat." Gomez said.

Curry sat in the chair next to Reinhardt, he was still wearing the shackles from his court appearance.

"Guard, you can remove the shackles, and wait outside, please." The warden said.

"Yes, sir." One of the guards said as he unlocked the prisoner's manacles and left the office.

Major Reinhardt stood and began pacing, "So, Herr Logan, I understand that we are going to be losing the pleasure of your company tomorrow."

"Yeah, that's what the judge said."

"I hope it's not because we haven't made you feel welcome, or haven't given you enough attention?"

"On the contrary Major Reinhardt, if anything you've given me more attention than I deserve."

"Nonsense, Herr Logan, I've really enjoyed our conversation about your country. I would like to hear more stories about the wild west."

Curry looked to the warden for any sign of hope or any sort of intervention, but there was none. The warden told the Kid that he would be transported to the county jail at 8am, so be ready. He then pressed a buzzer on his desk, and the two guards that brought the Kid to and from court entered the office.

"Guards, take Mr. Logan back to his cell."

As Kid was leaving the office, Reinhardt said, "I hope to see you before you go, Herr Logan."

The Kid sat in his cell all day just waiting for a couple guards to come and escort him back down to Major Reinhardt's torture chamber. They didn't show up until four o'clock in the afternoon, Curry had fallen asleep and was startled awake when his cell door opened. The two guards stood outside his cell. They were the same ones that had taken him to court. They said nothing, just waited for him to come to them.

Reinhardt was dressed in his white lab coat, standing by a straight back wooden chair, he held out his hand as to invite his victim to have a seat.

"Welcome, Herr Logan. I'm sorry it has taken so long, but I was busy."

The Kid saw that there was blood on the Majors lab coat and said, "I can see."

Reinhardt looked down at his tunic, "Oh, well, things did get out of hand."

From down the corridor, there was whimpering and sobbing of an inmate who had been in the room minutes before.

"Doesn't that bother you?" The Kid asked.

"No, its music to my ears. Makes me feel good knowing that I'm doing my job."

"And what exactly is your job, Major."

"Bringing suffering and misery to those who deserve it."

"And who decides who deserves it?"

"Why, I do, Herr Logan. It's God's will that I should inflict anguish, torment, and even death to such weak, and contemptuous vermin. These aren't humans, they're animals, and they all get what they deserve. The Jews, the communists, the gypsies, criminals, and the parasites of society like you, Herr Logan get what they deserve."

"So, are you going to kill me?"

"Heavens no, Herr Logan. Although I do have something special in mind for you. But, all in good time. I first want to hear more about your experiences growing up in the American west."

"What would you like to know?"

"What outlaws did you personally know?"

"Before coming to South America, I rode with Butch Cassidy and the Wild Bunch."

"Butch Cassidy, yes he hid in the Crack-in-the-Wall."

"That's Hole-in-the-Wall."

"Ah, Hole-in-the-Wall. Was it as impenetrable as they say?"

"No one ever got thru that we didn't want to."

"Who else?"

"Let's see, there was the Sundance Kid, Wild Bill Hickok, Wyatt Earp, and even Belle Starr, she rode with the Dalton Gang until she was shot and killed while robbing a train."

They talked well into the night, the Kid sharing mostly true stories and some tall tales of the old west. It seemed to the Kid that he just might survive the evening unscathed, as it looked to him that they were getting along, Hell, they even had a few laughs.

Just when the Kid thought he just might escape whatever evil that Reinhardt had planned for him, it was not meant to be. Reinhardt did what all Nazis do, get you to believe that they will treat you fairly, that you can trust them, that is until they get what they want from you and when you have nothing more of value for you, then you are expendable.

Abruptly Reinhardt stood up from his chair and said, "Herr Logan, I want you to come sit in this chair."

Reinhardt indicated that the Kid should move to sit in what looked to be a dental chair. As Curry stood up, the two guards closed in on him, making sure that he did as instructed. There were leather restraints for the hands, feet, chest, and head.

Once he was securely fastened in the chair, Reinhardt rolled a silver tray with several dozen medical instruments next to the chair.

The Kid's whole body was immobile, his head was sandwiched in between two blocks of wood so he could not move his head from side to side. He knew he was in deep trouble. Just as he was about to speak Reinhardt stuffed a cloth rag attached to a leather strap in his mouth, so he was unable to speak.

The Major held up what looked like an ice pick with a hook on the end in front of the Kid and said softly, "Herr Logan, have you ever heard of a lobotomy?"

"Arrrrgggggh."

"No, well it's a type of surgery performed on the brain. Now, I've never done one before, so this will be a first for both of us.

"I have heard that it's rather painless. Basically, I'm going to take this tool, called an orbitoclast, slide it under your eyelids, and lightly tap it with a hammer and break through the thin layer of bone of your eye sockets. Then I will slide it around using the hook on the end to remove parts of your brain.

"Afterwards, you're going to be a new man, depending on how much of your brain I remove. Since I've never done this before it will be interesting to see what happens, don't you think?

"Are you ready?"

"Argggh! Arrgggh!"

"Oh, yeah, I don't have any anesthesia, but it shouldn't hurt too much. And if it does, so much the better, you American schweinehund!"

Reinhardt slid the ice pick tool under the Kid's right eyelid, he then slowly raised the hammer above his head and in a swift motion swung the hammer around and brought it up to hit the handle of the ice pick.

Klonk!

"We'll need three months to accomplish the job, we're going to tunnel in." Butch said.

Che asked. "Can't you just go in and hold it up?"

"That's the way you do it if you just want what's in the cash drawers, but the real money's in the vault. And unless you want to start killing people and having a standoff with the police, this is the smarter way to go. We'll break thru on a late Friday night, which will give us two days."

"But, three months?"

"Look, Che, you can have it done fast, cheap or good, but you can only pick two. So, if you want it fast and cheap, it won't be good. If you want it fast and good, it won't be cheap. See what I'm saying?"

"I understand, you're the professionals, I trust you."

"Now, I will need some setup money, I figure three hundred thousand dollars should take care of it."

"Any men?"

"I will need at least twenty-four men, who aren't afraid of putting in a full day of back-breaking work."

"But, Butch how are you going to get rid of all that dirt, won't that raise suspicions?"

"We've got it all well in hand. Now, once I get the money, I can start right away.

"You will have it tonight."

"When do you head off for the Congo?"

"Tomorrow afternoon, so, I'll plan on coming back in three months to collect the fruits of our labors."

"Ve con Dios, amigo."

"Good morning, Monsieur Moulin, I hope you had a pleasant night." Barbie chirped.

Moulin was sitting the same chair with his hands and feet still restrained. His fingers were so swollen they looked like sausages, Barbie took a riding crop and whipped both of his hands with all of his might, causing Moulin to scream out in agony.

Barbie had two Gestapo goons take the prisoner over to the door and had his fingers forced thru the space between the hinges of the door and the wall, then the door was repeatedly slammed shut until all his knuckles were broken.

"Care to talk Moulin, if you do, all this suffering will stop. I promise you a swift death if you talk, what say you?"

Moulin lifted his head and whispered, "I have nothing to say."

Barbie looked at the larger of the agents, "Günter, just don't kill him."

Günter Müller, was a heavyweight boxer before the war, having fought for the World Championship only to have suffered a defeat by the American King Levinsky, a Jew. Müller and the rest of Germany thought that his loss was all part of an international Jewish conspiracy.

In the red corner, currently weighing in at a solid 225 pounds, at six-foot-two, blonde hair and blue eyes, Ladies and Gentlemen, the Beast of Berlin, Günter Müller.

And in the Blue corner, the challenger, weighing in at 155 pounds, five-foot-eight, brown hair and brown eyes, all the way from France, the martyr saint Jean Moulin.

Günter Müller used Moulin as a punching bag, broke both his cheekbones, broke six ribs, destroyed his kidneys, and literally gouged both eyes out.

Barbie was so impressed by Günter Müller's work he had Moulin's unconscious body placed on the chaise lounge in his office during the day. It served as a display to show off to other prisoners what awaited them, if they did not cooperate.

At night, they would carry him back down to the basement where they would continue to brutalize him, Barbie used screw-handcuffs that were tightened until they bit thru his flesh and broke the bones in his wrists.

Hitler was so impressed with Barbie's cruelty, especially when it came to Moulin, that he personally awarded him with the Iron Cross. Moulin never did reveal any information. He was tortured for three weeks and eventually succumbed to his injuries, dying while being transported to Germany.

Klaus Barbie left Lyon France and went back to Germany to be treated for venereal disease. As the war was coming to an end, he was recruited by the Americans to spy on the German Communist Party. He was eventually relocated to Bolivia with the help of the CIA.

"Harvey Logan! Pack up your gear, you're leaving. Now!" A guard was shouting at him at his cell door.

Kid Curry woke up earlier with a gargantuan pounding headache, it seemed that everything he was looking at, he was looking at thru a fog. Nothing was coming into focus, and he felt that he was moving in slow motion. He had a vision of being tied down and something terrible happening to him, but he couldn't remember exactly what it was. Had it really happened or was it all just a bad dream?

He was taken to Warden Gomez's office where his attorney Mr. Dipierri met him, as well as two county police officers that were to transport him to the county jail.

"What the Hell is going on here warden, Mr. Logan looks as if he's been severely beaten!"

The Kid's face was all swollen, and he had two black eyes. He looked as if he had gone ten rounds with Sonny Liston, plus his speech was slurred.

"Mr. Logan, can you tell us what happened?"

The Kid's mind was trying to form words, but all that emerged was mush. He was trying to tell them that Reinhardt had hurt him, but it was just gibberish.

The warden pressed the button on the intercom on his desk, "Maria, have Major Reinhardt come to my office, immediately."

Within minutes there was a knock on the door, Major Reinhardt entered the room, "You wanted to see me, warden?"

"Major Reinhardt, can you tell us what has happened to this man?"

"I was told that Herr Logan was attacked by several prisoners who hate Americans. I have the men in custody and am currently in the process of investigating the matter."

"Warden Gomez and Major Reinhardt, I will be lodging a formal complaint with the court against you both for negligence against my client."

With that, the two-county police took the Kid into custody and drove him to the county jail to be processed.

Once there, Mr. Dipierri had a private doctor examine his client as soon as he was finished being booked into jail.

While the doctor was examining the Kid, Mr. Dipierri called Butch and told him what had happened. Butch thanked him and asked that he keep us apprised as to the Kids condition.

"Sundance, News, this fucking Nazi Reinhardt has beaten up the Kid really bad, I think it's payback time."

As we were going over the plan how to handle Reinhardt, we got a call from Mr. Dipierri, he said the doctor had determined that the Kid had been brutalized and tortured by that Nazi who performed a lobotomy on the Kid. He said that it looks like he may be suffering from an infection. The doc doesn't think the Kid will make it, and if he does, he'll never be the same.

We all sat in silence, deep in thought, the Kid may have been stupid for trying to rob a bank by himself, but he, nor anyone else deserved this. This son of a bitch Reinhardt was going to get a taste of good old American revenge, wild west style.

Reinhardt's apartment was totally dark when he entered it after a hard day of tormenting and torturing prisoners. Before he could turn on a light, we set upon him, forcing him down on the ground. Butch and Sundance hogtied him while I stuffed a gag in his mouth. It only took a matter of seconds to have Reinhardt rendered helpless.

I turned on the lights, and there on the wooden floor was one of the so-called master race lying on his stomach, with his hands tied behind his back and legs in the air struggling to get up and trying to speak, but to no avail.

Sundance grabbed him by his necktie and dragged him into the living room. Butch grabbed him by his hair and tilted his back so Reinhardt could see his face, "Greetings Major Reinhardt, or should I say Obertsturmführer Karl Albin Rauff. Remember me? Please allow me to introduce myself, I'm Butch Cassidy, this here is the Sundance Kid, and that fella over there is News Carver. We're the last of what's left of the Wild Bunch, ever heard of us?"

"Mmmmmfffggghhh!"

"I'll take that as a yes. Harvey told me that you had this fascination with the American wild west, is that right?"

"Mmfffttghaat!"

"Well, you're in luck, because we're going to give you a history lesson about the wild west. Do you know anything about the American Indians, Major?"

"Wwwaamfffgggtt!"

"No? Well, I think you're going to find this really interesting, considering how you like going around torturing folks and all."

Butch reached behind his back and produced a Bowie knife with a 12" blade and waved it in front of Reinhardt's face. Still holding the Major by the hair, Butch said, "This is what the injuns liked to do to their enemies back in the ole days."

Butch made several quick semicircle cuts on either side of Reinhardt's head, and then vigorously yanked at the nearly severed scalp, ripping all the hair and skin off from the top of his head.

"Aaaaarrrrgggggghhhhhh!"

Butch held Reinhardt's bloody scalp in front of him smiling; unfortunately, the Major had passed out from the excruciating pain.

"News, go get some water to bring this piece crap around." Butch said.

As I went looking for something to help revive the Nazi, Butch and Sundance carried the Major into the bathroom, tied his hands over the shower rod, bound his feet together, then stripped him naked.

I brought in a large glass of water and threw it in his face, and slapped him hard on both cheeks, I was getting ready to slap him again when he blinked his eyes several times, then became totally conscience. He quickly looked all around and assessed his situation, he knew from first-hand experience that whenever the victim is naked, it's never going to end well.

Butch held up his scalp and said, "You know I hadn't done that in decades."

"You still got the touch, Butch." Sundance said.

"Yeah, I learned that from an old Sioux warrior named, Red Cloud. He would have hung this trophy on his lodgepole as a badge of honor. Since I don't have a lodgepole, I'm just going to flush it down the toilet." Butch said as he tossed the scalp into the commode and flushed it.

"Mmggrraafffh!"

"I know, I know you're anxious to know what the next history lesson is going to be. Well, this is something that the Apaches were famous for, skinning their enemies alive."

"Auurggggghhh!"

"Now, Major the secret to making a perfect "suit" is for you not to squirm around, or else you'll mess it up. Sundance would you mind assisting me?"

"It would be my pleasure, Butch."

Butch took the razor-sharp Bowie knife and made a quick motion across Reinhardt's chest from his right shoulder to his left just under his collar bone. The blade was so sharp Reinhardt hardly felt anything, he looked down and didn't see anything right away, then a thin pencil line of blood appeared. Butch then made two swift flicks with the knife on either side of the bloodline creating two small flaps.

"Now, Major, are you ready?" Butch asked.

Butch took hold of the left flap and Sundance grabbed hold of the right, in unison, they began to slowly peel the skin down off of Reinhardt's chest.

"Aaaaarrrrrgggggghhhhhh!"

Reinhardt was found barely alive two days later, still hanging from the shower rod by Colonel Karl Altmann aka Klaus Barbie. Warden Gomez had alerted the Colonel when the Reinhardt hadn't shown up for work to the prison on the second day. It wasn't like Reinhardt to miss out on a day of torture, much less two.

The "Butcher of Lyon" Klaus Barbie, was genuinely impressed with the workmanship of the flaying of Obertsturmführer Rauff, a technique that he had used on several members of the French Resistance during his time in Lyon.

Obertsturmführer Rauff aka Major Reinhardt had less than 20% of his skin left on his body, and he had been castrated, his skin and genitals were nailed on to the living room wall with a Nazi swastika painted above them in Reinhardt's own blood.

Reinhardt died two days later from hypothermia, he never regained total consciousness, he did however muttered a single word, *"sonnentanz"* (sundance), which Colonel Altmann thought was just gibberish.

Kid Curry did recover from his infection, but due to the butchering that he had suffered at the hands of Major Reinhardt, it was decided that he wouldn't be prosecuted for the failed bank robbery, and subsequently, he was released.

He was sent back to the United States, where due to his diminished mental capacity, the U.S. also declined to prosecute him for past crimes. Kid Curry spent the rest of his life bagging groceries in the Bozeman A&P. We never did see him again; I understand that ironically a stray bullet fired during the commission of a robbery while he was standing in line at a Wells Fargo Bank waiting to make a deposit killed him.

Che's collaboration with the Congolese guerrilla leader Laurent-Désiré Kabila proved to be an unmitigated disaster. Together they tried to lead an unsuccessful revolt, over the course of the next seven months, but with failure, after failure, Che grew ever more disillusioned with the poor discipline of Kabila's troops.

On top of that, there was a massive influx of white mercenary troops into the Congo National Army, which was supported by anti-Castro Cuban pilots and the CIA. They thwarted their movements from their base camp in the mountains by Lake Tanganyika in southeast Congo.

Although Che's presence in the Congo was supposed to be a secret, the United States government knew of his location and activities, by using the NSA's intercepting all his incoming and outgoing transmissions were tracked via a ghost ship floating off the coast.

It was Che's wish to export the revolution to the people of the Congo by instructing the local anti-Mobutu Simba fighters in Marxist ideology and guerrilla warfare strategies. But due to the incompetence, intransigence, and infighting among the Congolese rebels, the revolution was doomed from the beginning.

Che retold a story to me on his return to La Paz of an encounter with a group of mercenaries working for the Congo National Army and their leader, a guy named Thomas Michael "Mad Mike" Hoare.

Mad Mike Hoare was a British mercenary and adventurer, whose motto was "You get more out of life by living dangerously."

Che and his men of the Cuban expeditionary force were taking refuge in the small village of Fizi on Lake Tanganyika. They just had a firefight with some of Congo National Army (CNA) undisciplined troops, virtually eliminating them. Things would change dramatically when Hoare and his mercenaries joined the fight.

The irony was not lost on Che, that it was primarily European mercenaries fighting Cuban mercenaries for the destiny and soul of the Congo. The Congolese army had no stomach for fighting and was happy to sit back and let the two foreign mercenary armies fight it out amongst themselves.

Che had heard rumors that CNA was bringing in mercenaries, as he was told about 1600 from all over Europe and South Africa. That meant that they were outnumbered

16 to 1. He wasn't overly concerned, as he had faced greater odds fighting in Cuba.

There were two missions that they had to win to establish a foothold against the government, the first was capture and hold Ndlili International Airport, and the second was take control of the state-owned radio & TV station, RNTC, located in Kinshasa, just an hours drive to the airport.

Che felt that they had the element of surprise on their side, plus he was hoping that Hoare would have his men spread out all over the country embedded with several different units. That would help him accomplish the two objectives.

He divided his 112-man outfit into two equal teams of 56 men each, Victor Dreke, his second in command would attack the airport, while he and his men would capture media stations.

May 14th, 1965, the coordinated assault on Ndlili Airport and RNTC broadcasting outlet began at precisely 6:10am.

Dreke radioed Che at 7:47am, that the taking of the airport was a success, in addition to occupying the airport, as well as the control tower. Several Congo Airways planes full of passengers were also hijacked. They were in the process of fortifying their positions in readiness for a counter-attack.

Che's troops were also victorious, as they met little or no resistance in taking control of both the radio and television studios. They also made preparations for an attack from the CIA.

Unbeknownst to Che and the Cuban fighters, the CIA had been eavesdropping on Che's communications for months and had devised a trap. It had occurred to Che that it all came too easy; unfortunately, he realized it too late. Within minutes of claiming victory, the attacks from Mad Mike's mercenaries began at both the airport and RNTC.

Because of the lackluster performance of the anti-Mobutu Simba fighters, both Che and Victor Dreke were lucky to escape with their lives. With the exception of the 12 Cuban expeditionaries, who fought heroically, the Congolese warriors were able to snatch defeat out of the jaws of victory.

Only six of the original Cuban twelve survived the bloody campaigns. They went into jungle guerrilla warfare, hit and run tactics, but they proved not to be all that effective.

Over the next seven months, they experienced one defeat after another, and on top of that, during that time most of them came down with bad cases of dysentery. Che developed a severe case of acute asthma. He had planned to send the six Cuban survivors back to Cuba, while he soldiered on alone. But after being urged by his comrades and two emissaries from Cuba, he reluctantly agreed to leave Africa.

Before crossing over into Tanzania, they dismantled their camp, burned their huts, and threw their weapons into Lake Tanganyika, under cover of the night.

Good evening this is Nigel Williams for BBC World News Tonight. This evening we start our coverage in Bolivia, where it is reported that the mutilated body of a suspected ex-Nazi war criminal was found at his home in the city of Cochabamba, Bolivia.

The victim is believed to be that of Nazi war criminal Obertsturmführer Karl Albin Rauff, known as the Beast of Auschwitz. Rauff was reportedly in charge of operations at the death camp, where he was personally brought in to manage the gassings of new transports by Heinrich Himmler himself.

After the war, Rauff was charged, with being personally responsible for the killing of over 15,000 women and children, mostly Jews and gypsies.

After the war, he was captured by the allies but managed to escape. During the Nuremberg trials, he was tried in absentia in 1945, found guilty and sentenced to death.

It is believed that he worked at the San Sebastian Penitentiary in Cochabamba, as head of security under the alias Major Josef Reinhardt.

The officials at San Sebastian Penitentiary and members of the Bolivian government have so far refused comment.

Israel denies any knowledge or involvement in the slaying of Rauff. Sources told BBC News that the manner of Rauff's killing isn't the Mossad's method of execution.

So far, Bolivian police say that no suspects have been identified.

SS Hauptsturmführer Klaus Barbie aka Colonel Klaus Altmann sat at a large conference room across from Generals Miranda and Tejada in the National Congress of Bolivia building in La Paz.

"Colonel Altmann, would you please explain the circumstances around Major Reinhardt's unusual demise?" General Miranda asked.

"General we are looking into several potential suspects, including ex-prisoners who we believe might have had a grudge against the Major."

"Can you tell us how the newspapers got hold of this story?" General Tejada queried.

"I believe that the killers contacted the news media."

"And why would they do that?" General Tejada asked.

"To embarrass the Bolivian government."

"And who do you think would benefit from such an act?"

"The communists. Someone like that Marxist revolutionary, Che Guevara. You've seen him here with your own eyes, trying to instigate the workers, trying to organize them, to unionize them. Wherever he goes, he's always trying to ferment and agitate the poor into revolt, just like he and that scum Fidel Castro did in Cuba."

General Miranda leaned forward and asked, "And what measures are you taking, Colonel?"

"Well, I have had my men round up the usual suspects and arrested a number of communist sympathizers. We are currently reviewing anyone that Reinhardt had interrogated and recently released, and we have started doing our own interviews and interrogations. We will have some answers very soon."

"What about that American that Reinhardt recently interrogated?" Miranda asked.

"Harvey Logan? After what Reinhardt did to the man, he's a walking vegetable. No, besides he is being processed to be released."

"How about the Americans? Maybe the FBI or maybe the CIA?" General Tejada inquired.

"Doubtful, not their style. Americans like to abduct and use conventional torture techniques. This was a rogue operation and personal. But, as I said, we'll find out who's responsible for this and make them pay."

"Colonel, we are not happy. We want results, and we want them quickly. Do you understand?" Tejada demanded.

"Yes, sir, General."

"Remember, Colonel, you are here to serve at our pleasure, understand?"

"Yes, General, I won't let you down.

Altmann rose from the table and gave both Generals a snappy salute and headed towards the door. Just as he was about to leave General Miranda said, " Colonel Altmann,"

"Sir!"

"We had a call from a Simon Wiesenthal requesting an audience."

"Have you ever heard of the man?"

"The man is a filthy little Jew. Did you see him?"

"Not yet, that depends on you, Colonel. Understand?

"Jawohl!" Altmann snapped.

Simon Wiesenthal, a holocaust survivor, had dedicated his life to raising public understanding of the need to hunt and prosecute Nazi war criminals.

He was responsible in part for the capture of Adolf Eichmann, the Nazi put in charge of transporting and deportation of millions of Jews in the Nazi Final Solution.

Mossad agents captured Eichmann in Argentina in 1960 and smuggled him back to Israel to stand trial. He was found guilty of multiple war crimes, sentenced to death and was hanged. He was cremated, and his ashes were dispersed in an unknown location.

He was responsible for the capture of Franz Stangl, the supervisor at the Hartheim Euthanasia Centre, this was an early euthanasia program that was responsible for the deaths of over 70,000 mentally ill or physically deformed people in Germany. He later became the commander of the

Sobibor and Treblinka extermination camps where he oversaw the deaths of over 900,000 people.

Stangl was arrested in São Paulo, Brazil and extradited back to Germany where he was sentenced to life in prison, where he died.

Then there was the case of Hermine Braunsteiner, better known as "the Mare of Majdanek," a guard at Majdanek and Ravensbrück concentration camps. Braunsteiner was a cruel and sadistic woman who earned her nickname by kicking her victims to death.

She immigrated to the United States and became a U.S. citizen. It took Wiesenthal ten years to have her deported back to Germany; finally, she was charged with the killing of 250,000 people at Majdanek, found guilty and sentenced to life in prison, where she died.

Simon Wiesenthal, a little Jewish man, struck terror into the hearts and minds of all Nazi war criminals all over the world. So, when General Bazner mentioned the name of Simon Wiesenthal, Klaus Barbie knew he had to get results and fast. For as much as he felt that he was vital in helping the Generals, everyone is expendable. It's one thing that being a Nazi under Hitler taught him, you either got the job done, or you got hung.

Barbie was not going to let some filthy, dirty, stinking little Jew destroy his life.

"Banco Nacional de Bolivia, located at 2072 Av. 20 de Octubre is our bank of choice." Butch said.

"And why that bank?" Che asked.

"Because right next door to the bank is a vacant lot."

"And?"

"And, we're going to start to construct a building in that vacant lot."

"Why?"

"So we can dig a big hole in the ground."

"And why would we want to…Ah Hah!"

"Sure, we could dig a tunnel from a building across the street or even next door, the problem is what to do with all the dirt so it won't raise suspicions."

"But, isn't constructing a building expensive?"

"I never said we were going to complete it, I said start to build one.

"Now we already have the permits, the architect plans and we're going to have to hire actual construction workers to make this look legit, I have News out now looking to lease a couple of dump trucks, a bulldozer and driver, and a small crane operator."

"How much of the three hundred thousand have you spent?"

"About fifty-thousand, I hadn't figured on all the palms that needed greasing."

"He's next door opening a large business account to check out the vault and security system."

"So, some of the money that we'll be stealing will be our own?"

"Right."

"How soon will be breaking ground, in a manner of speaking?"

"In about a week, we're still ironing out some details."

"Can you explain exactly how and when we'll actually break into the vault?"

"I'm thinking once we know the exact location of the vault, we'll place steel beams nearby, so when we start using the acetylene torch on the vault, people will think we're using a welding torch to place structural beams. This has to appear to be the real thing. I don't want some armchair construction worker calling the cops because we don't know what we're doing. We'll start working on the opposite side of the building to have a good start. We don't want to be too eager and mess this up.

"The other thing is we'll be working on weekends and into the night, just enough so when we do hit the bank on a Saturday or Sunday, it won't look suspicious. As far as the when, that is to be determined."

"Sounds well thought out Butch, of course, I expected nothing less. When can I visit the site?"

"Maybe tonight, I don't want to take the chance of somebody recognizing you, and by the way, plan on being sequestered. You're too well known to be traipsing about like some sort of movie star."

"Butch, I'll go crazy just sitting in this room all day and night."

"Read a book."

"What book?"

"Marx?"

"Read it."

"Lenin?"

"Read it."

"Engels?"

"Read it."

"Mao?"

"Read it."

"Kennedy?"

"Rea… Kennedy?"

"Yeah, try reading someone from the other team for a change; you might learn something. I'll go out and get you a copy of Profiles in Courage today."

"How bourgeois!"

Colonel Altmann/Klaus Barbie was kind of enjoying getting back into the swing of torturing people, he didn't realize how much enjoyment it gave him.

The contorting faces in pain, the convulsions, the twisting of the bodies that seem to strain almost to the breaking point and sometimes they do. The screams, the whimpering, the crying, and the begging. Oh how he loved it when those poor wretched souls pleaded and begged for mercy. That's when he would turn the thumbscrews a little bit tighter or elevate the electricity a couple more volts.

He loves this part of the job. It was almost like being back in the Reich, where he had an open hand to do whatever he wanted, whatever he desired. He tortured each victim differently, never two the same way; that to him was boring and uncreative. After all, he was an artist, a master of agony, distress, and torment.

Down in the bowels of the Ministry of Justice building, Colonel Altmann had the entire sub-basement to practice his enhanced interrogation techniques

"Who's next, Ramon?" Altmann asked his assistant.

"It's Xavier Abastoflor, head of the Bolivian communist party. He's in room four."

"Very good. Are my dental tools all set up?"

"Yes, sir."

"Excellent."

Room four was totally dark, except for a small overhead dental light. The "patient" had been beaten up prior to being strapped down to the pseudo-dental chair, a block was wedged into his mouth so that it would stay open while Barbie infected severe unencumbered pain.

"Good evening Xavier. I hope you don't mind that I call you Xavier, I feel that torturer and the tortured should have a friendly rapport, don't you?"

"Grraaphff"

"I'll take that as a yes. Now before I ask you a question, I'm just going to do a quick dental exam, is that alright with you, Xavier? Good. Here goes."

Barbie picked up a sickle probe, the tool with a sharp point at the end to enhance tactile sensation, it's used to probe for cavities.

At first, Barbie was gently probing and scraping the teeth and gums looking for weak spots. He found what he was looking for, a large cavity back on the bottom left side, his second molar.

Barbie shook his head, "Tisk, tisk, Xavier, I can see that you haven't been practicing good dental hygiene. Now that is a shame, here let me show you."

Barbie took the sharp metal point of the probe and jammed it deep into the tooth, touching the nerve, sending an intense white light pain shooting thru his entire body.

"Aaaaahgrraaaffff!!!!"

Tears were running down the man's face as he began to sob.

Barbie placed the sickle probe down and picked up a pair of extracting forceps, he held them in front of Xavier's face.

"You know Xavier, it seems that that molar is giving you some trouble, so why don't I just yank that troublesome tooth out. That should give you some relief. What do you say?"

"Nnnnnaaaaaawwww." Xavier uttered as he tried to shake his head no.

"Well, I'm glad that we're in agreement. Here goes." Barbie said as he began to go for the tooth, but he abruptly stopped.

"Oh, there is just one thing Xavier, seems that I'm all out of Novocain." Barbie grabbed hold of the molar and began to twist and pull, twist and pull for over a minute and finally with a mighty tug, pulled the bloody tooth out and held it up to his victims face.

Barbie could have taken the tooth out with just a simple twist, but that wouldn't have induced the maximum pain that Klaus was going for.

Holding the tooth in front of Xavier, Barbie said in mocking shock, "Oh dear, silly me, I've taken the wrong tooth out. Here let me correct that."

He made the second extraction even more laborious and painful, so much so that Xavier passed out. Throwing the tooth on the floor, Barbie turned to his assistant Ramon and said, "Damn it, I hate when they pass out. Pick up that bucket and throw the water on him and bring him around."

"Yes, Colonel."

"Oh, and Ramon, is his wife here?"

"Yes, Colonel."

"Good, after you revive this pig, I want you to gag her, strip her naked and strap her face down on the bench, then wheel her in when I tell you."

"Yes, Colonel."

Ramon then picked up the bucket full of dirty water that had been recently used to mop up blood from the previous victim. Ramon threw the water on an angle so as not to get too much water down the unconscious man's throat.

SPLASH!

Xavier was brought to consciousness by feeling like he was drowning. He had no choice but to swallow the filthy water mixed with his own blood that was oozing from his open wounds.

Barbie approached the man bound to the dental chair; he was smoking a Cuban cigar, "Ah, good you're awake. Now, Xavier, I 'm going to ask you a question, and I want an honest answer. If I feel that you are truthful, I promise you a quick and painless death. However, if I feel you're lying to me, I shall slowly pull every tooth out of your head. Do you understand, me Xavier?"

The man nodded as best he could.

Barbie turned his head and shouted, "Bring her in, will you Ramon?"

From out of Xavier's peripheral vision, he could see what looked to be something or someone being wheeled into the room on a metal bench. His vision was still unfocused from the pain and the dirty water that had been splashed on him. Finally, he could see, it was his wife Maria. She was bound face down and bent over onto a metal bench, and she was naked.

Anger and rage-filled Xavier, so much so that he tried with all his might to break free from his bonds and kill his tormentor. He even prayed to the God he doesn't believe in to give him the strength, but to no avail.

"See, now that's good Xavier. Hate is a powerful emotion, and I feel your hate; you want to kill me, but you are powerless. However, love is even stronger. Your love for your wife is the most important thing right now, and you'll do anything to save her, isn't that right?

"Well, if you answer truthfully, I shall spare your wife's life, understand?"

Xavier gurgled, *"Si."*

"I want to know who killed Major Reinhardt. Was it Che Guevara?"

Tears began to well up in Xavier's eyes as he croaked, *"Ah doont ggnnooww."*

"Not that's not the answer I wanted to hear, Xavier. I'm afraid that's going to cost you a tooth."

Barbie reached into Xavier's mouth and rocked the back molar on the other side of his mouth back and forth for several minutes and finally pulled it out. Thankfully, by now, his mouth was becoming numb, and the pain was becoming almost bearable.

Barbie took a big drag on his cigar and blew a cloud of smoke into Xavier's mouth, causing him to gag and cough. He then walked over to Maria and leaned his body on her backside, took another drag on the cigar, so the ash was bright red and touched her buttocks with the lit cigar. Maria let out a woeful muffled scream, as did Xavier.

Barbie was a most sadistic man, and there was nothing he enjoyed more than seeing others in agony. He was actually smiling when he walked back to his helpless quarry bound to the dental chair.

"See! Do you see what happens when you don't tell the truth?" He said, pointing to his wife.

"Now, tell me the truth. If you do, I promise to let your wife go, you have my word as an officer and a gentleman. Did Che Guevara have anything to do with the murder of Major Reinhardt?"

Xavier had never met Che Guevara, but this Colonel Altmann thinks that all communists must know each other. Sure he had heard of him, he even admired him, but right now his only concern was saving his wife Maria, so he nodded and said, *"Si. Guavaaa."*

"Now, wasn't that easy? All I ever wanted Xavier was for you to tell the truth. We could have avoided so much pain if only you had been forthright with me."

Xavier tried to communicate about letting his wife go free, *"gaana lllleet Maarreea gaa."*

"Maria? I'm a man of my word, and Maria shall be released just as I promised. However, since you weren't completely honest with me, Maria will have to do her penance."

Altmann walked back to Maria and again touched his red hot cigar ash to her other buttock, and laughing he said, "Maria is going to spend the next hour entertaining some boys from my special unit."

He walked over to the door and shouted, "Ramon, will you be so kind as to bring Sabastián and the others into room four, por favor."

Moments later, eight men followed Ramon into the room.

"Gentleman, Maria here has so kindly agreed service you all, for as long as you like. All she asks is that you enjoy yourselves. Ramon, you may be the first."

As the men, one by one raped her, Altmann stood by Xavier laughing and whispering vulgar remarks in his ear until after each man had his way with her. He told Ramon, "Ramon, untie her and see that she is released. You see Xavier, I am a man of my word."

As Maria, still naked, was stumbling toward the door, Barbie stopped her, "Maria, wait, I want you to see this."

Barbie then pulled a Luger from under his lab coat, cocked it and shot Xavier in the mouth, blowing a large hole in the back of his skull, bits of Xavier's skull and brains splattered onto Maria's naked body.

Barbie smiled and said, "Now, you may go."

A half hour later, Maria was seen walking just north of the market called Cancha where the bus station is located. It was reported that she apparently stepped in front of a bus that was headed to Santa Cruz. She was killed instantly.

With the proper permits and using a shell company Butch Cassidy and the Wild Bunch were on their way to the biggest bank heist of their career. The possibility of scoring over 90 million dollars according to the bank president speaking with the Sundance Kid aka Tommy St. John. Not too bad for a group of septuagenarians, men in their 70s.

On the first day of construction, Sundance and Butch went into the bank to meet with the bank president, a Senõr Morales.

"Senõr Morales, thank you for taking time out from your busy schedule to met with us." Sundance said.

"It is my pleasure, Senõrs St. John and Thomas. Please have a seat. Now, what can I do for you?"

"Well, we just wanted to come by and tell you that we will be starting construction on our new building today, and hope that we won't inconvenience you too much with the noise and any vibrations," Butch said.

"Thank you for your consideration, but I have already alerted our employees that there might be some minor disruption and disturbance due to construction."

"We will try to be mindful of your business hours. Most of the heavy work, we will do after your closing time and on weekends." Sundance noted.

"Gracias, that is very considerate of you."

"It's the least we can do since you were so kind as to help get our loan. Well, we've taken up way too much of your time. So again thank you, Senõr Morales. Adiós." Butch said as he and Sundance rose.

"Thank you both for stopping by, it was very thoughtful of you, Adiós and que tengas un buen día."

"You have a nice day, too." Butch said.

When they got outside the bank, Butch said, "What a nice fella."

"Yeah, too bad we're going to steal all his money."

"Hey, he's not that nice."

Colonel Altmann / Klaus Barbie was about to interrogate his last subject. He had interrogated over twenty men and women and they all signed confession and statements claiming that Che Guevara was indeed the culprit that tortured and killed Major Reinhardt.

This last subject to be "interviewed" was Kid Curry's cellmate, Juan López, serving 10 to 20 years for armed robbery and assaulting a police officer.

Hauptsturmführer Barbie hated Americans almost as much as he hated communists and maybe, just maybe they were all working together with those Jewish vermin, Mossad.

Juan López was strapped down lying spread eagle prone on a wooden table with his arms and legs outstretched. He resembled Christ on the cross.

"Good evening, Senõr Lõpez, so glad you could join me. I understand that you were the cellmate of the American Harvey Logan, is that correct?"

"Si, but only for a short time."

"How long?"

"Maybe six weeks."

"Did you two ever talk?"

"No, senõr."

"Come, come Juan. May I call you Juan?"

"Si,"

"Come, come, Juan, you mean to tell me you shared a cell together for six weeks and you never spoke to one and other?"

"He's Spanish was poor, as is my English."

"I see, and you can't remember ever speaking to Senõr Logan, is that what you're telling me?"

"Si, senõr."

"Well, Juan, let me see if I can help you jog your memory."

Altmann turned to his assistant, Ramon and said, "Ramon, would you be so kind as to set up the fire pit?"

"Yes, Colonel."

Lõpez watched as Ramon brought in a large metal dish filled with white-hot coals, and several iron pokers and placed them into the bowl.

"Now, you'll have to be patient Juan for my irons to get up to temperature, so just lie there and try to relax."

"Please, senõr, no! I remember!"

"Oh, I'm sorry, Juan. Once I have my fire pit set up I have to use it, you had your chance. This will be fun, I promise, not for you, but for me."

Altmann looked thru the red hot pokers and found one he was looking for, a swastika branding iron, the swastika was 3" X 3".

"Ramon, would you please remove Juan's clothing? I'd hate to ruin his prison uniform."

His assistant did as he was told, leaving Juan naked spread eagle on the table.

"Now, the question for you, Juan, is where would you like your swastika?"

"Please, no senõr, please that won't be needed, I remember clearly what the gringo said, every word. Please!"

"Yes, yes, we'll get to that in a minute. Now, how about we place this right here." And with that, he touched the branding iron to Juan's lower right side. The stench of burning flesh filled the room along with screams.

"My, my that does make the most unpleasant smell, but I must admit, and I think you'll agree, that it is rather striking. Do you think we should do another one on your left side?"

"No! Por el amor de Dios, no!"

"Okay, well we'll just leave it for now. So, Juan tell me what Logan had to say."

"He talked about how he hated that Major Reinhardt."

"Go on, did he ever mention anyone else?"

"He did mention his lawyer, I can't remember his name, also the American Consulate William Ackley, some assistant Lester and some friend last name Cassidy."

"Did he mention anyone else? Think, it's important."

"No, senõr, I swear it."

"What did he say about Reinhardt?"

"He said that the major liked to hear stories about Logan's wild days in the west, cowboy and Indian stories."

"Interesting. Did he ever mention the name, Che Guevara?"

"The revolutionary?"

"Yes."

"No, he never did."

"You're a communist, aren't you, Juan?"

"No senõr, I am pro-General Banzr, I swear."

"I don't believe you, Juan."

"Please, just tell me what you want me to say."

"Are you willing to sign a statement stating that the prisoner Harvey Logan told you that he and Che Guevara conspired to kill Major Reinhardt?"

"Si, anything, I will sign whatever you tell me to."

Colonel Altmann had Juan Lõpez sign a formal statement declaring that Che Guevara was responsible for the death and torture of Major Reinhardt.

As his reward for signing was that Altmann spared his life, but not before he branded his left side with the swastika branding iron, blinded him in one eye, crushed his left hand and castrated him with an old pair of sheep shears and then cauterized the wound with a hot poker.

Juan Lõpez was a lucky man; of the twenty-two people that Barbie "interviewed" only three survived.

The prisoners of San Sebastian Penitentiary call Juan Lõpez, Lucky Lõpez.

Unlike construction in American, construction workers in Bolivia don't start the day at 5 or 6am in the morning, usually between 9 and 10am, leaning more towards the 10 than the 9. So, not wanting to draw attention to our site we had out crews start their days around 10am. Most of the crews were local construction workers. When it would come to the actual robbery, we would schedule that when the real workers were off-site. We didn't want any of them getting into trouble with the law.

I don't know why, but me and one of Che's men, who actually knew construction, were acting as project managers. Butch and Sundance would show up every day just to check-in.

For the first six weeks, it appeared to me that the guys were mostly rearranging, adding, or removing dirt. We had a bulldozer and dozens of dump trucks coming in and out of the site, clogging up traffic, and pissing lots of people off, but hey, that's progress.

It wasn't until our eighth week when we started pounding the giant iron I-beams into the ground that it really began to look like a building was being built.

The architect, Raúl Márquez, is one of Che's men. I could tell he was really wanting to see the project completed. Every week we'd have to remind him that we were more interested in robbing the bank than completing the building.

We wanted him to find things that would slow down the progress. Our target date is Monday, August 6th, Independence Day, the annual celebration of the signing of the Declaration of Independence on August 6th, 1825.

That will give us three days when the bank will be abandoned. Today is July 16th, and it feels like winter since we're below the equator. That whole equator thing is always throwing me off. Even after all these years.

According to Raúl, we will have enough of the building completed to shield us from breaking into the bank vault.

We are presently putting more effort completing the left side of the building. So that way when we're working on the vault, it will give the appearance that we're working to catch up.

While we're in La Paz, Che has been traveling under the name Adolfo Mena González. He's pretending he's a middle-aged Uruguayan businessman working for the Organization of American States. He shaved off his beard and much of his hair, also dyed it grey. He shows little resemblance of the image people have of the revolutionary Che Guevara.

He has been trying to form his guerrilla army located in the montane dry forest in the remote Ñancahuazú region. Setting up a training camp proved to be hazardous with little to show for the effort in the way of building a guerrilla army.

His guerrilla force only numbered about 50 men, they operated under as the ELN (Ejército de Liberación de Bolivia; National Liberation Army of Bolivia). They were well equipped and scored a number of early victories against the Bolivian army regulars. Most of their successes took place in the rugged mountainous terrain of the Camiri region. After their latest skirmish, Che made his way back to La Paz to check our progress. We met him at a small hotel not far from the construction site, the El Rey Palace.

When we all went up to his room, we were shocked to see the once robust, energetic revolutionary looking like an old man, and it wasn't just his disguise either.

He looked haggard and tired. Combat will do that to you, that plus sleeping out in the wild and always on the run, and not eating properly. That sort of life takes its toll, war is not an old man's game.

"Che, it's really good to see you, we been reading of your successes." Butch said.

"Yeah, you're getting a lot of positive press. Is it helping in recruiting men?" I asked.

"It's encouraging to see what we can accomplish with a handful of well-trained men against a larger force. It boosts our morale. Hopefully, more people will be attracted to the cause with more victories." Che said with pride.

"How long are you here for?" Sundance asked.

"Only two days, we have to keep on the move. Tomorrow I will be meeting with a representative from Cuba and the new leader of the Bolivian Communist Party. They will be delivering supplies and much-needed equipment.

"How's the construction going, are we still on schedule?"

"According to Raúl, everything is going according to plan; August 6th, arc you planning on being here for the robbery?" I asked.

"Yes, if I can. At this point, I really can't say. That money will really help in the cause, I know you guys aren't doing it for the struggle, but are you just doing it for the money?"

"Che, of course, we're doing it for the money, and for the challenge, but mostly we're doing it to help you. You've been like the son we never had, and yes, I guess we're doing it for the cause, too." Butch said as he walked over to where Che was standing and gave him a big hug.

"We just hope we won't let you down." Sundance said.

"No matter how this turns out, you guys will never let me down."

Buzzzzz. The doorbell rang, everyone reached for their guns.

"Everyone just relax, I ordered some Chinese and some beers before we came over." I said.

A young Chinese man stood in the doorway holding two large paper bags, one full of Chinese food and the other full of beer.

"I got this." I said.

"I hope it's good." Che said.

"Just like Chairman Mao likes it." I quipped

Generals Miranda and Tejada were once again sitting at one end of the conference table when Colonel Altmann entered the great room.

"Sit down, Colonel." Miranda said.

"We've heard that you've been a busy boy, Colonel. What have you found out?" Tejada asked.

"From my investigations, I have found that I was right. It was indeed Che Guevara who was behind the killing and torture of Major Reinhardt, I have proof." He stated as he held up copies of the signed statements.

"We are familiar with your "investigation" techniques, Colonel. In the end, don't people say whatever you want them to say?" Again it was General Tejada who raised the question.

"General, it's all in the approach, I pride myself in my ability and years of experience to ascertain and glean unbiased and factual data from the people I interview, while still enjoying the process."

"And by the process, you mean the torture and suffering that you inflict on people, correct? I'm not criticizing you, Colonel, God knows we've all done our share of interviews. But I don't know anyone who enjoys this type of work as much as Nazis. And of the Nazis, that at least that I've met, no one enjoys it more than you." Tejada stated.

"Thank you, sir, I'll take that as a compliment."

General Miranda asked, "May we see those statements, Colonel?"

Barbie rose from his seat and walked them down to the other end of the table where the Generals were sitting.

"Here you are."

He placed copies on the table in front of them, walked back to his place, sat down, and waited with his hands together in front of him.

Each of the Generals took half the stack and began reading them, passing each other the statements that they had read, until finally after whispering to each other and appearing to come to some sort of consensus. General Miranda asked, "What is your next course of action, Colonel?"

"With your permission, I would like to head a special unit of Rangers to pursue, capture, or kill this enemy of the state. I have had reports that Che Guevara, himself is in Bolivia and is heading up the ELN, which has claimed several victories over regular army troops, as I'm sure you both are well aware."

"We are." Tejada said.

"What makes you think that you can take this man down, Colonel?" Miranda asked.

"All I need is to capture one man. Then I can, let's say, convince him to turn on this Marxist scum."

"How long do you think it will take?" Tejada inquired.

"I believe that I can have him by the end of the year, maybe before."

"Colonel, you'll have your Rangers." Miranda said.

"Thank you, I won't let you down."

"Colonel, of course you know, failure is not an option." Tejada warned.

"As I said, I won't let you down."

By the time Che got back to the jungle, he had found that the Bolivian Army managed to eliminate two of his guerrilla groups in a violent battle, and reportedly killed or captured one of the leaders, Félix Espinosa.

The day before, at the meeting with the Cuban representative, Julio Almeida and the new head of the Bolivian Communist Party, Mario Monje, Che had received bad news.

The Bolivian Communist Party told Che that they had decided to throw in with Moscow rather than Havana. So, they could not count on them for any support.

"Comrade Che, we sympathize with your struggles brother, but we just don't feel that revolution is right at this time."

"It's not my struggle, comrade. It's the poor and oppressed struggle; it's the workers and the peasant's struggle. If not, now, when?"

"Moscow doesn't feel…"

"Moscow! They've already had their revolution, comrade. And they sure as Hell didn't discuss their timing with you."

"Look, we just don't think…"

"That's exactly your problem Comrade Monje, you don't think. I'm going back to my men and fight against the imperial capitalistic masters who continue to keep their boot on the necks of the workers. You'll see, once they see our struggle, they will join our cause."

And with that Che stormed out of the room. Later in Che's own diary, he described the Bolivian Communist Party as, "distrustful, disloyal and stupid."

After that disastrous meeting, he went to meet the Cuban representative Julio Almeida, who Che had fought alongside in the Cuban Revolution.

"Che, we can't give you as much as we promised now, but certainly more will come, and soon."

"I understand."

"So, how's the fight going? We hear many good reports from our sources."

"It is true, we have had much success, but recently some losses and we still haven't won over the peasants to our side. It's not like Cuba, where the people were behind us. Here there is apathy, a weariness, an unwilling to make a commitment."

"Brother, they will come around, you'll see. You must be patient. These are uneducated people, simple people, you just need patience."

"How are things in Cuba these days."

"Like you, we are making slow progress, but we will persevere."

"And Fidel?"

"He sends his love. He has his own struggles establishing the government, dealing with so much, as they say, 'Heavy is the head that wears the crown.'

"Send him my regards."

"I will."

"When can we expect our supplies?"

"Within the next week."

"The sooner, the better, the rainy season is fast approaching."

"Soon."

As he was traveling back to his troops, Che wondered, when did Julio, Fidel, and the others go from revolutionaries to bureaucrats.

Frank Williams rose to the rank of Captain in the Office of Strategic Services (OSS) in World War II, he was one of the best in keeping tabs on all of the German High Command.

Captain Williams was personally responsible after German surrendered in tracking down and capturing most of the people who were wanted for war crimes.

There were a few that escaped Frank's squad either with the help of sympatric government, sheer luck or suicide. Of the three, Frank preferred the latter.

There were those times when the "Big Brass" decided to make exceptions. Those that our government thought were guilty of war crimes could be overlooked if those people could somehow be beneficial to us.

Like German V2 rocket engineer and SS Major, Wernher Von Braun, who was given a free pass on his war crimes if he would help us with our rocket and space program.

The fact that tens of thousands of Jews, Roma, Soviet soldiers, and French resistance fighters died while constructing his rocket sites for the V2 Buzz Bombs, and that it was rumored that he went to concentration camps to help select the slave workers who were beaten and starved while he went on about the business building the rockets that killed thousands of women and children in the air blitz of London.

Then there was Klaus Barbie, Frank Williams and his team captured Barbie in 1947. But instead of facing war crime charges, he was recruited as an agent for the 66th Detachment of the U.S. Army Counterintelligence Corps. The U.S. used Barbie and other Nazi criminals to further their anti-communist efforts in Europe.

But, once the French found out that the U.S. had Barbie, they demanded that they turn him over to them to stand trial for the murder of 14,000 people for whom he was directly responsible.

Well, that didn't happen. When the French made a plea to John J. McCloy, the U.S. High Commissioner for Germany at the time. McCloy refused; instead, he helped Barbie flee to Bolivia.

Now, I don't know if McCloy particularly didn't like the French, or the Jews or both, and maybe he just felt he had an obligation to a Nazi war criminal because they made a deal with him. But whatever the reason, he let him getaway.

It was assigned to Frank Williams to assist Barbie to get established in Bolivia. It didn't take long once the dictator, General Rogelio Miranda discovered the diamond he possessed. He put Barbie to work right away fighting his opposition and aiding the Bolivian military by forming the Fiances of Death, also known as the infamous death squads. Most of them were from Germany, Italy, and France, and many wore Nazi swastikas on their uniforms, just old times.

In 1967, Captain Frank Williams, now a captain in the CIA, got a call from a high ranking Bolivian official, asked if it were possible for Williams to meet him in La Paz at his earliest connivance.

"Could you tell me what this is in reference to?" Williams asked.

"I'd rather not say over the phone."

"Well, you 've got to give me something to justify my traveling to La Paz."

"Che Guevara."

"I'll be down tomorrow."

Che Guevara had been a thorn in the side of the CIA ever since he helped Castro take power in Cuba. They had been looking for him, but their operations reached a dead-end when it was thought that he had been murdered and buried in an unmarked grave in the Dominican Republic; a rumor perpetrated by Che himself to keep his whereabouts unknown. But, if this turned out to be accurate, it certainly would be a big feather in William's cap.

William's was on the first plane to La Paz out of D.C the next morning. Little did he know or suspect that he would again be working with the Nazi war criminal, Klaus Barbie.

The building site was really starting to take shape. The four corner vertical I-beams were set in concrete yesterday. Today, we'll be setting four more beams between them and begin to attach the I-beams with horizontal beams.

It's starting to look somewhat like the skeleton for a building. Although we don't officially have the specific area of the bank vault, we have designated the space where we have our project desk. Here all the blueprints are laid out, as sort of a command center. We added a little wooden shack that butted up against the wall where the vault was so we would be able to break into the bank undetected.

Most of the work and construction is being done on the opposite side where the vault sits. Butch and Sundance have had several companies inquire about leasing space in the building. A couple of companies have already placed deposits with us, which give us even more credibility, especially with the bank. It gives the impression that we're legit when Butch and Sundance go in and deposit money into our account, money that we're eventually going to withdraw along with several million dollars that aren't ours.

The three of us have been talking about what we're going to do and where we'd like to go after this last big heist. Over the years, our robbing banks outside of Bolivia has proven to be very lucrative. I don't know about the others, but I've been able to squirrel away close to a half a million dollars.

Butch keeps talking to us about heading down to Australia. Sundance really has no opinion about it, but he'll go wherever Butch goes. I might go with them, I don't know. I am pushing 70 like Butch and Sundance, although you'd never know it, except for a little stiffness from some old gunshot wounds, I think the three of us are still pretty spry.

I'll either go with them, or I just might head back to the States, although Butch and Sundance are like family, Hell we've been together for over fifty years, and I don't know what I'd do without them.

It's been a month since Che was here, and I've been reading about his exploits, The papers say that he doesn't seem to attract inhabitants of the local area to join his militia. Many have willingly informed the Bolivian authorities and military about the guerrillas and their movements.

We have sent word that we're still planning on breaking in on August 6th, just two weeks from now.

Che had expected to stay in radio contact with Havana, but the two shortwave radio transmitters given to him by Cuba were faulty; consequently, they were unable to communicate and get resupplies, they were basically isolated and stranded.

Che would always choose confrontation rather than compromise, but it, unfortunately, contributed to his inability to develop a good working relationship with local rebel leaders just as he did in the Congo. Che, was like so many others, they couldn't see that it was them and not others that help create failures.

Part of Che's problem was because he wasn't able to communicate with Cuba, he was under that false impression that was dealing with the Bolivian military, who were for the most part poorly trained and equipped.

We would all be in for a rude awaking.

"Frank Williams?" Asked a young man wearing a black suit, white shirt, black tie and aviator sunglasses standing at the terminal gate of Pan American flight 226.

"And you would be?"

"I am General Tejada's assistant. Please follow me, do you have any luggage?"

"No, I'm not planning on staying overnight."

"Please, right this way, sir."

The young man led Williams out of the terminal and outside to a parked black limo with Bolivian flags on both sides of the front fenders. The young man opened the passenger's rear door and shut the door once Williams was seated. He then got into the front passenger side door.

"Where are we going?" Williams asked.

"To the capital, General Tejada's office." The man said without turning around.

The driver was wearing the exact same "uniform" as the kid who met him at the airport. Must be all those spy movies that these kids are watching and want to emulate.

Not another word was spoken the rest of the ride. This was the first time Williams had been back in La Paz since he dropped off that Nazi Barbie back in '57. A lot has changed in ten years.

"Come in, come in Mr. Williams, it is good to see you again. Please come, have a seat." General Tejada said.

"Thank you, General, it is good to see you. too."

The General waved his hand, and his assistant left the room, closing the door behind him.

"Did you have a good flight?"

"Yes, sir. A little long, but pleasant."

"Well, I suspect you're wondering why I asked that you to come meet with me."

"I was told it has to do with Che Guevara."

"Yes, that is so. Che is here in Bolivia trying to stir the peasants up into a revolution.

"But, so far, he has failed to do so. However, he has been wreaking havoc with our army, and he has been succeeding.

"It is bad for morale, and eventually it might incite some to come and join him,"

"Where do I come in?"

General held up his hand as to indicate a pause, then he picked up one of three telephones on his desk and said, "Theresa, send him in."

The door opened and in walked Klaus Barbie wearing, what looked to be a Bolivian Colonel's uniform. He approached Williams, who remained seated, held out his hand and said, "Captain Williams, it is good to see you after all these years."

Williams didn't shake Barbie's hand; instead, he looked past him at the General and said, "Like I said, where do I come in."

Tejada looked at Barbie and offered him the seat next to Williams.

"Have a seat Colonel."

"Thank you, sir."

"Captain Williams the reason I asked you here is that we, and by we I mean Colonel Altmann, is heading up a special unit that has been assigned to capture or kill Che Guevara.

"I am assuming that you know, or at least know of Félix Rodriguez, the Cuban exile turned CIA Special Activities Division operative."

"Yes, I know him."

"Well, he has been advising Colonel Altmann in his endeavor to get Guevara."

"Yeah?"

"Captain Williams, I am hoping that you want Che Guevara as much as we do, so I'm asking for your help."

Without looking at Barbie, Williams asked, "Will I have to work with him?"

"I'm afraid so, will that be an insurmountable obstacle for you?"

"No, if it means getting rid of Guevara, but I call the shots."

"Colonel?"

"I'm agreeable." Barbie said.

"Excellent, excellent." General Miranda chortled.

"What exactly do you need from me?" Williams asked.

Barbie thought for a moment then said, "Frank, may I call you Frank. Frank, is it possible to have a team of your Special Activities Division commandos aid us in our anti-insurrection efforts?"

"No."

"No?"

"No, you may not call me Frank."

"Sorry. Captain Williams, is it possible to have a team of your Special Activities Division commandos aid us in our anti-insurrection efforts?"

"I'll have a team of U.S. Army Special Forces and a battalion of U.S. Rangers that are trained in jungle warfare sent down to set up camp near Guevara's last know encampment."

"That would be La Esperanza."

"They'll be there within a week."

"Thank you, Captain."

"Look Altmann or whatever you're calling yourself these days. I don't like you. If it were up to me, you would have hung years ago along with all of the other Nazi scum at Nuremberg. So, don't thank me, I'm not doing this for you, I'm doing this to get rid of just another annoyance on the world stage."

Williams stood up, "General, you'll have American boots on the ground within the week, and with any luck Che Guevara will be caught or killed within a month.

"Colonel, you'll be hearing from one of my men by the end of the day tomorrow."

The revolution, such as it was, wasn't going as planned. Che was down to only fifty men, and the people weren't rallying to the cause. He heard rumors that the U.S. was planning on sending special units to start tracking him down, and Klaus Barbie, the notorious Nazi war criminal, was leading the search.

He suffered several desertions, morale was low, and the local peasants were spying on them and even turning them in for rewards. He desperately needed that money from the bank heist to buy equipment, purchase the latest weapons, and offer pay for mercenaries to join the fight.

Unfortunately, he didn't think he could afford to leave his men, so he sent one of his lieutenants to represent him at the robbery. It wasn't that he didn't trust Butch and Sundance, but money does have a funny way of making one forget your friends.

"I am Lieutenant Gomez, Che sent me to represent him in this endeavor. Here is a letter from Che."

Butch read the letter, "Seems in order, here take a look News. Whadda think?"

"Looks like the real deal to me." I said.

"Lieutenant Gomez, come with me." Butch said as he walked towards the shack. Butch opened the door to reveal the outer brick wall was gone, only the metal of the vault was exposed.

"This time tomorrow, we should be starting to torch our way in."

"How long do you think it shall take to be inside?"

"We're thinking at least four hours. If all goes well, we shall be long gone by eight in the evening."

"Che asked me to ask you about the split."

"We've discussed that amongst ourselves, We're only going to take the U.S. currency, Che can have everything else.

"Now, we're out of here once we get our cut, so if you want to fool around with the safety deposit boxes, that's on you. But, we're going to deliver the cash to Che, and then we're gone.

"We recommend that you just take the money and run. It's the greedy that gets caught."

"Yes, I understand."

"Meet us back here tomorrow at 10am, and wear work clothes, nothing new or you'll stick out like a sore thumb."

"I do not understand, sore thumb."

"Just wear dirty clothes tomorrow."

"So, you are Félix Espinosa, I understand that you're one of Che Guevara's top lieutenants. It is a great honor to meet you, sir, may I call you Félix? Félix, over the next couple hours we're going to get to know each other very well. You're going to tell me things that you've never have told another living soul, and you're going to find out things about me that you'd wish to God you didn't know.

"My name is Colonel Altmann, have you ever heard of me?" Altmann asked.

Espinosa didn't say anything, he just shook his head no. He was bound naked to a wooden armchair bolted to the floor, the chair seat had been modified so that his legs were spread apart, exposing his genitals and his ankles were bound to the bottom of the chair legs.

"Now, Félix, I'm going to ask you a straightforward question. If you answer me truthfully, you'll find that I'm a reasonable man, but if you lie to me, I am going to hurt you very badly. Do you understand?"

Again, Félix said nothing, this time he nodded, yes."

"Do you know Che Guevara?"

Félix shook his head no.

"Mmmmmm, that was the wrong answer Félix. Now I'm going to have to hurt you. Ramon, would you lean Félix's head back for me?"

Ramon came up from behind, grabbed the prisoner's hair and yanked it hard, forcing Félix's head to snap backward.

"Hold it back, please."

Altmann reached over to a tray nearby and took a small bottle with an eyedropper, forced Félix's eyes apart and placed several drops of a liquid into each eye. At first, the drops felt cool and soothing, but seconds later, a fierce burning developed, and soon his eyes felt on fire.

Altmann had used Hydrochloric acid, which is a corrosive acid that causes severe burning and produced irreparable damage to Félix's eyes, causing blindness.

The man let out an agonizing scream, he was in so much pain that he twisted and turned, begging for relief.

"Ramon, go get some water in that bucket over there and splash it in the poor man's eyes, can't you see he's suffering."

The bucket that Altmann was referring to was a bucket of urine left over from the previous prisoner's torture session. As Ramon readied the bucket, Altmann said, "Open your eye real wide, Félix."

Blood was streaming from his eyes when Ramon threw the bucket of urine into the man's face, it only made the pain even worse, causing him to scream even more.

Altmann just stood there laughing, "Félix, did you have an accident, you smell like piss, Ramon go get some water, this man reeks, I can't work with him when he smells so vile."

This time Ramon did bring over a couple buckets of water and threw them on the man bound and in agony.

Blinded and suffering, Félix knew there was no way that this maniac was going to let him live, he knew he was going to experience a living Hell before he was murdered. He could either try and make it easy on himself and maybe get an early death by telling partial truths or suffer thru the worst torture saying nothing.

From deep down inside there grew an immense hatred that far exceeded his fears, Félix decided that he would be damned if this Nazi piece of shit was going to break him.

Barbie had tortured hundreds maybe thousands of poor souls, very few of them could totally resist, they all broke, it was just a matter of when. Oh, there were a few like that leader of the French Resistance leader, Moulin who never gave in, and maybe one or two others, but overall, he felt that he was the master of extracting information, and even if he didn't, he so enjoyed the process, of thinking up new and more devious ways to inflict pain on people.

"Félix, feeling better?"

Félix said nothing. He just sat silently, a mixture of blood and tears streaming from his eyes.

"So, you're not going to talk to me, is that right?"

Silence.

"I will give you one more chance to speak. If you do not, then I will cut out your tongue and just continue to brutalize you for the sheer pleasure of it. And let me tell you that it shall go on for days, maybe, if I'm careful even a week. Do you think you can handle that?"

Silence.

"Good, I love a challenge."

He walked over to a table where he kept a variety of implements of torture, none of which had ever been washed or sterilized. He picked up a pair of sheep shears. He randomly walked around his quarry to confuse and torment him, since the man was blind, he knew he was relying on his hearing to guess which direction his attacker would come from.

Barbie stopped walking and stood still for a few minutes, then he and Ramon rushed him from behind, forcing his head back and prying his mouth open Barbie started snipping off bits and chunks of Félix's tongue piece by piece.

"There, that wasn't too bad was it Ramon?"

"No, sir." Ramon answered,

"Well, I think that's all for today, we'll let Félix just relax and have a go at it again tomorrow."

Barbie indicated the Ramon should go and close the door. Once Ramon had left, Barbie stealthily walked over to the fire pit where there were several red-hot irons of all different shapes and sizes. He selected two small rods and slowly crept up behind Félix, whose head was slumped over, mouth oozing blood and saliva, he was in a daze of semi-consciousness when Barbie shoved the two red-hot irons into his ears.

Félix let out a thunderous scream and then collapsed unconscious from shock.

Barbie feeling incredibly proud of himself, opened the door to leave as he did, he turned and whispered, "Sleep well, I'll see you tomorrow, Félix."

There comes a time where small circumstances, can have a significant impact or even change the course of history. I believe that is what happened, at least to me on the morning of August 6th, the day of what was to be known as the "Great Bolivian Bank Robbery."

Butch, Sundance and me had decided that we were going to take our share of the loot and fly, that night on to Lima, Peru. The following day we were to set sail to Australia on the SS Rijndam.

We were preparing to start the process of firing up the acetylene torches to burn our way into the bank vault. I was standing outside the small shack talking to Butch when from the scaffolding above us, a worker slipped and dropped a wheelbarrow full of broken metal bits and nails raining down on us.

I happened to look up and saw all of the debris falling down towards Butch. Instinct took over, and I rushed to push Butch out of the way, since he was unaware of the imminent danger. In the process of shoving Butch out of harm's way, I slipped and fell, resulting in a hundred pounds of rubble landed on my ankle. In spite of the noise of all that metal hitting the ground, I swear I heard the bones in my ankle snap, crackle, and pop, to coin a phrase.

"News, are you alright?" Butch shouted.

"Motherfucker, it hurts like Hell." I screamed.

They got my leg out from under the rubble, and Butch rushed me to Obrero Hospital emergency room. Three hours later, I hobbled out with a plaster cast that went halfway up my leg, I also sported a real spiffy wooden cane. Butch said it gave me a certain air of sophistication.

On the way back to the construction site, Butch kept thanking me for saving his life.

"Butch, stop it. You would have done the same for me, I just feel bad that I'm now a hindrance rather than a help."

"You know, News it might work out to our advantage."

"Whatta mean?"

"Well, ya think you should go and gather the bags and come back here. Once we get our share, we'll pack into the steamer truck and you can head over to the airport and check in all the luggage. Then after me and Sundance deliver Che's share, we'll meet you at the airport."

"I just feel like I'm letting you and Sundance down."

"Don't be silly, News. Honestly, except for you getting hurt, this is a good thing, it will work out better."

"Really?"

"Really."

Butch dropped me back at the house, where all the luggage was packed and ready to go. We decided that we would each only take one small suitcase since we figured anything we didn't have we would get when we get to Australia.

"How's News?" Sundance asked.

"Not bad, a couple of broken bones in his ankle; he's walking with a cast and a cane?" Butch answered.

"Bet he looks very sophisticated."

"Yeah, that's what I told him. How's it going here?"

"Good. Go take a peek."

Butch stuck his head into the small shack where two of Che's men were cutting thru the bank vault with torches. Due to the enclosed space, the temperature inside was sweltering. The men were working shirtless, and every hour we would have to swap men out in order not to have them collapse from heat exhaustion.

Butch went up to Sundance and said, "It looks like about another hour."

"That's what I was thinking."

Raúl Márquez, the building's architect and Che's representative, was still directing the construction crews, even as the bank was in the process of being robbed.

"Raúl, we're thinking about an hour or so." Butch said.

"Si, I agree."

"So, when we break thru, Sundance and I are only interested in U.S. currency which we're going to pack up in that steamer trunk over there and give it to News to take to the airport. We'll join him later after we drop off Che's share."

"Si, I understand, and we will gather up all other currency in these canvas banks, load them into a truck and go to the rendezvous point to deliver the money to Che."

"Is everything ready with Che?"

"Si, we are to meet Che and six of our men just off Highway One in Villa Ramedios."

One of the men working inside the shack came running out, excited, and said, "Está hecho!"

Raúl said, "We're in."

"Let's go!" Butch said.

Sundance went to call me and tell me to come to the sight. By the time I got there they would have the money all packed up and ready to go.

"I'm on my way." I said.

When Butch and Sundance entered the vault, off to their left was a palette with stacks of assorted U.S. currency: ones, fives, tens, twenties, fifties, hundreds and even a couple stacks of William McKinley five hundred dollar bills and thousand dollar bills, with President Grover Cleveland gracing the front.

As Butch and Sundance started loading the steamer trunk, they loaded the bigger bills first, and by the time they filled the chest, the only bills they didn't have room for were the fives and ones. They estimated that the trunk was filled with at least seven million dollars.

While they finished up with our portion of the heist, Che's men were filling up over twenty-six large canvas bags, Raúl estimated that they cleared over one hundred and seventy million Bolivian Bolívianos, which works out to be over 25 million U.S. Dollars.

When I got to the site, Butch and Sundance were sitting on the trunk, waiting for me on the sidewalk. The cabbie popped the automobile trunk so Butch and Sundance could load the chest inside.

"Listen, News; you head on to the airport and check-in. We'll get there as soon as we can. Now listen, if we're not there by take off, you go on ahead, and we'll catch the next available flight out. We'll meet you at the Gran Hotel Bolivar, as soon as we can, okay." Butch said.

"Say, maybe I should stick around for you guys, and we all go together."

"No, no, this is better. No one is going to suspect you to have been involved with that cast on. Right now, it's important that you get this trunk out of Bolivia, understand?"

"I guess, I just feel like I'm not doing my share."

"News stop talking crazy, why you just saved Butch's life today and you have been and always be an equal partner. Hell, we're the Wild Bunch! "

Now, get your ass outta here and take good care of that trunk, and we'll see you if not tonight, then probably tomorrow in Lima. Now vamonos!" Sundance said.

And with that, I headed off to La Paz's El Alto International airport. The airport wasn't busy on a Monday night; everyone was celebrating Bolivian Independence Day. The night was going to be chaotic with people celebrating, shooting off fireworks and dancing in the streets.

As it turned out, robbing the bank on Independence Day was a good idea and a bad idea.

Félix Espinosa floated in and out of consensus. He had no concept of time. Barbie had rendered him deaf, dumb, and blind thru torture, Félix Espinosa was ready for this to be over as he was prepared to die.

Barbie knew plenty of bullies within his "special" squad who he planned to call on to do whatever they would like to do to Félix to entertain themselves. The first man he sent in was Paulo Guzman, an ex-heavyweight boxer who was kicked out of professional boxing for his vicious illegal punches. Barbie and Guzman entered the room; Barbie sat in a chair opposite the prisoner as if sitting ringside for one of Guzman's fights.

"Can I kill him?"

"No! You get you to hit him one punch at a time. You wait till I tell you that you can hit him again. I want to enjoy each punch. Do you understand?"

Guzman nodded.

His first punch was to Félix's stomach; he hit him so hard that Félix threw up the little he had in his stomach. He gasped for air, to try and catch his breath.

PLOF!

Barbie began directing him. "That was very good, Paulo. Now hit him in the face."

SMASH!

Several teeth were instantly dislodged and flew out of Félix's mouth, crashing against the wall eight feet away.

"Nice. Now you get one more. Hit him in the groin."

Hitting men below the belt was a Guzman specialty. Since the prisoner was sitting down, Paulo got down on one knee and gave a pseudo uppercut to Félix's testicles.

THWACK!

Barbie stood up, clapping, "Bravo, bravo, nice work, Paulo."

"Why can't I kill him?"

"Maybe later, but there's so much more I want to do with this pig. You may go, oh and here's 700 Bolivianos."

The big goon walked out of the room, counting his reward. Barbie watched him leave then he turned to Félix, who was crying and convulsing in pain and said, knowing he couldn't hear him, "Oh, we've just begun my dear Félix. I've got a lot more surprises for you."

"Captain Williams, I hope you have good news for me." General Miranda said.

"General, I have been authorized to send you a dozen Green Berets advisors, and a battalion of elite U.S. Rangers specialized in jungle warfare. They are being deployed as we speak."

"Excellent, and will you be personally heading up the campaign, Captain?"

"Yes, I'll be flying down tomorrow morning."

"I'll inform Colonel Altmann of your arrival."

"Thank you, General, I shall see you soon."

"Goodbye, Captain."

Williams hung up the phone and pressed the call button to his intercom, "Sergeant, would you have Lieutenant Ackley come in."

"Yes, sir."

Moments later, there was a knock on the door, "Enter." Williams said, not bothering to look up. In walked the young lieutenant who smartly marched to the front of Captain William's desk snapped to attention and struck a near-perfect salute and announced, "Lieutenant Ackley reporting, sir!"

"At ease, Lieutenant."

"Sir!"

Lieutenant Robert Ackley, son of William Ackley, Charge d'Affaire of Bolivia, was to be William's number two man on this assignment as code name "Amquack." Ackley was a recent graduate from West Point. He had never experienced any actual combat assignments; he had been attached to Williams outfit by some top brass upstairs who was friends with the kid's old man.

"Lieutenant, I've been going over your service record, recent graduate from the Point, I see that you weren't exactly top of your class, were you?"

"No, sir."

"From what I can tell, you're a bit of a goof-off and a slacker, or am I reading this wrong?"

"No, sir."

"And you volunteered for this assignment, is that correct?"

"Yes, sir."

"Why?"

"Why, sir?"

"Yeah, why did you volunteer for this duty?"

"Well, sir, I was…"

"Does it have anything to do with the fact that your father is Charge d'Affaire of Bolivia?"

"I was told that it would be an easy mission, and that that it could be a career booster, sir."

"Okay, Lieutenant here's the skinny. I'm going to approve your assignment to the mission, but know this, we're going after a cunning fox, one who has been fighting guerrilla-style warfare for over ten years, so this isn't going to be a walk in the park. You're going to be slogging thru muck up to your balls. There will be blood-sucking leeches, malaria-ridden mosquitoes, booby traps, and combat-hardened troops.

"You'll be fighting alongside our elite Ranger unit who don't suffer fools, so you better bring your A-game, do you read me, soldier?"

"Yes, sir, loud and clear."

"Because I don't give a rat's ass who your old man is, it could be Lyndon Baines fucking Johnson, for all I give a shit. If you fuck up and put any of my men in danger, or cause a man's death, I'll shoot you myself. Understood?"

"Sir, yes, sir!"

"Good, now get out of here and gear up, we leave in an hour."

"Aye, aye sir

"How was your day, dear" Regina Barbie, Klaus's wife asked her husband.

"Wonderful, I'm working with a subject that's quite the challenge."

"Is he telling you everything you want to know?"

"Actually, no."

"Oh, I'm sorry, I know how much pleasure you get from forcing them to tell you all their dirty little secrets."

"That's normally true, but with Félix, I'm just enjoying myself."

"Really?"

"You see, on day one, I blinded him, cut out his tongue, and drove red hot pokers into his ears. So, he's deaf, dumb and blind. I can't exact any information from him, so I now have to think of unique ways to torment the man. It's marvelous. I have taken some films of our sessions, would you like to see?"

"Yes, I do so enjoy seeing you at your work."

"Regina, my love, let's go to the den. I have my projector all set up."

They went into their den where Altmann first turned off the lights, closed the shades, then threaded the projector and hit play.

The film as 16mm black and white, a bit on the grainy side, but not enough to distract the Barbie's from the sheer entertainment of seeing poor Félix Espinosa being tortured and brutalized.

Regina got so aroused that she stripped naked, laid on the floor moaning "Fick mich Klaus, fick mich," begging Klaus to fuck her. As he was, she kept watching the screen and moaning with pleasure, "Schwerer! Schwerer!"

Later, at dinner, Regina said, "Klaus, do you think I could come and observe your session with this man, Félix? I promise not to interfere. I'd like to watch."

"Of course, my dear, if that's what you'd like."

"I find it all quite exhilarating, but you know what the one thing that would make it even more pleasurable?"

"What is that my dear?"

"If he was a Jew."

It was just after three in the afternoon when all the canvas bags with the money were packed up into an unmarked Ford Box Truck. Butch, Sundance and Raúl

Márquez jumped into the cab and drove off, heading to Villa Ramedios to meet up with Che.

Raúl instructed the men who cut thru the vault to repair the brick wall, so any people passing by wouldn't see the hole and call the cops. They were told that once that was done, they should all head down to Villa Ramedios to hook up with Che and their unit.

Raúl was driving the box truck, going along at a pretty good clip.

"Hey, Raúl, slow down. The last thing we need is to get stopped by a cop for speeding. We've got plenty of time." Butch said.

Wheeooooww Wheeooooww Wheeooooww

"Great! It's the fucking police! " Sundance said.

There were two motorcycle police flashing their lights and running their sirens. We pulled over off the highway onto the dirt shoulder.

"Don't worry. I can handle this. " Raúl said.

One of the officers stood by his motorcycle, while the other approached the driver's side of the truck. The officer peered into the truck, Butch and Sundance just stared ahead, Raúl smiled and asked, "¿Que pasa, ofical?"

"Estabas haciendo 80 en un 60."

"Lo siento."

"Hablas Ingles, official" Butch asked.

"No señor."

 "Que hay em la parte de atras?"

"He wants to know what's in the back." Raúl said.

"Tell him; you're helping me move."

"Estoy ayudando a mis amigos a mudarse."

The officer looked at Butch, Sundance, and Raúl and figured that something wasn't right.

"Abre la espalda, por favor."

"He wants me to open the back."

Sundance asked, "Think he'd take a bribe?"

"I don't think so." Raúl said.

The police officer placed his hand on his gun and said, "Señor, necesito que abra laparte de atrás. Ahora."

"He's demanding that I open the back." Raúl said as he started to open the door. He pulled a pistol out from his belt and shot the officer in the chest. He slammed the truck into reverse and backed up over the other officer who was trying to get on his motorcycle. Then he dropped it into drive and screeched out back onto the highway.

The officer who had been run over wasn't killed, he had enough forethought to radio in for assistance and the description of the truck.

It wasn't long before the police were on their trail. It was just before they reached the Villa Ramedios turn off when the first patrol car spotted them. Once they turned off the highway, they saw the three-parked vehicles with Che sitting in the front seat of car number one.

Che could see that four police cars were chasing them. He jumped out of the vehicle holding a BAR automatic rifle and shouted, "Prepárate para abrir fuego!"

Eleven guerrillas rolled out of the cars and aimed their weapons and waited for the command to open fire. As soon as the truck passed by, Che gave the command, "Fuego!"

The automatic fire seemed to go on forever, until Che gave the command to stop, "Cesar el fuego!"

When the smoke cleared, there were four bullet-riddled cars with two police officers lying dead in each one. Che walked up to the truck, opened the door, and asked, "What the Hell happened?"

"Raúl got pulled over for speeding." Sundance said.

"Then he shot a cop and ran over another." Butch added.

"Estúpido!" Che snarled as he pulled Raúl out of the truck, throwing him to the ground and shooting him point-blank with the BAR.

Che got everyone to start unloading the canvas bags filled with money into the back of a Volkswagen micro-bus when it was all loaded up he said, "Butch, Sundance you come with me. The rest of you follow."

He got into the driver's side, and we all started caravanning south towards his encampment in the Yuro ravine.

"So, how'd we do?" Che asked.

"We estimate about seventy million Bolivian Bolívianos, which works out to be over 25 million U.S. Dollars." Butch said.

"Dios Mio! That's incredible. How did you guys do?"

"We think we got close to seven million."

"Where's News?"

"He went on ahead; he got injured at the site today. Injured his leg, so we didn't think it was smart to have him tag along."

"Nothing serious, I hope."

"A broken ankle."

"A small price to pay in the scheme of things, I guess."

"That was our thinking."

"I know you were hoping to leave after the drop-off today, but I think it best that you wait until things cool down. Hell, they don't even know about the bank yet. Once they do, all Hell's going to break loose. You might have to lay low for a couple of days."

"Yeah, we figured as much, it's no big deal."

As I was boarding the plane to Lima, I saw on the TV in the airport bar, a report about a police shooting involving three men in a truck.

My first inclination was to cash in my ticket and either see if I could help or at least stay in Bolivia, I felt like such a deserter, abandoning my friends in their time of need.

Even though reports didn't sound good, I knew that Butch and Sundance had always had a way to get out of even the toughest scrapes. Like that time in El Paso.

It was early in their cattle rustling days, Sundance had come across a large cattle ranch named the KO rancho whose brand was the KO. Well Butch and Sundance claimed that they were selling cattle from the O Double-K O ranch from just outside of Las Cruces, whose brand looked like this

ØЖØ. Well it took almost a year before the folks at the KO ranch figured out that they had been buying their own beef.

The folks at the KO ranch sent out all of their ranch hands to hunt down these two hombres that had been rustling their cattle and selling them back to them.

They thought they had them trapped not far from the little town of Truth or Consequences, New Mexico. There had been rumors that they were held up in the small ranch. As they were on the road to the ranch, they passed a couple traveling with their baby in a covered wagon. A clean-shaved man and a rather plain-looking woman, who looked like farmers. They were heading south towards El Paso to visit their kinfolk. They wished them well and rode on to the ranch where Butch and Sundance were thought to be hiding out.

Once they got there, they found that there weren't nobody there but an old man and his wife. The old man told them that a couple of fellas had bought their old wagon and some of their clothes, and a baby piglet. The old rancher told them, "It was the darnedest thing we ever saw. One of them young men dressing up in my wife clothes."

By the time the ranch-hands caught up with the abandoned wagon, Butch, Sundance and the piglet were long gone.

Butch and Sundance did have a way about them of avoiding capture. Call it luck, cunning or divine intervention, but those two always seemed to get away when others weren't so fortunate.

Colonel Altmann had kept Félix alive and tortured for six days. He had a vicious dog attack him and mutilate his genitals, he nailed all ten fingers to the wooden chair he was bound to, he force-fed him spoiled meat and dairy, causing him to throw up. Today he was going to have Ramon smash each of his toes with a sledgehammer.

Altmann was planning on keeping Félix alive for another week with blood transfusions, but his old CIA buddy, Captain Williams was flying in today to start the campaign of finding and killing Che Guevara. So after Ramon finished breaking his toes, he was going to kill him.

Altmann and Regina entered the room where Félix sat. The man was nothing more than gobs of flesh and bits of bone dripping and oozing blood. Altmann positioned two chairs to have a good view of Félix Espinosa's face. He always got great pleasure and satisfaction from seeing the tortured looks of his victims faces. Recently Félix's facial expressions were becoming less and less expressive as his body was shutting down. Altmann was hoping that the crushing of the toes would bring some agony.

Ramon picked up the hand hammer, knelt and hit the big toe on Félix's right foot with so much velocity that it burst like a pimple. There was less than a minor grimace on the battered man's face.

"Stop!" Altmann shouted.

Ramon stopped, stood up, and waited for further instructions.

"I'm sorry, my dear, but this has become rather boring. Ramon, get me that barbers straight razor. Ramon did as he was told and handed Altmann the razor. He then grabbed Félix by the hair and tilted his head back to give Altmann a clear view of his intended target. But, Altmann stopped, thought a moment, looked at his wife, then said, "Ramon, give me that hacksaw."

Regina's eyes lit up, she smiled and nodded approval, and she even gave a small clap of her hands

As Altmann started to saw the head off of Félix Espinosa, he was hoping for some sign of pain, agony, but Félix gave him none. Félix had given up the ghost long ago. It was almost a relief to have this nightmare over. And as Félix was slipping away, his mind was traveling to that pure white light of eternal peace; his last conscious feeling was one of rapture and bliss, then nothingness.

Good evening this is Nigel Williams for BBC World News Tonight. This evening we again start our coverage with Breaking News from Bolivia.

Police have disclosed details of the largest bank robbery in Bolivia's history. It had been reported that South America's notorious "Banditos Yanquis" in league with Che Guevara's National Liberation Army of Bolivia perpetrated the robbery of Banco Nacional De Bolivia.

It is believed that the robbers got away with more than thirty million dollars. The ingenious plan was devised by what police believe were two Americans who went by the names, Brad Thomas and Tommy St. John. A third American is believed to be involved, but his identity is unknown at this time.

The robbers apparently, secured a building loan from Banco Nacional De Bolivia to start construction of a four-story office building next door to the bank, which was originally a vacant lot. According to the bank's general manager, Señor Cajero, the robbers had obtained all the proper government documents and permits, along with professional blueprints done by a professionally licensed architect. Cajero told police that the loan went thru all the proper channels and committees for approval. It is not believed that anyone within the bank was involved.

The body of Raúl Márquez, a known member of Che Guevara's National Liberation Army of Bolivia was found by the side of the road shot dead at close range. It's believed Márquez was involved in the traffic stop that resulted in his shooting and killing of one officer and running over another with a truck.

Marquez's body was found next to an abandoned truck believed to be the getaway vehicle. The Ford Box truck was located not far from the small town of Villa Ramedios.

Police and the Bolivian Army are in pursuit of these criminals. Colonel Altmann of the elite Bolivian Rangers is heading up the special task force of Rangers, with the aid of American Special Forces to hunt down the robbers and Che Guevara.

Colonel Altmann, when asked for comment, said, "It is time that we put an end to these Marxist criminal thugs. They will find that they can't steal from the good people of Bolivia, or kill our brave police, and spread their communist lies and get away with it. We will hunt Che Guevara down like the dog he is, and as far as the Banditos Yanquis, they have gotten away too long stealing from our neighboring countries. Today they robbed the wrong bank, and we will show no mercy."

That was Colonel Altmann of the Bolivian Rangers.

In other news, wildfires in California are still raging out of control, the governor....

I managed to pass thru Lima customs without incident. I got a taxi to the Gran Hotel Bolivar, checked in under my real name, William Carver. I hadn't used my real name in over twenty-five years, and it felt strange, I was half expecting for the FBI to come crashing into my room with a warrant. But, I guess they have bigger fish to fry than a seventy-year-old desperado.

When I got all settled in, I turned on the television, and saw the news about the robbery, the killing of the policeman and that Colonel Altmann was talking about capturing and killing Che Guevara and the Banditos Yanquis.

I remembered Kid Curry talking about Reinhardt and this guy Altmann being ex-Nazis. When I saw Altmann interviewed on TV, it made my blood run cold. I had a premonition that Butch and Sundance were in for a rough time. I felt lost, and I didn't know what to do.

Now I'm in a plush hotel sitting on seven million dollars in cash, and my oldest and dearest friends, Butch and Sundance are down in the jungles of Bolivia fighting for their lives. I'm not ashamed to tell you I was scared.

The next morning, after checking the BBC news channel on television, I decided to start moving ahead with our plans to book our passage on the SS Rijndam to Sydney, Australia. Downstairs in the hotel lobby, they had a travel agent office. There was an attractive woman, in her fifties typing a letter when I walked in.

"Buenos días, señor."

"Good morning, Miss."

"How may I help you?"

"I'm interested in booking passage on the SS Rijndam to Australia."

She stopped her typing and gave her full attention to me. I noticed that her nametag said her name was Maria.

"Yes, sir. When are you thinking of traveling?"

"Well, Maria, when does she set sail?"

The young woman smiled and opened the desk drawer and found the ship's brochure and began to thumb thru it. When she found the schedule, she said, "The next cruise to Sydney Australia will be in two days. Would you like me to book your passage?"

"Actually, Maria, I would like to book three first-class staterooms if that's alright. Say you don't mind me calling you Maria, do you?"

"Oh, no, I prefer that to people calling me Miss."

"I find it more friendly, don't you agree? By the way, my name is William."

"Well, William, may I have the names of the people traveling?"

"There's me, William Carver, Mr. Butch Cassidy, and Mr. Harry Longabaugh."

"Very good, and you say you wanted to book three first-class staterooms, is that correct?"

"Yes."

"Round trip?"

"No, just one way."

"Alright, that comes out to be six thousand five hundred each, or nineteen thousand five hundred total."

"What happens if I go ahead and pay for the rooms and for some reason the other two fellas can't go?"

"Let me see what the policy is for last-minute cancellations."

The young woman spent several minutes reading the fine print of the brochure. Then she picked up the telephone, and said to me, "William, I'm going to call them just make sure I'm reading this right."

"I appreciated it."

Maria talked to several people over at the cruise ship company in Spanish. Now and then I'd pick a couple of phrases. I'm embarrassed to say that after all this time living in South America, I can barely get by.

Maria hung up the phone and smiled, "William, they have a 24-hour cancellation policy, so you can cancel up to 24 hours before departure and get your money back, but after that, you lose the entire amount. Do you still want to book the rooms?"

"Sure, what the Hell, it's only money. Is cash alright, Maria?" I said as I pulled out my wallet and counted out $19,500 in cash.

Well, you should have seen Maria's face, "Señor William, should not carry all that money; it is not safe."

"I don't normally carry this much, but I knew I was going to booking the staterooms."

"Are you an American, William?"

"Yes, I guess I'm that obvious."

"Only when you speak." She said, laughing.

"Ouch, the truth hurts, but you're right."

She typed up the order and printed my receipt and three first-class stateroom tickets.

"Here you are, William. Now, remember to bring these tickets and your passport when you check-in at Dock 17, no later than 6 pm."

"Thank you, Maria, for all your help."
"Bon voyage, Señor William."

"Butch, I have a bad feeling about this, I don't think we're going to make it to Lima and hook up with News. I have no idea where the fuck we are, and to be honest I don't think Che knows where we are either or how we're going to get out of here." Sundance said.

It was about two in the morning after the bank robbery when they reached the guerrilla's encampment in the Yuro ravine. The camp was pretty crude, old army surplus tents, men dressed in a hodge-podge of uniforms, the weapons seemed antiquated, some had AK-47's, others old farmer's shotguns. It was overall a rag-tag army at best.

"You guys can bunk in here. It's my tent. I'll sleep outside on the ground." Che said.

"Don't be silly, Che. We can all sleep in there; it's big enough to sleep six." Butch insisted.

"Well, I'm going to help the men unload the van and set up the guard duty. You go on to bed. I'll see you later."

"Say, me and Sundance need to get to Lima, as soon as we can. How soon do you think we can be own our way?" Butch asked.

"I'll know more tomorrow, first things first. I have to make sure that we're secure here for the night. We'll talk tomorrow, alright?"

"Sure thing Che, didn't mean to trouble you."

"Butch, I owe you and Sundance more than I can ever repay since you have possibly helped save the revolution. I promise, we'll get you to Lima, as soon as possible."

Butch and Sundance went into the tent and tried to convince themselves that somehow they were going to make it out of this mess.

"Damn that Raúl!" Sundance cursed.

Butch had just laid down and was starting to drift off to sleep when Che burst into the tent shouting, "Butch, Sundance get up we have to move, now!"

Butch and Sundance had been smart enough not to undress and to sleep with their shoes on. They had been thru this kind of drill on many occasions before.

'What's up?" Sundance asked as they were grabbing anything and everything they could and throwing it into the van.

"There's a squad of Rangers heading our way, and we've set up some booby traps which should slow them down. I'm keeping a dozen men here to ambush them so we can get away."

They were very efficient in packing up an escaping quickly. You have to be nimble when you're fighting guerrilla-style.

"Where we headed?" Butch asked Che.

"We're going up into the hills of Santa Cruz. It's tougher terrain, which makes it harder for them to track us, plus we'll have the high ground." Che answered.

As they were driving, the sun started to peek up over the horizon. Butch and Sundance were sitting asleep in the backseat surrounded by bags and bags of Bolivian Bolívianos worth millions.

They were almost to the small town of Villa Serrano when Che noticed that his amigos in the backseat were awake.

"You fellas sleep well?" Che asked.

Butch looked around at the bags of money and said, "It would be hard *not* to sleep well surrounded by twenty-five million dollars."

"Listen, Butch, Sundance, I'm sorry that your plans to escape to Lima haven't exactly worked out as you planned, but I promise to as soon as we can get you out safely.

"In the meantime, I think it might be best that you put on these army fatigues; it will help you two from sticking out like sore thumbs."

"Hey, I'm not going to be a private am I? I want to at least be a general, and Butch too."

"Sure, you two are hereby appointed the honorary rank of Generals. Now put these on before I court marshal you both." Che tossed them each a pair of faded green fatigues, boots and field caps, then stepped outside the tent to set up scouting patrols.

"I like it. General Sundance, kinda catchy." Sundance said.

"Yeah, we'll see how much you like it when you're pulling K.P. duty, sitting around the fire peeling a mountain of potatoes, Generalissimo."

"That's when I desert."

"They shoot deserters."

"Man, you're such a kill-joy

Captain Frank Williams along with Lieutenant Ackley met up with Colonel Altmann and his staff to go over the Intel that the CIA brought with them. Williams brought satellite images of the whole Santa Cruz area, with detail maps of the entire region. They had photo images of Guevara's past camps and had pictures that told them of his manpower strength, which Altmann estimated to be well over two hundred men, but they now knew there to be a little over fifty men, total.

"Excellent news, Captain. I think we can probably sweep these vermin away without too much trouble."

"You think so, Colonel?"

"Of yes, I believe that I can wrap this up in less than a week."

"Okay, that's fine by me. However, I would like Lieutenant Ackley to accompany you, he's fresh out of the Academy, and I'd like for him to gain some field experience; he'll only act as an observer. You don't mind, do you, Colonel?"

"Mind? Not at all, seeing combat firsthand will be an invaluable experience for the young Lieutenant."

"Colonel, me and my men will bivouac with the army's aviation company, the 292 at Santa Cruz, just in case you could use a little extra help."

"I thank you; Captain and I certainly will contact you if I need the backup. Lieutenant Ackley, please be ready to move out at first light."

Ackley snapped to attention and saluted the Colonel as he left. "Aye, aye sir!"

"Ackley keep an eye on Colonel Altmann. Report to me every evening unless you're engaged with the enemy. Understand?"

"Yes, sir."

"Good, and one more thing don't get your ass shot off. Unlike what Altmann thinks, these fifty men are hardened troops and there may be only fifty, but you can bet they'll fight like five hundred. And Che Guevara likes confrontation over compromise; he's one Hell of a fighter, which he proved in Cuba. Well, good luck, Lieutenant."

"Thank you, sir."

Williams headed back to the army base at Santa Cruz. He would have his men on standby, knowing that Colonel Altmann will believe that, just by having a superior force in numbers that he will win the day.

It was evident to Williams that Altmann isn't a student of history or warfare; if he were he'd know that bigger isn't always better. There are hundreds of examples where small, highly trained brave men can hold off and even defeat a more significant force.

The Battle of Thermopylae is a perfect example. It's the story of 300 Spartans holding off nearly 100,000 to 150,000 Persians for three days, inflicting heavy casualties on the Persians.

Colonel Altmann was about to suffer his Battle of Thermopylae, and unfortunately for him, he was going to be playing the part of the Persians.

I was getting nervous, it's been two days since I had heard anything, and there wasn't anything in the newspapers or on television. If I didn't hear anything from Butch or Sundance by tonight, I was going to cancel the cruise tickets.

I sat in the hotel bar, drinking beers, and watching soccer all day. I still don't understand the fascination with soccer, gimme baseball any day. I'm a big Yankees fan, love that Mickey Mantle.

Well, at 6 pm I went back to the hotel travel agent. There sat Maria looking just as lovely as I had remembered.

"Good evening, Maria."

"Good evening Mr. Carver, how can I help you?"

"Well, it looks like my two friends are going to be no-shows, so I'd like to cancel these tickets and see about booking the later cruise."

"To Australia?"

"Yes, Australia."

"Alright, let's see when the next cruise is."

Maria first canceled the tickets for the next day's cruise. Then she looked up when the next ship sails to Australia.

"It looks like the next cruise to set sail for Australia will be in two weeks. How does it work for you?"

"I guess it'll have to do, can you just use the credit from this cruise for the next one?"

"That shouldn't be a problem, Mr. Carver. Is all the information still correct?"

"Yes, and its William"

"That's right, I'm sorry, William."

It seemed to me that she was busy typing all the forms at lightning speed. She could type faster than I could speak. When she finished, she pulled the pages out of the typewriter and had me sign several copies.

"There, you're all set."

"Thank you, Maria. Say, could I buy you dinner? After all, you've been so nice and all."

"Oh, I don't know."

"It's just that I'm here in Lima all alone and after a while, it gets a bit lonely not having anyone to talk to."

"Well…"

"Look, I understand, you probably got dozens of young fellas wanting to take you out for dinner, not some old coot like me. It's okay, I understand."

I started to walk out when Maria called out, "William, wait. I'd love to have dinner."

"Would tonight be good for you?"

"Sure, I close up at 7 pm, why don't you stop by then."

"Great, I'll see you at seven."

Colonel Altmann, his two hundred men, and Lieutenant Ackley were about to get their first taste of fighting guerrilla warfare.

Altmann had, in theory, surrounded Che Guevara and his fifty men, but when the shooting started it was experience that carried the day for the guerrillas. They not only created an opening from which they were able to escape, Che also then forced Altmann's troops into a box canyon in which they found themselves trapped. To Che and his men, it was like shooting fish in a barrel.

If it weren't for the cool head of Lieutenant Ackley, all might have been lost. He radioed Captain Williams and requested some air cover to force the rebels to scatter.

Williams sent in four Bell UH-1 Iroquois, better known as Hueys to light up some air to ground missiles and lay some machine gun cover so Altmann and his men could escape.

It wasn't too long before the Hueys were buzzing overhead lighting up the sky with their M134D Gatling machine guns. These fire at an incredible rate of 3000 rounds per minute, that's 50 rounds per second.

Fortunately for Che and his men, he had scouts out watching for just such an eventuality so by the time the Hueys reached Altmann's position the guerrillas were long gone.

Eight of Altmann's men were killed, six wounded and one man missing, probably deserted. Meanwhile, for the opposition, only two men wounded, none seriously. If it weren't for Williams and his Hueys instead of a minor skirmish, it could have turned into a massacre.

Ackley later told Williams that although Altmann was the senior officer, his knowledge of field tactics was woefully lacking, and this coming from a snot-nosed kid from West Point. He said that Altmann never really took command, instead let the three non-coms make the decisions and take command. It was like he never had any real combat experience, as he was always reacting rather than being proactive.

It was after the first battle that Williams told Ackley the truth about Altmann.

"So that you know, Altmann is a German. He's an escaped Nazi war criminal, by the name of Klaus Barbie. The Americans recruited him after the war to spy on the Communists in East Germany. Once the French found out that he was working for us, they demanded that we turn him over to stand trial for all kinds of heinous war crimes. But in our infinite wisdom we allowed and moreover helped him escape, here to Bolivia where he ingratiated himself with the ruling fascist general, Rogelio Miranda.

"Barbie wasn't a combat veteran. He was a member of the SS and Gestapo, who was in charge of rounding up Jews and others in southern France that the Nazis thought were undesirables. He earned the nickname as the Butcher of Lyon. Hitler pinned the Iron Cross on him for torturing and killing a leader of the French Resistance and sending 44 Jewish orphans to Auschwitz.

"Barbie couldn't fight his way out of a wet paper bag, but you put him in a dark, dank basement with a frightened person bound to a chair with implements of torture, well his right in his element.

"He's still wanted in France. They would love to get their hands on him and put him on trial. The folks here use him as an 'Interrogator' of sorts; his primary function is to torture the government's enemies and to set up and to oversee death squads.

"You watch at any minute the phone will ring; it will be General Miranda requesting that I take the lead on this mission."

And just like Williams predicted, ten minutes later the phone rang, it was General Miranda requesting that Williams take the lead in tracking down Guevara.

Butch and Sundance weren't involved in the firefight with Colonel Altmann and his men; they were back at the base camp. Che had asked them to stay behind and keep an eye on the money, both Butch and Sundance thought it to be a bit ironic, asking a fox to guard the henhouse.

When Che and his men got back to camp, the radio operator informed Che that Fidel Castro wanted to talk to him.

Che's mood brightened, this could be the call that changes everything. Now that he had the money, he could afford to hire more men and purchase better weapons. This could be a real game-changer, his amigo Fidel could help facilitate and procure getting all the things they needed.

"Che, this is Fidel, how is it going?"

"Fidel, it is so good to hear your voice. How are you, my friend?"

"I am well, how is the campaign going?"

"It has been going slow, but we now have money to help supply the cause; money enough to attract skilled mercenaries, to buy better weapons, and much-needed equipment. But I need your help."

"You know I will do whatever you need. That is wonderful news. How much money are you talking about, you know good fighters and weapons aren't cheap."

"Twenty-five million."

"Bolívianos?"

"Dollars."

"My God, Che, what did you do rob a bank?" Fidel said, half-joking.

"Yes, that's exactly what we did."

"Ah, of course. The robbery of the Banco Nacional de Bolivia. Brilliant, congratulations."

"So, you'll help us?"

"Si, si, but first I need to get the money, hold on."

Che could hear the muffled sound of Fidel talking to someone, and at one point Castro raised his voice in anger.

"Listen, Che let me contact you later today. I need to work the logistics for a pickup of the money. For now, try not to engage with the enemy until we work this out. I will get back to you within a couple of hours. Adiós."

"Adiós, amigo."

"I hear this place is very good. I'm sure you've heard of it, Cordano. What do you think?" News asked.

"Oh, yes, it is an excellent choice." Maria said.

Cordano is one of the oldest bars in Lima. It is considered an institution. Because it is at the corner of the Government's Palace, all past Presidents have eaten there, also artists, writers, and world leaders as well.

It has been around for well over a hundred years, and according to regulars, the place hasn't changed a bit since it opened its doors. It still has the original floors, tiles, the dark wooden cabinets and counter, and looking at the wait staff you might think that some of them were there on opening day.

They were seated in the front by the window where they could watch all the people walk by. Maria suggested that they order the house specialty.

As their waiter was shuffling his way over to them, she smiled and said, "Just repeat what I say, okay?"

"Yeah, okay."

The waiter, holding his little pad and pencil, asked, "¿Puedo tomar su orden?"

Maria said, "Uno Del país, porfa."

The waiter then looked at me, "¿Y para tí?"

Maria looked at me and nodded for me to order.

"Uno Del país, porfa." I said.

As the old man was walking away, I shouted, "Dos Cervezas por favor."

I looked at Maria and asked, "What did we just order?"

"A Butifarra, it's a sandwich on a French baguette filled with slices of pork with onions, lime, and peppers. It's the best in town."

I have to admit that that darn Butitfarra was one damn good sandwich. There's nothing like a good sandwich, an ice-cold beer and sitting next to a beautiful woman.

She took a drink of beer and asked me, "What do you do for a living, William."

"Oh, I'm retired."

"Well, what kind of work did you do?"

"Well, for the most part, I was a cowboy."

"Oh, like John Wayne?"

"John Wayne weren't no cowboy, he just playacted. Hell, we'd laugh him out of town if he'd ever come into town all duded up like that. No, in the real west, it wasn't like they make it out to be in the picture shows."

"No?"

"It was hard living, and times was hard, the people was hard, had to be to survive. Back then, there wasn't much law in a lot of places, that's one reason we all carried sidearms. Many a time you'd have to rely on yourself for protection. They called it the Wild West for a reason."

"You ever kill a man, William?"

"There was a time or two, back then, when I did have to defend myself. But, I never did kill somebody that didn't deserve it, and that's the truth."

Except it wasn't the truth, I had killed several good and decent men who were on the right side of the law, but as someone wiser than me once said, "It's the victors that get to write history."

"I guess you probably want to go home and not associate with the likes of me, being that I'm a killer and all."

"But, you said it was self-defense, and it was a different time. I don't get the sense that you're a cold-blooded killer."

"I was never that."

We sat there looking out the window just watching all the people walking by, some in a hurry, some slowly strolling.

"It appears to me that it's the single folks are the ones in a rush, whereas the couples, the ones in love are the ones that are in no hurry. Do you have a boyfriend, Maria?"

"I used to, but we broke up. He has found another."

"Why he must be a dern fool."

"That's very kind of you to say so."

"Say, would you care for another beer?"

"No, I better not, I have work tomorrow."

I paid the check, and we went outside to grab a taxi.

"It's alright, William, I can see myself home." She said.

"Certainly not, I insist on seeing you home."

"Oh, but it's late."

"No matter, I guess I'm just old fashion, but a gentleman always sees a lady home."

When we got to her apartment, I told the cabbie to wait, and I walked her to her door.

She said, "Thank you, William, for a lovely evening."

"It was my pleasure, and I want to thank you for being so kind to spend some time with this old cowboy, it meant a lot to me. Goodnight."

"Goodnight, William." She said and then gave me a little kiss.

Che had begun pacing the minute Castro ended the radio call.

Butch shouted, "Hey, Che, you're driving everyone crazy, sit down and relax, he said he'd get back to you."

"Yeah, it takes time to formulate a foolproof plan." Sundance added.

Che stopped, looked at his watch, "It's been over three hours." Then he began to pace again.

"Papa, Papa, this is Ruz, come in Papa, over."

"Comandante! It is the call you've been waiting for!" The radioman shouted.

Che ran over to the radio, grabbed the receiver and said, "Papa, here. Over."

It was the voice of his comrade Fidel, "Sorry, it took so long, but we have a plan to receive the money. Once we do we will be able to help you with everything you require, my brother."

"When can we expect to make the drop-off?"

"Tomorrow evening. Bring the packages to these coordinates: -18.786498, -64.206711. There is a large clearing where the helicopter will arrive at precisely twenty-two hundred hours. Fire off a yellow roadside flare if everything is good, a red flare if aborted. The code name is perro diamante. Over."

"Message received, will contact you after the drop is made. Over."

"Affirmative, good luck. Over."

Che handed the receiver back to the radioman and looked at the map to see where the drop off would be. All the men were standing around, waiting for instructions.

"We will be making a drop off of the money with our comrades from Cuba tomorrow at 22:00 hours, until then we will not, I repeat, not engage with the enemy. We will move camp to the coordinates where the drop off will take place. According to the map, the drop off location is not far from the village of La Higuera. So, let's break camp, grab our gear, and get started."

It was a full day march thru the mountains to reach the drop-off area. They set up camp and sent out sentries. Che gave orders that everyone was to stay in camp, and no one was to make contact with any of the villagers until after the drop off was made.

Butch and Sundance found Che inside his tent, going over the map coordinates with his noncoms. He peered up and saw them standing outside.

"Butch, Sundance come in, come in."

"Che, when you get a minute, we need to talk."

"Of course. I know that you're anxious to leave, and I promise as soon as we make the drop tomorrow night, I will help you make your way to catch a flight to Lima.

"I can't thank you both enough for helping me. Just be patient, and you'll be on your way."

"It's okay. We know you've got a revolution to run." Butch said.

"Yeah, what's one more day, anyway?" Sundance added.

As Butch and Sundance headed back to their tent, Butch said, "What difference could one more day make?"

Sundance looked like he was going to answer, but before he could, Butch held up his hand and said, "Don't!"

Captain Williams made a few phone calls back to Langley and had Félix Ismael Rodríguez Mendigutia flown down to Bolivia to infiltrate Che's guerrillas. Mendigutia was CIA Paramilitary Operations Officer in the famed Special Activities Division; he was instrumental in the Bay of Pigs Invasion.

"Félix, welcome aboard."

"Thank you, sir. How can I be of assistance?"

"We need a man on the inside of Guevara's guerrillas. He has become a real thorn in our side. We want him dead. And I felt that you're just the man for the job."

"Do you have any idea where they are?"

"Our latest intelligence is that he's up in the Santa Cruz Mountains, we think near the village of La Higuera. Our best guess is that there are about fifty men total, and he's desperate for volunteers."

"Is there anything to the rumors about him being involved in the multimillion-dollar bank robbery with the so-called Banditos Yanquis?"

"I wouldn't put it past him, as they are desperate for cash to be able to recruit men and arms. But he's not going to be able to lug around twenty-five million in cash while fighting a revolution. He's going to need to get it to someone like Castro who can act as a broker."

"Well, if you drop me into the area, I'm sure I can find him and hopefully join his merry band of men."

"How will I be able to communicate with you?"

Williams handed him what looked to be old beat-up tin tobacco can, a pipe, and a red bandana.

"The pipe has a small tracking device in it, so we will be able to see where you are. Now, built into the bottom of the tobacco tin is a small transmitter/receiver with a range of three miles. You'll be able to communicate with us, but unfortunately, for security reasons we won't be able to communicate with you."

"Understood. Is there anything else, sir?"

"Yes, the homing device in the pipe will start to activate the first time you begin to smoke, so don't use it until you join up with Guevara. That's when we'll know to start tracking you. As soon as we know where you're at, we'll start moving troops into the area."

"One more thing sir, once you engage Guevara in battle, how will I avoid getting killed?"

"Ah, that's where the red bandana comes in. Colonel Altmann's troops were under strict orders to avoid shooting anyone wearing a red bandana."

"Not the most reassuring solution I heard of. But, I'll make it work, I've been in tougher spots."

"I know, that's why I asked for you."

"When do I move out?"

"Head on over to see the quartermaster to get fitted out. He's got some clothes and a weapon for you to change into."

"Very good, sir."

"Good luck."

"Thank you, sir."

Mendigutia went over to get dressed for his role as a volunteer. His "outfit" was old army fatigue pants, a tattered chambray shirt, worn-out shoes, a ragged poncho, and a beat-up fedora. He was given an old 12-gauge double-barrel shotgun.

Sergeant Vasquez, in the quartermaster's corps, handed him a small envelope and said, "These are your identification papers. Your name is Poncho Diaz, you're forty-two years old, you lived in Coro Coro, and you worked in the Compania Corocoro de Bolivia's copper mines. You are a widower, and you have no children, and you're sick and tired of all the inequality of the rich getting richer on the backs of the countries workers."

"Thanks, sergeant."

"Your Jeep and driver are outside ready to take you on your mission. Good luck, Señor. Mendigutia."

"Diaz."

"Right, Diaz!"

The ship was to sail in just two days and still no word from Butch or Sundance. I was getting prepared to cancel our tickets again. I have until tomorrow at midnight to be able to cancel and reschedule for a later trip.

Over these last couple of weeks, I have been seeing a lot of the hotel's travel agent, Maria Cortez. I have gotten to know her pretty well. She's an only child, both her parents have passed away. She was born and raised in Lima and has never traveled outside of the country. Maria has a Bachelor of Arts degree in Art History from the Universidad Peruana Cayetano Heredia.

Aside from working at the travel agency, she works part-time at the Museo de Arte Contemporáneo. We went there one day and I have to admit that most of the paintings looked to me to have been painted by children, with big canvases that filled an entire wall painted the color blue, or a giant picture of nothing but paint splatters and drippings.

"Say, don't you have any painting of cows or cowboys?" I asked.

"As a matter of fact, we do have one." She said and took my hand and walked me to a room that had some drawing from this Spanish fella, Pablo Picasso.

And by golly, this Picasso had drawn some bulls that looked just like bulls, then he drew the same bull with fewer lines, but it still looked like a bull. Eventually he drew the bull with only six thin lines and you still could tell it was a bull.

"Do you see how Picasso could make the image of the bull with only a few lines?" She asked.

I said, "Yeah, he's pretty dern good, but I still don't get the guy with the paint splatter."

"Well, William that's why they say that art is in the eye of the beholder."

I like Maria. She's not like any of the women that I've ever met before. Like most of the women that I knew when I was young. All I cared about was having sex with them. It wasn't until I met Della Moore that I had a real relationship with a woman. I guess you could say that Della was my first true love, before that it was only about one night stands. I did love Della and could have seen myself spending the rest of my life with her, but she was killed during that robbery, I still do miss her to this day.

Having met Maria has sparked feelings in me that had been long forgotten, and for that, I am grateful. If and when I do set sail for Australia, I'm thinking of asking her if she'd like to go with me. I'm sure Butch and Sundance won't mind since I'm sure that they'll like her right off.

I wish I'd hear something from them. I miss my friends. !"

They heard the helicopter before they saw it's red running lights. Che gave the order to light up the yellow flares, giving the all-clear signal.

The helicopter, a Russian built Kamov Ka-25 anti-submarine helicopter developed for the Soviet Navy in 1958 had taken off from the Russian aircraft carrier, the Admiral Kuznetsov steaming off the coast of Peru.

As the chopper settled down, Che and a small contingent of men stood off to one side. An old friend of Che's emerged from the helicopter. Roberto Sánchez was a fellow freedom fighter who fought alongside Che in the Congo several years ago in support of the Marxist Simba movement.

"Che, mi Viejo amigo, es bueno verte de muevo." Sánchez said.

"Roberto, it is good to see you, too."

"Fidel asked me personally to come."

"I'm glad you did."

Che waved to his men to start loading the canvas bags filled with money onto the helicopter.

"I wish you could stay. I could use a good man like you here." Che said.

"I wish I could, but they have me helping to rebuild the Cuban infrastructure."

"A worthy cause, I'm sure. I am entrusting you with all this money. It will help in our struggle."

"Mi amigo, you can trust me."

"I know I can. Well, you better take off now. Ve con Dios."

"And to you."

They gave each other a hug and moments later they were gone. The area was eerily quiet, made even more so by the iridescent glow of the dying yellow flares.

Che had held back two bags of money, about 2.5 million dollars for unexpected expenditures, weapons, uniforms, food, drink, and women. Now that the money had been sent back to Cuba, hopefully, there will be an influx of mercenaries to help fight against the current fascist regime.

When Che had returned from the drop-off, he called his men together and told them tomorrow they would go into the village of La Higuera for recruiting and a little well-deserved R & R!"

Félix Ismael Rodríguez Mendigutia sat quietly drinking his Chicha de colla, a drink that has been traced back to the Inca empire. It's made from fermented corn. Mendigutia was sitting in the courtyard of the cantina near a fire pit, his shotgun leaning against the stone wall when Che and his men came strolling by.

"Hola." Mendigutia said nonchalantly.

"Hola, mind if we join you, it's such a nice day." Che said.

"Not at all, I would welcome the company. Please have a seat."

As they sat down the owner came out to see what they might like to drink.

Che held up four fingers and said, "Cuatro cervezas por favor."

"Can I buy you a drink, señor?" Che asked Mendigutia.

"Thank you. I'll have another Chicha, please."

The owner nodded and walked back into the cantina to get the drinks.

Mendigutia said, "Thank you, señor, my name is Poncho Diaz."

"I am Che Guevara, and these are some of my men, Luis, Jose, and Diego."

"Che Guevara, I have heard of you, señor."

"Oh si, que has escuchado?"

"I have heard that you are trying to help the peasants and the workers, is that not so?"

"Si, we are fighting for the oppressed, just like we did for Cuba where everyone is equal. No more ruling class, equality for everyone."

"That is what I have heard."

"We are looking for men Señor Diaz, men who are willing to fight for a noble cause."

The owner came with the drinks, Che gave the owner a Two Hundred Boliviano bill. The owner said, "Señor, I cannot make change for such a large bill."

"I don't want change, señor. It is all for you." Che replied.

"Muchas gracias, señor."

"De nada."

Mendigutia pulled out his pipe and tobacco canister and began to fill his pipe. He noticed that Guevara had a pipe sticking out of the top pocket of his fatigue field jacket.

"Would you care for some tobacco, Señor Guevara? It is not an expensive blend, but I like it." Mendigutia said.

"Gracias, Señor Diaz, and please call me Che."

"And you must call me Poncho."

As Mendigutia lit his pipe the transmitter in the bowl of the pipe started, sending a signal to Colonel Altmann, letting him know the location of Che Guevara.

Sitting there each man smoking their pipes and drinking their drinks, Mendigutia said, "You know I have only this old shotgun, I don't think it would be much good in combat."

"Do not worry Poncho, if you decided to join us you will be given a new rifle. But first, maybe you should go and discuss it with your wife. This is a dangerous fight, we are up against the Bolivian Army, but I believe that once the people get to know what we are fighting for, they, like you will want to come to join our cause because it is their cause."

"I do not have a wife. I am a widower."

"I am sorry to hear that, children?"

"No, we were never blessed."

"What do you do, Poncho?

"I used to work in the copper mines outside of Coro Coro, but since my wife has passed, I just have been doing odd jobs. I want to join you if you'll have me?"

"Have you ever killed anyone, Poncho?"

"I have not, I guess no one knows if they can kill a man until the time comes, but I do believe in the cause."

"Welcome to the National Liberation Army of Bolivia."

Mendigutia held up his cup and said, "Viva la revolución!"

Lieutenant Ackley came running down the hall to Colonel Altmann's office. He gave three solid knocks and then entered, "Sir! We have the signal. They're at La Higuera."

"Excellent, Lieutenant. Alert the troops."

"Yes, sir!"

The alarm sounded, and two hundred Bolivian elite Rangers scrambled out of the barracks and into twelve waiting Bell UH-1 Huey helicopters. They were all airborne in minutes and headed for La Higuera.

The flight time would be about an hour; the men on this mission weren't the usual troops that Che had tangled with before. These were a mixture of American Green Berets, US Army Rangers, and a couple of American trained Bolivian Rangers. Each man sat quietly going over in their minds every scenario, knowing that in combat, there are no planned scenarios.

One thing everyone did know was that this wasn't going to be a day in the park, they were going up against a group of fierce battle harden troops who aren't getting paid to fight, they're fighting for something they believe in, which makes them true zealots. And nobody fights harder than a zealot. !"

When Che and his men got back to camp, he found Butch and Sundance all packed and ready to go.

"You fellas going somewhere?" Che said jokingly

"Che, it's been a real thrill working with you, but enough is enough, we have a date with a steamship." Butch said.

"Okay, I know I've taken advantage of your good nature, and as I said before, I appreciate everything you both have done for me and the cause."

"Now, don't go getting all sentimental on us, or I'm going to cry." Sundance quipped sarcastically.

"No, no nothing like that. So, the Bus doesn't come until 18:00 hours, so if you want you can stay with us until then, or I can have Luis drop you off, and you can sit on a rock until the bus comes in six hours."

"If it's all the same to you, Butch, I'm tired of sitting on rocks, why don't we just stay here until it's time to go." Sundance said.

"Sounds good to me. Che, we'll try and not get in the way."

"Okay, why don't you go hang out in the mess tent and relax."

Butch and Sundance meandered over to what Che called the mess tent, but what was more like a lean-to with two benches, a small table and an open fire pit with two coffee pots. They were each having a cup of coffee when this guy walked in, someone they hadn't seen before walked over to get a cup of coffee.

Butch looked at the guy and said, "You new here?"

"Si, I am Poncho, Poncho Diaz."

"Nice to meet ya, I'm Butch Cassidy, and this here is the Sundance Kid. You a new volunteer?"

"Si, yes, I am. Are you Americans?"

"That's right."

"I did not know that Americans were volunteering to fight for Bolivia."

"It's a long story, we're amigos of Che for many years, and we just did him a huge favor," Butch said.

"Yeah, and now we're going." Sundance added.

"Favor? Que es al favor?"

"A favor is something one does because someone needs something that only you have or could do." Butch explained.

"Yeah, you see Che needed money to help finance his revolution, so Butch and I robbed a bank and gave Che the money, ya see." Sundance said proudly.

"You did that for Che? You two are very good amigos."

Butch grinned and said, "I'll tell you a little secret, Sundance and I are the Banditos Yanquis."

"No! I have heard of the Banditos Yanquis ever since I was a small boy."

"Yeah, we've been at it a long, long time. But, now we're done, this was our last job." Butch admitted.

"Yeah, we're officially retired. Once we catch tonight's bus, we're gone." Sundance said with a smile in his voice.

"I wish you both good luck, but I don't think you'll be catching tonight's bus."

"Why would you say that Poncho?" Sundance asked.

"Do you not hear the helicopters?"

Way off in the distance, if you strained, you could hear the sounds of a dozen chopper's motors.

Whuh! Whuh! Whuh! Whuh! Whuh! Whuh! Whuh!

Seconds later, one of Guevara's men shouted, "Incoming! Choppers at two o'clock!"

Che took command and started barking orders. They were to head down the hill into the village of La Higuera, where the cover would be better than fighting out in the open.

It looked like the dozen choppers were splitting into two groups, one would be to their right flank and the other to their left. They were taking casualties as they were making their way to the village. The choppers were flying over the guerrillas, shooting down on them; it's like shooting at fish in a barrel. That was until Che fired off the ground to air missile and brought one of those big old Huey's crashing down in flames. Then the helicopters backed off.

They made it to the village and started taking up positions. There were civilians in the village when the government troops set siege to the town. It didn't seem to matter to them if they killed the innocent or not, as they say nowadays, acceptable collateral damage.

Butch and Sundance were trying to stay with Che, but with all the chaos, they got separated. They ended up in the cantina with six other rebels, bullets whizzing all around them, really tearing the place up pretty good.

"Butch, we're going get chewed up in here, let's make a break for it out the back, before they box us in."

"I'm with you. I wonder where the rest of Che's men are, cause they aren't down here."

"Maybe, he's using the rest of them for a counter-offensive. Ready?"

Butch and Sundance cracked open the side door that led to a cattle pen, where several cows were freaking out. One had already been shot and killed. Sundance tied a couple together with just enough room for the two of them to squeeze in between them.

The plan was to use the cows as shields. Walk them to the gulch that ran alongside the town to work their way out of this mess. By the time they got to the gulch, Altmann's men had figured out that somebody was trying to escape, so they started shooting the cows.

By the time Butch and Sundance extricated themselves from their cow shields, they both were wounded. As the cows collapsed to the ground, they rolled down into the ditch and laid there catching their breaths.

The incoming fire was increasing, Butch shouted out, "Che! Where the Hell is the rest of your men!" trying to be heard over the gunfire.

They had gotten separated from Che and his men, Butch, and Sundance when they had taken refuge in the cantina when the ambush started. Che and his fifteen men were also pinned down all along the small ravine. They were being picked off one by one, by the 200 Bolivian Rangers surrounding them. The Rangers had the high ground, which made picking off the guerrillas' child's play.

Both Butch and Sundance laid there in the ravine assessing their wounds. Butch had been shot in the left shoulder and right thigh, Sundance had sustained a bullet to his left side, a grazing wound to his right forearm, and a minor laceration to his forehead.

They both knew deep down they weren't going to survive, that this was the end of the line.

"Hey, we've been in tougher jams than this, right Butch?"

"Ah, piece of cake."

"It reminds me of that time when we had that posse and General Miles, and his troops surround us outside Las Cruces."

"Yeah, we held out until dark and then gave them the slip."

"And, they were a tougher outfit than these guys."

"There can't be more than a couple dozen of them out there."

"How you doing on ammo, Butch? I'm down to fifty rounds for the BAR and four clips for the pistol, you?"

"Bout the same, plus I have two grenades."

"Hell, that should last us until it gets dark. What time is it anyway?"

"9 am."

"Damn, seems later."

"Listen, Sundance. We got to meet up with News and head down to Australia."

"I like the sound of Australia."

"Yeah, they love Americans, and they speak English. You know we've been down here over twenty years, and we still have trouble speaking Spanish, plus we stick out like a couple of gringos."

"We are a couple of gringos."

The bullets started up again. They were taking fire from all sides.

"Butch, we gotta move! See those fig trees on the edge of the forest, let's make a break for them, we can probably lose the soldiers in the jungle."

"Man, I'm getting too old for this shit."

"You and me both, brother? Ready?"

"No, but let's go!"

They both starting firing in all directions, as they started running Butch lobbed the two grenades, one to his left and one to his right.

As a result of their wounds and their age they fell short of making their goal by ten feet, a group of twelve Bolivian Rangers had been hiding in the thicket of fig trees and opened fire point-blank, killing Butch Cassidy and the Sundance Kid.

Not far away, down in the ravine, surrounded by his dead comrades, Che had been wounded twice, with his gun out of ammunition, he surrendered.

He put up his arms and shouted to the Rangers, "Do not shoot! I am Che Guevara, and I am worth more to you alive than Dead."

Lieutenant Ackley saw Félix Mendigutia standing with the other prisoners, "Nice job, Félix."

Che looked at the man he befriended earlier in the day, "Ah, just like Christ, I to was betrayed by a Judas."

Félix replied sharply, "Ah, but Jesus wasn't a communist."

"Oh, but he was, reread your Bible, Judas!"

"Maria, have you given any more thought to my proposal?"

"William, you are such a romantic, to be married by the ship's captain on our way to Australia."

'I know that this is all very sudden, but I do love you."

"And I love you, too."

"So, does that mean you'll marry this old fool,"

"Yes, of course."

"Well, I guess you better contact the cruise ship people and add one."

"William, what about your friends?"

"I guess we might have to push back our departure another two weeks if I don't hear something today. They should have been here by now."

"Maybe you should go talk to someone at the American Consultant. Maybe they might be able to help you."

"That's a good idea, thanks, babe."

So, that's what I did. I had to do something. It was the not knowing that was driving me crazy. I talked to several people at the consultant, and I gave them the names that Butch and Sundance had been using, Brad Thomas and Tommy St. John. They said it could take a couple of days or maybe a couple of weeks, but they would be in touch with me. Now, it was just a matter of waiting.

I got back to the hotel around 6 pm, Maria was going to come up to my room after she got through with work, and then we were going to go out to dinner.

I turned on the television to catch the BBC News, and there it was, scenes of the shoot out at La Higuera and the capture of Che Guevara!"

Good evening this is Nigel Williams for BBC World News Tonight. This evening we again start our coverage with Breaking News from Bolivia.

Tonight Bolivian authorities disclose new information on the capture of Ernesto "Che" Guevara; the beret-wearing communist guerrilla leader was captured after an intense gun battle with Bolivian Rangers today.

In the stifling Bolivian jungle 75 miles north of Camiri in the village of La Higuera is a steep gulch covered with dense foliage. It was there that Bolivian Rangers totaling 200 men split into two columns encountered the handful of guerrillas. Shortly after noon, the Rangers spotted their quarry and opened fire. After a lengthy firefight, four Rangers, three guerrillas, and two Americans lay dead, and four other guerrillas captured.

Che was dressed in dirty, faded, torn green fatigues wearing high-top sandals. He had been wounded in his left thigh as he and his men were advancing towards the Rangers.

He was loaded onto a stretcher and taken into La Higuera where he was locked in a dilapidated mud schoolhouse where he was tied up and heavily guarded.

A spokesman for the Rangers, Colonel Altmann told BBC News that he interviewed Guevara and that the prisoner revealed valuable information about the rebel's plans.

Later, he was stood up and placed against the wall and was shot nine times, five times in the legs, once in his right shoulder and arm and once in the throat and chest.

His last words were: "I know you've come to kill me. Shoot, coward! You are only going to kill a man!"

As we had reported earlier, two Americans were also killed in the battle. They are believed to be the infamous Banditos Yanquis that were responsible for the largest bank robbery in Bolivian history. They have tentatively been identified as Butch Cassidy and Harry Longabuagh, better known as the Sundance Kid. Two American outlaws who have eluded police on two continents. Their connection with Che Guevara is still unknown. !"

I just sat there stunned, Butch and Sundance gone. I didn't seem real. For the first time in my life, I felt alone. I mean, truly alone. And as I was feeling sorry for myself, there came a knock on the door. It was Maria. She could tell that I was upset. I told her that my two friends were not going to join us after all, so we should go ahead and go on the cruise as planned.

And that's what we did. We got married by the captain of the SS Rijndam. We settled down in a small town called Alice Springs, Australia, where I started my own business, a newspaper, The Alice Springs Gazette. Every day I got to see my name in the paper, granted it's as the editor, but even so.

Funny thing, to this day, nobody knows whatever happened to that twenty-five million dollars that Che sent back to Cuba to help with his Bolivian revolution, it seems to have disappeared.

Before leaving Chile, I took time to write a letter to a Mister Simon Wiesenthal and to let him know that he might be interested in investigating Colonel Altmann of the Bolivian Army as he just might be surprised at what he finds.

And sure enough, in 1983 Colonel Altmann, aka Klaus Barbie, was arrested and extradited to France to stand trial for crimes committed as Gestapo chief in Lyon between 1942 and 1944.

Barbie was convicted and sentenced to life in prison, where he died a painful death from cancer.

Today, I'm one hundred and three years old, my wife, Maria passed on many years ago. After her passing I sold the paper and moved back to the United States, I'm now living in Yuma, Arizona, it reminds me a little of Alice Springs, they're both hot and boring.

And, if you're wondering whatever happened to the seven million dollars that we stole from that bank in Bolivia, well, I brought back one million to the States with me and the rest I buried in the outback, it's yours if'n you can find it.

I'll give you a clue, stand atop Uluru at sunset, face due west, just as the sun touches the horizon, you'll see a glimmer way off in the distance. It's a billabong and six miles south by southwest there's a rock formation that resembles a man standing. Forty paces from that rock are buried five million dollars in an old steamer trunk

Sometimes looking back, it hits me, that I am the last surviving member of the Hole-in-the-Wall Gang. Butch and Sundance went out like the legends they were, and for that, I am grateful. As for me, I was little more than a footnote, and I know it.

The other members of the Wild Bunch were much more colorful than I was: Bronco Bill Walters, William Ellsworth "Elzy" Lay, Black Jack Ketchum, Harvey "Kid Curry" Logan, Ben (the Tall Texan) Kilpatrick, "Laughing" Sam Carey, George "Flat Nose" Curry, and of course Butch Cassidy and the Sundance Kid. I wrote this book because I felt that I had a duty to Butch, Sundance, and the rest of the boys to set the record straight.

I feel privileged to have been a part of what was once the most historical outlaw gang of the Wild West. The stuff that legends are made of

<u>Obituary</u>

William "News" Carver (September 12, 1892 – April 2, 1998)

Carver was born in Coryell County, Texas, in 1892. He worked for a time as a cowboy, before venturing west to Wyoming and Utah where he met up and threw in with Butch Cassidy and his Hole-in-the-Wall Gang.

Said to have been a superior marksman, Carver's criminal record was mostly unremarkable, becoming famous for riding with more famous outlaws. He enjoyed the notoriety, earning himself the nickname "News" because he liked seeing his name in the newspaper stories of the gang's exploits.

William "News" Carver was 103 years old.

The End